SOMETHING STIRS

TOR BOOKS BY CHARLES L. GRANT

After Midnight
The Bloodwind
Dialing the Wind
Doom City
For Fear of the Night
The Grave
Greystone Bay
The Hour of the Oxrun Dead
In a Dark Dream
The Last Call of Mourning
Midnight
Nightmare Seasons
The Orchard
The Pet
Seaharp Hotel
The Sound of Midnight
Stunts
Tales from the Nightside

CHARLES L. GRANT

SOMETHING
STIRS

A TOM DOHERTY ASSOCIATES BOOK   NEW YORK

SOMETHING STIRS

Copyright © 1991 by Charles L. Grant

Book design by Judith A. Stagnitto

A Tor Book
Published by Tom Doherty Associates, Inc.
49 West 24th Street
New York, N.Y. 10010

Library of Congress Cataloging-in-Publication Data

Grant, Charles L.
    Something stirs / Charles L. Grant.
        p.   cm.
    ISBN 0-312-85152-9
    I. Title.
    PS3557.R265S63   1991
    813'.54—dc20   91-21770
                                                    CIP

First edition: November 1991
Printed in the United States of America
0 9 8 7 6 5 4 3 2 1

For the Little Bird.

With love.

The bright-eyed lad becomes a man,
The bonny lass a woman shines,
And leave behind both doll and dream.

It matters not that you grow old,
That ghoul and witch are night-told tales;
It matters not for anything.

Believe it then.

Believe it now.

It matters not what you believe.
What matters is what you forgot:

The sun will shine on loch and kirk,
But in the dark, child,
Someting stirs.

PART ONE

WHEN WE
WERE YOUNG

ONE

Nobody died until Eddie Roman screamed.

TWO

A mild night in November, though not so mild that the season
was forgotten. Dead leaves stirred in gutters at the touch of a
breeze, dead leaves on branches just waiting for a wind. The air
still damp after a sudden day-long rain. Puddles quivering.
Neon hissing. A small dog, muddy and white with a wire tail
and pointed snout, rooting in the garbage left in an alley behind
a closed Chinese restaurant. A large cat, bedraggled and white
with a puffed tail and flattened muzzle, tightroping the chain-
link fence around the Little League field. A car backfiring, and
several young voices in it laughing hysterically, a beer can
spinning into the gutter, rattling across the bars of a storm drain
before settling against the curb. A wheezing bus stalling at a
traffic light, the driver swearing, his four passengers saying
nothing, only staring out the windows at the shops long since
emptied. On a poncho behind the high school, in the middle of
the gridiron, a boy and a girl playing out a dare, though the girl
had less qualms about finally taking off her clothes.

A haze that blurred all the lights, even the stars, especially the
low and hazy hanging moon.

On a dark street a boy in a black leather jacket, collar turned
up, hands jammed into his black jeans pockets with thumbs
hanging out, walking slowly, turning around every ten yards or

so and looking back, into the dark, turning around and kicking morosely at the shadows. His boots, bulky and black, made too much noise, their pointed chrome studs catching too much of the diffused light when he glanced down at the pavement. His jeans were too thin, too cold when a breeze swung out of a driveway and slapped against his calves. And he should have listened to his mother's nagging, should have worn some kind of sweater; but no, not him, he was tough, he was cool, he knew he could stand it when the unseasonable warmth finally deserted the night, he could take the chill as the warmth bled from concrete and blacktop and wood and his bones, he didn't need any damn sweater. He was tough. He could take it.

He shivered.

He was a jerk.

He looked back again, this time only over his shoulder, and resigned himself to the fact that Laine wasn't going to be there. She wouldn't follow him. She wouldn't chase him. She wouldn't throw herself at his feet and beg his forgiveness. She wouldn't call out his name, from back there in the dark, and make him feel less like a total jackass. She was going to see this anger thing through, make him suffer.

He stopped at an intersection and looked east, toward Summit Boulevard, thinking maybe he should walk up there and catch a bus. Otherwise he'd have to walk all the way to the South End, another half hour at least, and probably freeze half to death before he got there. Plus which, he'd catch holy hell from his father for being out so late on a school night. Which would serve her right. Serve them all right. On the other hand, walking would give him time to cool off, think a little, and give *her* a long chance to change her mind and chase him.

Frustrated, he scratched angrily through his ducktailed black hair, sniffed hard, and turned down Lamb Street, heels forcefully loud, his whistle less a recognizable tune than a series of dares to the neighborhood to complain.

It made him feel better.

Not much, but better, and by the time he had gone three blocks more he had almost forgotten why he was being stupid enough to walk when all he had to do was drop a quarter in the damn collection box and let the bus driver take him practically to his door.

Almost.

"Idiot!" he whispered to his shadow. "Costello, you're a goddamn idiot."

He lashed out at a tree trunk, pulling his punch just in time.

She always did this to him, all the time, always made him feel one thing, then another, and left him hanging like a jerk, not knowing which way to turn. Eddie was right. Women, sometimes, just don't understand guys. They read some books, they listen to some teachers, they figure they got it all nailed. Especially guys. But they can't get into a guy's head, that's for damn sure. So they play games, brain games, and sometimes they're lucky and everybody's cool, and sometimes they just drive him up the goddamn wall.

Eddie was right.

Women aren't human.

Another street, a third, and the breeze kicked him again, blew hair into his eyes, made him hunch his shoulders.

He wasn't so sure about this part of town, wasn't sure he liked it so late at night. His own neighborhood was almost entirely rowhouses, old and faded, with one or two regular homes so narrow they looked like the rest. Here in the Manor, all the houses were settled behind fences, hedges, shrubs, trees, once in a while a low fieldstone or brick wall tangling with ivy. A place so neat it didn't seem real. Most of the windows were dark, cars in their garages or, on those rare blocks where the houses were too close together, settled at the curbs, reflecting the streetlights and giving back false color.

His street had a voice most nights of the year, guys hanging out, girls hanging with them, radios and televisions, couples screaming at each other, old people screaming back, cars racing, cats spitting and screaming. It had a life, he thought; this place is like a graveyard.

It's too quiet.

He paused for a moment, to listen to some birds arguing in an evergreen.

Quiet.

He looked behind him.

Nothing back there but the dark.

Maybe this wasn't such a good idea after all.

He came abreast of a tall barberry hedge, taller than he, and he did his best to ignore it, thinking instead about how he would give Laine tomorrow morning to make up her mind to catch up with him in school, to apologize, before he tried to find a date for Friday night. Maybe Tang Porter. A quick grin. Boy, would Laine be pissed. Worse; she'd raise hell, want to know what the hell he thought he was doing, going out with someone else, didn't he love her anymore?

He rubbed the back of his neck.

Well, he wasn't so sure about the love part, but he definitely didn't want to see anyone but her. Not regular. Teach her a lesson, was all. Like Eddie says, you gotta keep 'em in line, don't let 'em take you for granted. That's the way they used to do it, before all this sensitive crap started and women started acting more weird than ever.

What was funny, though, was that Eddie Roman didn't have a steady. Not since he had called at the beginning of the summer, said he had this humongously great idea out of which, within a week, the Pack had been born. Since then, the guy had been pretty much on his own. Oh, he dated now and then, always had a girl when the Pack went down to the movies on the boulevard Strip, or to the Starlite Diner just to hang. But there wasn't anyone special.

"Like to spread myself around, Joey," he explained once, before school started. "Keep one to myself, all the others tear my throat out, you know what I mean?"

"Jealous?"

"You got it."

"Bullshit."

Eddie had laughed, slapped and grabbed his shoulder. Hard. "Yeah. But what the hell, at least I don't have no stupid ring through my nose."

Joey didn't like that. Laine didn't have a ring through his nose, his ears, his balls, any damn place. He did what he wanted. It just happened that, most of the time, what he wanted happened to be what Laine wanted. No big deal.

A gust rattled the trees, and droplets spattered his head, his face. He danced into the open, slapping the water away, cursing until he found himself facing the hedge.

A rustle.

Quick; nothing more.

Not exactly a footstep.

More like a gliding.

Cat, he decided, and moved on.

Heard it following.

Rustle. Snap.

On the far side of a driveway, the hedge higher, not really trimmed, a twig snagging his jacket until he slapped it away.

Something on the other side, untouched by a streetlamp that created black caves between the tiny black leaves.

One of the Pack out to tease him.

Furtive. Quick.

Quiet.

It wasn't them. They never would have been able to stop from laughing for so long.

A breeze carried something light and wet to tickle his neck, and he yelped, spun wildly, spun again and ran a few stumbling steps, giggling when he finally passed the ragged end of the hedging, turning and laughing once he'd run another ten yards.

A cat.

It had been a cat.

He hadn't seen it, but he knew it.

It had only been a cat.

Now listen, Costello, he said to his shadow, hands back in his pockets, you're being a jerk-off here, man. You get into a little fight, you're letting a stupid damn cat spook you, for god's sake. You're a big boy now, right? Like Momma says, practically a man, and men don't let things like cats in hedges spook them.

Right?

He nodded sharply.

Right.

So get your ass home before your mother tears if off and hangs it in the hall.

Grinning, he walked, and yawned unexpectedly, laughed aloud when his jaw popped.

Quiet.

The creak of a branch.

A wink of light, low to the ground.

You're spooking yourself, pal.

Damn right.

He passed another hedgewall, trimmed low this time, and glanced at it warily.

Something was behind it.

No there wasn't.

"Damn."

The soft sound of a leaf pressed under a careful foot.

Yes there was.

When his pace quickened, boots too loud, he tried to slow down, telling himself that this was his town, damnit, it wasn't so damn big there wasn't anything in it he couldn't recognize, even in the damn dark.

The air stirred into a breeze he could barely feel against his cheek, but the top of the hedge shook for a moment as if someone, something, was trying to climb over.

He stared.

The shaking stopped.

Damnit, it's a cat.

Another leaf crushed.

Not it isn't.

Of course it is.

When the hedge was left behind, the noise stopped.

Nothing there.

Yes there is.

"Ha!" he said loudly.

Scare it away; make it vanish.

He didn't look back.

Instead, he moved faster, thinking it would be the weekend before he got home if he didn't haul ass, and his old man would ground him for the next hundred years just for grins. He grunted. Actually, not much chance of that, practically no way in hell. Grounding would mean he'd have to stay home, wouldn't be able to work at the old man's truck yard after school and on weekends, and his father depended too much on his free labor to do that. He didn't much care, not all the time, because it gave him the chance to work his magic. What Laine called his magic. Look at an engine, dare it to screw up, and when it did, take out his tools and do a surgeon job on it. No motor, no engine, not a goddamn thing that had moving parts died while Joseph Francis Costello was on duty.

Soon he'd be able to do it to his own motorcycle; as soon, that is, as Momma got over her thinking that only punks and ex-cons and drug dealers used them these days. Soon he'd have his own bike to work his magic on, turn it into a frigging rocket, take him out of this frigging place.

"Laine, don't say that, okay? It isn't magic."

"It is," she insisted. "Some people do magic with numbers, some do it with rabbits and hats, you do it with motors. I don't care what you say, it's magic."

Okay, he had conceded, so it's magic.

He bowed to the houses, to the street, turned around and bowed to the dark. When he straightened, he stopped, a slight frown nearly closing one eye.

He was on Eddie's block.

Now how the hell had he managed that?

A police siren cried, and was almost immediately followed by a fire engine's high and low wailing.

A quick crossing of his fingers—please, God, let it be the school—and he hurried on.

There was no temptation to stop at the Romans' and say hi. None at all. For one thing, he saw enough of Mr. Roman in school. Though he never had him for any history classes, Jon Roman seemed like he was everywhere—in the halls, in the cafeteria, out in the yard—just when Joey was about to do something the school didn't like. Like breathe, for god's sake.

For another, for the last couple of weeks, Eddie had been acting really strange. Bizarre. When he was with the Pack, he stayed in the background, not saying much, not laughing, not teasing Tang about all her hair or Pancho about his gut, not doing much of anything except standing there; and when they were alone, walking home from school, he acted like he was walking on a bed of exposed wires that someone every so often sent some juice through. He was jumpy, sweaty, and nothing Joey could say would coax an explanation. If it was dope, Joey might understand it, but Eddie, like the others, wasn't that far gone.

Dumb but not stupid, like his old man always said.

Okay, a little peculiar maybe, that's all. Just this side of a little bit weird. They had to be, though, right, dressing like they'd been warped back to the Fifties, listening to the Big Bopper and Little Richard, telling elephant and knock-knock jokes, Barnaby even going so far as to try to corner the market on anything and everything that had to do with James Dean. Katie spending all her allowance on what she called atom-bomb-bug movies and scaring herself shitless once a week and twice on Sundays. Laine letting Fern make her a poodle skirt even.

Peculiar.

But not that bad.

So what the hell was wrong with Eddie?

He didn't know, and it had begun to make him uncomfortable just to be near the guy. He looked, in fact, like that nut case on cable, on the old TV show, who was running away, every week for damn ever, from the cop who never, ever, stopped coming.

He looked like he was being chased.

He looked like he was haunted.

Oh Christ, Costello, knock it the hell off.

He decided to take the next corner, the hell with it, and go on to Summit, catch a bus. If, by some miserable miracle, Eddie was looking out a window or something, he didn't want to be spotted. Not tonight. Tonight was—

He froze when he heard the scream.

"Jesus!"

So high and shrill it was sexless.

He swallowed hard and looked around, hands opening and closing, opening and closing.

He didn't know how, but he knew it was Eddie.

Another scream that hung in the dark; it didn't fade, it had been cut off.

That one wasn't Eddie at all.

Immediately, Joey sprinted down the sidewalk, willing himself not to think, swerving at last into the Romans' driveway and slowing as he stared up at a lighted window on the second floor. Shades down. Curtain drawn. That was Eddie's father's room. He told himself he didn't belong here, that someone else must have heard it and was calling the cops right now. But he couldn't get rid of the scream, and, when he noticed other lights in other houses snapping on, he ran around the side of the house toward the back.

Someone screamed.

Fear and anger.

An unpainted stockade fence stretched from the side of the house to the neighbor's rose hedge. The gate was unlocked, and he shoved it open, ran a few steps, and in trying to stop, skidded on the wet grass to his hands and knees.

Sonofabitch, he thought, looked up, and didn't move.

The back door was open, kitchen light escaping over a concrete stoop and three concrete steps, falling on the lawn, turning the air and the grass grey.

Eddie stood in the middle of the glow, stringy black hair in glistening tangles over his face and shoulders, his black leather jacket torn at both shoulders. He had no pants on, no shoes, no shirt.

"I got him!" the boy declared hoarsely, panting, pointing at the open door.

His face was mottled with exertion.

He carried a hatchet in one hand.

"Got him, Joey. Oh man, I got him."

Joey almost threw up he was so scared, but he held up a hand instead, palm out. "Okay, Eddie, okay. It's cool man, it's cool."

Eddie stepped back, swung the hatchet lazily in front of him. The blade was dark, and dark dripped from the steel, the haft, and the hand that held it.

"Got him," Eddie whispered.

Joey moved to stand, and the boy glared at him, freezing him with one knee off the ground. Again he raised his hand. "Okay, Eddie, okay, take it easy. It's me, all right? It's Joey, man, don't do anything stupid."

The hatchet swung side to side.

Pendulum.

Catching the light, sliding into shadow.

"Eddie, where's your dad?"

Eddie sniffed, wiped a sleeve over his face. Something dark smeared over his lips and chin. "In there."

Side to side.

Joey looked at the door. He could see a corner of the table, part of the refrigerator, a length of the counter and the cabinets over it. "Where?"

Catching the light.

The boy sniffed again. "There."

Joey felt a cramp threaten his right leg; he shifted, and when Eddie scowled, he said, "Aw, c'mon, man, it's cold down here, okay? I'm not gonna hurt you, you know that. I ain't gonna do anything." He swallowed hard, his throat felt packed with sand. "Look, I'm standing up, right? You got the ax, what the hell you figure I'm going to do, pull a damn cannon?"

He stood.

Nothing moved in the doorway.

Beyond the light the back yard was black.

"Mr. Roman?" he called. "Hey, Mr. Roman, can you hear me?"

"Got him," Eddie whispered.

"What?"

"Not me." Eddie shook his head quickly, twice. "Not me." He pointed at the house with the hatchet. "I told him not to come in, see, but he wouldn't listen. Big man. Christ, I told him, but he did anyway." He pulled the weapon to his chest and hugged it. "I had to save myself."

"Sure, sure you did." Joey wanted to spit but his mouth was too dry. Wishing to hell someone would come and get him out of here. Now.

In the distance, a siren.

Eddie's head snapped up, and Joey braced himself.

Then Eddie said, "Son of a bitch, they'll all get killed, they're all gonna die," and ran into the house.

Oh man, Joey thought, rubbing his fingertips hard against his jeans; oh man, Jesus help me.

Indecision forced him to take a hesitant step toward the street, made him shift his weight from one foot to the other, made him take a deep breath and finally charge up the steps, bursting through the kitchen entrance just in time to see Eddie spin around the newel post and vanish up the hall staircase. He took a step, whirled, yanked open several drawers and clawed through them before he found a knife.

It wasn't much better, but he felt better.

He didn't bother to move cautiously because he could hear his friend up in the hall, running, slamming doors, yelling incoherently; he took the stairs to the midway landing two at a time, and crouched there, a hand trembling on the banister, looking up just as all the lights went out.

Damn, he thought.

Then Eddie screamed.

Screamed again.

Run! Joey thought; Jesus God, run!

He moved upward, knowing that he was too slow and feeling as if he were running too damn fast. Listening. Straining, but hearing nothing.

He licked his lips.

Scraping; something sharp digging into wood, or bone.

He reached the top step and eased himself up against the wall.

Laine's gonna kill me; Momma's gonna skin me.

His vision adjusted from dark to shadow and, still pressed against the wall, he switched the knife to his other hand, scrubbed his palm against his leg, and made his way along the carpeted hallway toward the room at the far end.

Eddie's.

The door was open.

He switched the knife again, nearly lost it, closed his eyes and held it close against his chest.

Okay, he thought; okay, there are two ways to do this, Joey: wait for the cops, or be a hero.

There was no sound in there. The scraping had stopped; he couldn't even hear his own breathing.

Sweat slipped into his eyes. He blinked furiously and tried to think. The light switch was just around the frame, shoulder high. No; no, it wasn't. Yes; yes, it was. He could reach in, then flip it up, turn on the Roy Rogers lamp Eddie kept on the dresser.

He raised his arm.

It was dark in there.

Reach in; flip it on; no sweat, no sweat.

He could smell something strong, too strong, and when he looked down, the light from Mr. Roman's room drifted across the floor and let him see over the threshold. Only a few inches, but it was enough to explode bile in his stomach.

Pressing harder against the wall, then, and breathing quick and shallow, almost panting; swallowing, choking, finally exploding with a soundless cry into a run, stumbling back down the stairs, tripping in the front hall and falling hard against the door, fumbling for the knob he couldn't get hold of because his hands were slick with sweat, his eyes were stinging, there were barbs in his chest that kept him from taking a breath that wouldn't stab him.

The door opened.

He ran outside, leapt off the small porch and fell onto the grass. Dropping the knife. Hands and knees. Throwing up and sobbing.

A hard hand grabbed his shoulder, someone giving him harsh orders while trying to yank him to his feet, but he couldn't stop his stomach from trying to climb into his throat and he kept falling back down. The hand was replaced by a gentler one, the voice softer, and he looked up, wiped his mouth with the back of his hand, and said, "Al? Oh Jesus, Al, Jesus God."

too much blood

he could hardly see anything because there was too much blood

• • •

Too much light; he couldn't see a thing because there was too much light, and it forced him to lower his head and stare at the kitchen table, wait for the light to fade so he could trace the erratic patterns in the worn Formica top until he had to close his eyes.

"Joseph, are you all right?"

For god's sake, no, Momma, he wanted to shout; I'm not all right Jesus Christ how the fuck do you think I am what kind of goddamn stupidass question is that?

"Okay," he whispered. And shrugged. And picked up the glass of water his mother had placed before him five minutes ago, drank, shuddered, he couldn't get rid of the sour taste, couldn't get rid of the smell.

The same hand rested on his shoulder, only this time it wasn't out there in the yard, people in overcoats over their bathrobes standing on their lawns, drifting to the sidewalks, the curbs, trying to see what was going on, lights flaring from cruisers and an ambulance and static that carried voices he couldn't understand. This time the hand telling him it was okay, take it easy, was right here in his own kitchen, and he looked gratefully at his brother, tilted his head slightly, quickly, and looked at the table again.

The glass was empty.

He didn't remember drinking.

Opposite him, his mother held a cup in her hands but didn't use it; to his right his father held a cup and sipped from it noisily. He looked at them all and almost smiled. Uniforms, he thought; god, they're all wearing uniforms, even in the middle of the stupid night.

His mother in her dark print dress covered the moment he walked into the house by a polka-dot apron loosely tied around her ample waist; his father in his rumpled plaid shirt opened midway down his chest, white T-shirt stained with grease and something else; and his brother in his cop suit, the hat squared on the table in front of him. No gunbelt here, though. Never a gunbelt. The first time he had walked into the house with it strapped around his waist and started for the kitchen, his mother, without raising her voice, screamed bloody murder.

"That . . . that thing," she had declared, for all she was proud of her oldest child, "does not go into my kitchen, Al. That's the family place, and that gun never goes in there while I'm alive."

On a wood peg specially placed in the hall by the front door, then. Murderers, thieves, terrorists, arsonists—guns were all right for them, but never in Momma's kitchen, not even if it was her son's.

"Joey," Al said, voice low. "Joey, are you sure?"

He shuddered air from his lungs—it seemed the only way to breathe anymore—and nodded.

"You sure?" his father asked hoarsely.

"Yes, Poppa," he said, tight with impatience. "I didn't see anything. Not straight out. It was pretty dark, remember?"

He hadn't.

Just glistening blood streaked like a worm's tail across the part of the bedroom carpet that he could see. Before he ran. Before he ran like hell, like a baby, and the whole goddamn neighborhood had seen him crying, blubbering in his brother's arms. A detective had talked to him, a guy called Jorgen, but he had been okay too. No yelling, not like the first guy. Just quiet questions until he told Al to take the kid home. With no blood on his clothes, no blood on the knife, Jorgen knew he was telling the truth. Which told him he was glad, thank you God, he hadn't seen anything more, hadn't seen how bad it really had been in that room.

He only knew that Eddie was dead. So was Mr. Roman. And no one had gotten out of that room past him.

"You did a brave thing, going in there, Joey," Al told him. "Not too bright, but brave."

"Brave?" his mother said. Coffee slopped from her cup; she wiped it up with her apron. "Brave?" Her eyes were puffed, bloodshot from crying. A curl of dark hair that wouldn't stay off her brow. "He could've been killed, Al! My baby could've been cut to pieces in there! Some maniac could've cut his heart out, maybe—"

"Ma, c'mon," Joey complained. He'd been listening to that song since his brother had brought him home. She was right, but god, she didn't have to keep at it. She was always keeping at it. Never let go.

"Alfred, tell him," she appealed to his father.

Brother was always Al, Poppa was always Alfred, he was Joseph when she decided he was in trouble, Joey when he was her baby.

"Anna, why don't you just let the boy alone. I think he's been through enough for one night."

"Poppa's right, Momma. It's done now. Okay? It's all over."

Joey agreed with a weary bowing of his head, and stared at his hands clasped on the table. They were clean. With all the work at the truck yard, they were a little scraped, a little bruised, but always clean. Even under the nails. Not like his father's. And sometimes he wondered if he was really part of this family. The three of them, and his sister too, married and moved away, they all had darker skin, all were stout while he was lean. The only thing they had in common were their tempers and their thick hair.

Laine liked his hair.

Oh god, he thought, how am I gonna tell her Eddie's dead and he probably killed his father?

too much blood
too much light

He lay on his bed, his mother at the door.

"You be all right?"

"Yes, Ma, I'll be okay."

"Al didn't mean to keep asking. It's his job. He's a cop. He's got to find out who did this terrible thing."

"I know, Ma, I know."

She was a shadow, the hall light behind her. "You shouldn't have gone in there." It wasn't a scold.

His hands lay still at his sides, trembling from the effort not to turn into fists. "You didn't see him, Momma. Before, I mean. He's my friend. He—"

"Okay," she said calmly. "You want the door open?"

He never left the door open while he slept. This was his room, his lair, only his mother came in without asking.

"Yeah. Sure. Just for a while, okay?" He smiled. "So you don't wake me later checking up on me."

He felt her smile without seeing it. "Sure." She started away, looked back. "You don't have to go to school tomorrow, Joey. It's okay if you don't."

And she was gone, dragging her shadow behind her.

He knew he should have called Laine and the others right away despite how late it had been when Al finally brought him home, but his father had made him drink some wine, strong wine, while his brother asked again the questions he couldn't begin to answer—*are you sure you didn't see anyone? did you see anything, anything at all? did you hear anything?*—until he suddenly realized he couldn't keep his eyes open, and he had started to yawn. His mother tried to get him to talk about what he wanted for Thanksgiving dinner next week. Al wanted to know if he could bring a date. His old man wanted to be sure they were having pumpkin pie. Joey had yawned again, so loudly his jaw popped, and his mother clapped her hands once, hustled Al out, made his father lock all the doors and windows, and took Joey upstairs, fussing without saying a thing.

In the morning, he decided; I'll call them in the morning.

Then he heard Eddie's scream.

He saw the blood on the carpet.

He looked at the ceiling and said, "Got who, Eddie?" before falling asleep without taking off his clothes.

THREE

Town Hall squatted in the center of the commercial district, set back from Summit Boulevard by a wide, paving-stone-and-oak-tree plaza marked with islands of redwood benches and tub-blooming flowers. The building itself was pale marble and arched iron-frame windows, built in the Thirties with steps too wide for its height, and ornate fluted columns flanking brass-framed entrance doors tall enough for a giant. There was no dome—the roof was flat—but the checkerboard lobby was called the Rotunda anyway, and in its center, in front of a staircase that fanned to the second floor, was a huge table upon which sat a glass-encased model titled *Foxriver Then And Now*.

A score of second-graders gathered around the display, shoving and poking as a guide in incongruous gaudy uniform explained what the children could see clearly for themselves— an oblong town on a low flat-topped hill whose slopes north and south were virtually nonexistent as they bled into neighboring communities, the western slope clearly steeper than the one facing east, and the river at the western base like twisted colored paper much more attractive than the real thing.

A park with a frozen-ripple pond, toy trees, toy ducks, toy people taking walks. Houses and blocks color-coded to depict the town's historical eras, the developments northwest and north gleaming white to accentuate the doubling, in less than half a century, of the town's expansion, though there was nothing to show that now, and forever, there was no place else to go.

Miniature pedestrians strolled the boulevard, miniature cars in the four lanes and parked at the curbs. Miniature buses. Miniature trucks.

Voices echoed softly.

Some of the children, bored with the droning lecture and not wanting to be here although it was marginally better than being in school, tried to find their own houses, whispering to their friends, tapping the glass, while the teacher tried to keep others from using the marble floor as an impromptu skating rink.

Scott Byrns knew how they felt. If you're going to miss school, you shouldn't have to have a lesson anyway. That wasn't fair. It should be a law. Otherwise, what was the point? No school was for sleeping late, forgetting about classes, and hanging out with friends. He stood by the entrance, beneath a large bronze plaque which listed the names of those who had served and died during the Second World War, and wished he weren't here. This place was too much like a funeral parlor— hushed, smelling funny, people moving around as though they were walking on eggs.

Eddie's dead.

He rubbed a hand over his eyes, rubbed the palm hard and fast over his cheek until he felt a burning.

Joey had called him just before he'd left the house, but Scott already knew about it. It had been on the radio while he had breakfast, it would probably be on TV tonight, and all through the local paper—but none of it made it real. Especially the part about Eddie being a killer. But then, Joey hadn't made much sense during the short conversation. Scott's mother had nearly freaked when she found out, freaked again when he told her he was going down to the police station to meet his friend.

"You're not," she said. "I don't mind you not going to school, dear, it's a terrible thing, but you are not going to the police station."

"Mom, for pete's sake, he didn't do anything."

"Of course not. Not Joey. Joey walks on water."

He glared at the floor instead of her, rolling his shoulders beneath his black jacket. It wasn't leather. Not even imitation. They couldn't afford the real thing until his mother graduated and got the job she wanted; but Eddie hadn't complained and so no one else had either.

"He's my friend," he said, careful not to let his voice get high.

"Scott, I didn't let you stay home just so you could wander around town. You don't even want to talk to me, so what good is it going to do seeing Joey if you don't even want your own mother?"

"Aw, c'mom, Mom, it's not that I don't want you," he said, this time looking at her, trying not to plead, trying to keep his voice steady. "Eddie's dead. He was my friend. Joey's, too. I just gotta see him."

He had walked out of the house without being stopped, hadn't looked back, hadn't said a word to anyone since or looked anyone in the eye.

The teacher clapped her hands.

Echoes, this time sharp.

The children thanked the guide in sweet unison, giggled when he clicked his heels and saluted them, and allowed themselves to be led up the stairs, the teacher sternly promising them a visit with the mayor if they were good.

Echoes fading.

The guide took off his cap and wiped his brow, walked away, vanishing into a room under the staircase.

Scott closed his eyes briefly, blew out a breath, blew out another, and pointedly did not look to his left, to the inside entrance to the police station—a pair of pebbled-glass doors used by those who didn't mind being seen. Six years ago, his father had gone in through those same doors and hadn't come out.

C'mon, Joey, he thought impatiently; come on, man, let's go.

A shadow behind the doors, profile distorted by the irregular contours of the panes.

He straightened quickly and lifted a hand when Joey stepped

into the Rotunda and yanked angrily at his suit jacket, yanked his knit tie away from his collar.

Wow, Scott thought.

"Hey," Joey said when he saw him.

Scott nodded, and they hurried outside, Joey three inches taller but not as broad across the shoulders, blinking once at the still-bright light, holding their breath against the damp chill. The plaza was empty, but the sidewalks and street were filled with traffic, some heading for the shops and offices here in town, most of the rest for the highway malls.

They paused on the top step, turned away from a clear-sky wind that wound around the pillars and slapped against their backs. When it was done, they faced the street again.

"I hate cops," Joey muttered, yanking at his tie again.

Scott figured the suit was his mother's idea, coming alone his father's. "So what'd you say?"

"What the hell could I say? I didn't see hardly anything." He grimaced. "A formality. Jesus. The first cop there threw up all over the damn place, and I'm a frigging formality."

"At least they don't think you did it."

Joey lifted a *who cares* shoulder and started down, Scott following a step behind. On the way across the plaza he heard it all, from the fight with Laine about her little brother, Dale, to the walk home, to the scream, and more. More than he wanted to hear, and he was guilty, and he was glad, that he hadn't been at the house. He snapped his collar up, fisted his hands in his pockets, watched the paving stones pass beneath his boots until they reached the sidewalk. Then he leaned back against the low retaining wall that raised the plaza above street level and waited until Joey lit a cigarette, blew smoke angrily at the sky, kicked at the wall.

"So now what?"

"I don't know."

"The cops say anything about a funeral, something like that?"

Joey shook his head. "But I gotta get out of these clothes, man. They're strangling me."

Scott smiled. One-sided. Something he'd picked up from a movie he'd seen. Unless you knew him, you couldn't tell if he

was being arrogant or not; he liked it that way. It was like
wearing a mask.

"You talk to Laine already?" he asked.

Joey blew smoke at him. "Yeah. She's stayed home too.
Gonna see her later."

"Good."

"Yeah."

He watched the traffic, watched the pedestrians, smiled at
those who glanced at him and Joey, standing there looking like
they were ready to rob a bank, mug an old lady, probably
figuring they were skipping classes or something and were just
waiting to be arrested. They hated that, the smiling nicely.
They didn't know what to do. Only the old ones smiled back.

"So," he said. "What about the others?"

"They already know."

"Oh." There was something different now, something not
right. "So, we gonna meet or what?"

"I don't know. How the hell should I know? I'll call you,
okay?"

"Sure, right."

Something . . .

Joey smoked.

Shock, Scott decided; nothing's different, it's just the shock of
hearing about one of your best friends. So what do they do
now? Stand here all day and freeze to death? Who would they
talk to? The guys, yeah, but who else? Not his mother, that's
for sure. She thought the Pack was an idiot idea in the first
place, kept calling him a sheep, making fun though she never
seriously tried to stop him. So who? There were no Romans
left. Nobody to call so he could say he was sorry, nobody to call
to find out about the viewing, the burying, the church, all that.
No one to tell him how he was supposed to feel.

Right now he felt empty.

Nothing inside.

No compulsion to cry, no desire to hit someone, no over-
whelming need for company or someone's shoulder.

Nothing.

Joey flicked the unfinished cigarette into the gutter and spat dryly, rubbed a sleeve under his nose. "Al said . . ." He cleared his throat, looked up and down the street.

Several pairs of brakes signaled a near-accident at the traffic light, and Scott realized how noisy it was downtown—all the cars, the buses, the trucks passing through, people talking, people calling, footsteps so loud you could hardly hear yourself think. Jeez, was it always this loud? If it was, why hadn't he heard it before?

"You listening to me, Byrns?"

Scott stared him, trying to focus on the shock of hair carefully furrowed down over Costello's forehead. He almost giggled. Eddie actually used a ton of hair grease to keep his wave and tail in place; Joey used his mother's unscented hairspray.

Used to use.

Eddie's dead.

"What the hell you looking at?"

He shook his head. His own hair was too fine, too light, to be worn that way. Long, yes, but not that way. And he'd be hanged first before he used hairspray just to force it the way the Pack thought it should be. Instead, it all just kind of lay there, falling naturally in long waves, drawing comments from the girls—*god, I wish mine looked like that*—and the guys—*oh, Scottie, I wish mine looked like that too*—and generally making his life miserable.

Joey shoved his shoulder, and held it. "Hey!"

"What?"

"You hear me?"

"Yeah," he said, pushing the hand away. "You were talking about your brother."

Joey looked at him as if he couldn't quite figure him out, then gestured in disgust. "Right. He said—I heard him talking to the old man before I left—he said that Jorgen told him—that's the detective I told you about—he said Jorgen said Eddie probably killed his father with that ax he had."

"Oh shit."

A shadow floated over the street, crawling over car roofs, crawling up and down the lampposts.

"Yeah, tell me about it. But he said they didn't know who killed Eddie."

Scott's eyes widened. "What? But on the phone you said something about killing himself." He stopped, swallowed hard. Suicide. "I mean, you said—"

"I know what I said, okay? I was wrong, so sue me." Joey hadn't noticed the hesitation; he blew into the wind, shaking his head. "But there wasn't anybody else there, Scottie." His voice was almost pleading. "I swear to God, there wasn't anybody else there but me and Eddie. All I can figure is, the guy that nailed him must've gotten out the window. Shit, I don't know." Before Scott could answer, could tell him that couldn't be, it was two stories up, the cops would've gotten him if he'd jumped, Joey grabbed his arm and pulled. "C'mon, walk me a little, all right? I just gotta get these clothes off before they kill me."

Scott knew, then, where he had to be.

"As far as the park, okay?"

"Sure. I don't care."

It was a long walk, and before they'd gone two blocks, Scott began to get annoyed that no one paid them any attention. Their best friend had just died, had just been *killed,* and no one seemed to care. They read it in the papers, and they went shopping anyway.

He felt something surge then.

He didn't like it.

And he didn't talk at all as they threaded in and out of pedestrian traffic, heads down, every so often shaking their heads as if they both knew they were walking through a nightmare that would end before Joey got out of his suit, and he got into the park. They both knew it, and when they reached the stone wall that surrounded it, overhung with barren tree branches and branches of shrubs long since without blossoms, they dragged their hands along it, feeling the cold, the ridges, the bits of dried mortar that pattered to the ground. At the entrance, nothing more than a wide gap flanked by unadorned pillars, Joey rubbed a hand under his nose.

"Don't do nothing until I call."

"Sure. No problem."

"You gonna be able to get out tonight?"

Scott resented the question, resented the implication. "Don't worry about it."

Joey nodded. "Right." He looked into the park and walked away, quickly gone, not looking back.

Scott turned quickly as well and followed the blacktop path that led toward the park's center. His breathing eased, the November scent of damp earth and dying trees, needles on the ground, brittle leaves in his way, made him feel better. His place, this was, and had been since the day his father had left. Foxriver Park, not quite one hundred acres of grass and trees, a small ballfield, shrub-lined tarmac paths that were seldom straight for more than twenty yards, and in the middle, at the heart of a slight depression, a large irregular pond where fathers sailed their kids' boats, and the kids threw bread balls at the fat ducks living there. From each prime compass direction the main paths left the surrounding trees and dropped gently to join another, this of inlaid brick, that followed the pond's slightly irregular bank, redwood benches and wire trash bins under chestnuts and willows on the easy slope, a few lingering office workers, and some kids playing soccer with a partially deflated basketball.

His place; where he could daydream, think, plan, without some teacher butting in, without his mother feeling his brow for a fever. The Pack knew it. When one of them found him here, they would leave him alone until he smiled that smile, or said something; they knew him; they were patient.

He found an empty bench at the north end and stared at the water, felt the chill, ignored a fly that buzzed his chin.

Okay, he thought, so now what, Byrns?

His left heel tapped the ground rapidly. His mother called it his cat's tail, always moving when he was tense and needed to do something and didn't know what it was. He allowed himself a quick grin. There were times when she wasn't all that bad, not really. He knew in his head she was doing the best she could, what with school and the house and his medical expenses and all. Yet there were times—god, were there times—when he wanted to scream at her, slap her, tell her he was sick and tired of hearing about when she was a kid too because the world out there wasn't the same anymore.

Like now—Eddie's dead. Killed his father and . . . what? Was murdered too? But how could that be? Joey said . . . Joey said . . . how could that be?

This is going to be one miserable Thanksgiving.

His right eye burned, and he pressed the heel of his hand to it, pushed it until he gasped at an unexpected sharp pain that filled the park with pinwheels. Dumb, he scolded himself; dumb. But he knew he was supposed to cry. God, isn't that what people did when their best friends died? Cry? Scream or something? Throw things around? So why couldn't he cry? Why couldn't he feel *something*?

"You're different," his mother told him. Forever. "You're not like those other kids."

She meant Joey and Laine and Tang and Pancho and Katie and Barnaby and Fern. And Eddie. Especially Eddie.

"You're going to get hurt, Scott. I just don't want you to get hurt."

She meant that, because most of his left leg wasn't real, he couldn't be normal; she meant that he couldn't, shouldn't, take chances. Risk was forbidden. Impulse had to be chained. He should stay home instead. Study hard. Graduate in eighteen months, get a scholarship, and go on to college, preferably close to home. Where she could watch him.

Absently he rubbed his thigh just above the place where the prosthetic fixed to his knee.

He waited for the tears.

On the other side of the circular path, where the grassy bank held a steeper angle down to the water, two women in floppy sunhats, loose cardigans, and stained garden pants knelt with a shopping bag between them. From it they pulled rolls and slices of bread to feed over a dozen ducks with caps sparkling like polished emeralds and who hadn't left yet for the winter, and two plump and vocal geese who seemed determined to snap off the women's fingers.

He'd seen the ladies before, lots of times. He had a feeling this was what they did all day, this was the way they made the time pass. They weren't like the others, though, the ones who lived on the streets. These people looked like they had a house to go home to; the others—like the little black guy who called himself Blade, and the artist, and the pretty woman who called herself a queen—they had a look about them. A mask like his smile. Eddie didn't like them; for some reason, though, they always talked to Scott.

"Hey!" one of the women complained when the gander suddenly spread its huge wings and frightened the ducks into noisy flight. "You mind your manners, you pillow bastard."

"Mazie!" the second scolded.

"Well, he's a pig, Erma," Mazie said, looked up at Scott and said, "You, boy, ain't he a pig?"

Startled, surprised they even knew he was there, he grinned and nodded.

A small cloud took away a corner of the sun, darkening the water, shade and weeds spreading across the shallows like dried blood. The illusion vanished when the cloud did, a scant second later, but it was enough to sit him up.

That feeling again—everything looked so normal that something couldn't be right. Dumb. Truly dumb. He bunched his hands in his pockets.

The gander honked his impatience at being served.

Mazie deftly shredded a roll and tossed him all the pieces.

The second goose was chased away.

Erma fed it with bread and a low gentle whistle that kept it from fleeing again.

Scott watched their hands as they worked, liver-spotted, long fingers; he watched their arms, whips when they threw the food; he heard something behind him and looked quickly, too quickly, and his neck muscles nearly cramped. The dense shrubbery—laurel, evergreen, something with thorns that had more than once snagged his hands—that blocked the main path quivered, a leaf fell, the sound of a small dog snuffling and searching and someone calling for it angrily, jingling a metal leash.

Another cloud, much larger, and the water turned to dull slate.

A short man in a well-worn cardigan stepped carefully off the path and stood above the women, leaning on a stained bamboo cane. His scalp where it showed through a few strands of grey was mottled and peeling.

The geese fled.

"Well, damn, Calvin, you scared them." Mazie pushed herself wheezing to her feet, and Scott noted her age in the jowls, the deep lines around her eyes, in the way her left hand shook as she reached for the bag. "You always do that. You always scare them away, you old fool."

"Hate 'em," the man grumbled. Licked his lips. Spat toward the water. "Nasty birds. Kill one, we'll have it for dinner next week. I don't want any dark meat, though. I hate dark meat. Stringy. Like Erma."

"That's turkey, you stupid old fart. You have a goose for Christmas, don't you know anything?"

"Turkey, goose, who cares, I hate 'em all."

Erma—Scott decided she could be Mazie's twin except that she was so thin—swept her lap clear of crumbs and held on to her hat as she stood. Easily. Gracefully. Without a word she took the man's elbow and guided him unprotesting back onto the path. Then she smiled at Scott. The man squinted at him, his lower lip trembling, his free hand swiping lightly at his chest as if he too had crumbs to scatter, until Mazie, from his other side, fumbled in his shirt pocket, pulled out a pair of glasses, and set them none-too-gently on his nose. A moment later, he reared back and frowned.

Triplets, Scott thought; man, they could be triplets.

"Hey, I know you," Calvin said, pointing shakily with the cane. "You work in the market, down the boulevard, yes?" His lips moved soundlessly, testing words; then: "Relbeth. Tom Relbeth's place, right?"

Scott was surprised. "That's right."

"Oh," exclaimed Erma. "That store next to the newspaper place, the one with all the dirty magazines!"

He grinned and nodded.

Another cloud merged with the second before the sun could escape.

"You're the kid, I know I know, hang on a minute, you're the kid whose father took all that money from the bank, am I right? Couple years back, eight, maybe ten?" The man flapped his cane, demanding an answer.

The grin became a strained smile.

A breeze rippled the pond.

"Knew it was you. Tom told me." He closed one eye. "Killed himself, right? In jail, right?"

Mazie reached for his arm; Calvin shook it away.

"So they trust you at the market, huh, boy? That Communist Relbeth trusts you, dressed like that? They don't figure you'll steal from—"

"Supper," said Mazie sharply, tugging Calvin free, pulling him down the walk. "We got to make supper." Her goodbye smile was quick, almost a grimace.

"Damnit, I'm not hungry," the old man complained loudly. "I got gas."

Mazie laughed and hugged his shoulders. "Honey, you haven't had gas in forty years, not with my cooking."

"Hell I haven't."

She laughed again and slapped at his leg with the bag.

Erma watched them, took a step up the slope as she fussed shyly with her blouse's collar. "Don't mind him," she apologized quietly, sincerely, looking at him sideways. "He still thinks boys your age should be wearing short pants." A look away, a glance back. "I knew your father a little, you know. I talked to him at the bank all the time."

He didn't know what to do; he nodded.

"The nicest one there," she told him, still quiet, as if she were afraid the others would hear. "You wouldn't remember, but I was at the funeral!"

Oh god, lady, go away, he begged silently; please go away.

A shy smile then, and he knew she wasn't trying to be mean.

"I went to another bank, you know. The rest of them weren't nearly as nice."

He couldn't help it—he smiled.

The wind came up; she clutched her hat and turned away.

"Nice talking to you," he said quickly, not knowing why he did.

"Thank you," she answered. "We'll meet again, I'm sure."

The pond rose; the geese flapped to the opposite shore.

Sure, he thought, until you find out that besides my dad being a crook, my best friend happens to be a murderer. Still, he decided that she, unlike the gander, was a nice old bird, maybe they would meet again.

What the heck, maybe not.

Several yards farther on, she looked over her shoulder and waved, took Calvin's other arm and, with Mazie, turned onto the walk that led up the slope.

He watched as they moved—deliberately but not stumbling, definitely not feeble, until a darker cloud dropped twilight over the park, over the water, and they slipped into shadow and were gone.

He shivered, rubbing his arms as he realized how chilly he was. A check of the sky told him there would probably be rain before he got home, maybe even some now, and he cursed himself for not paying more attention to the weather. With his luck he'd be drenched by the time he reached the house, and his mother would strap him to his bed until she was sure he wouldn't catch pneumonia.

"Look," Katie had told him once, "she's just scared, that's all. Makes her a little weird about you, you know what I mean?"

He wasn't sure. He thought so. But he wasn't quite sure what his mother was supposed to be afraid of. How could she be afraid anyway? They'd been alone for over eight years now, and she worked all day, went to school at night, this June was going to get her law degree and make them both richer than God. How could a woman like that be scared?

Sometimes Katie and her atom-bomb-bug movies didn't make any sense at all.

The wind; whitecaps flashed on the pond.

Getting too cold to sit here, but he didn't know where else to
go. There was always the bookstore, listen to Mr. Tobin's
horrible jokes and watch Miss Bingham's chest bounce under
her sweater; he could grab a soda at the diner; he could always
go home; he could even go to the school, hang out in the yard,
hear what the kids had to say. He rubbed his leg again, a prick
of cautionary pain telling him he'd already walked too far too
quickly for one afternoon, and decided just to walk anyway.
Take his time. Sooner or later he'd get someplace, it didn't
matter where. As long as he ended up at the house in time to
catch Joey's call.

An unnecessary groan followed him as he stood, stretched
extravagantly, let the wind push him up the slope, into the
sudden dark the path had become. Overhead branches snapped
at him. Leaves were torn away and flung scratching at his face.
First it's like July; now it's like March. Why doesn't the weather
make up its stupid mind? He swore at it all the way to the park
entrance, then began to move northward when a drop of rain
struck his cheek.

Terrific, he thought; terrific.

Traffic was heavy on the boulevard, headlamps on, a few
wipers already working.

With none of the downtown buildings more than six stories
tall, their facades grey- and brownstone, some of the newer
ones in aged brick, the clouds seemed much lower, heavier,
moving more swiftly. His shoulders hunched as, not waiting
for the traffic light to go his way, he darted across the boulevard
and paused beneath an awning snapping its fringe and billow-
ing, its metal ribs creaking softly as a gust became the wind.

His left hand reached down to rub his leg absently.

A sudden downpour startled him, straightened him, as it
exploded off the sidewalk, pummeled parked cars, and rushed
along the gutters like an arroyo's raging flash flood. Mist rose
and was shredded. Under awnings up and down the street he
saw others trapped and waiting, none with an umbrella, all of
them huddled, all of them blurred as the rain came down even
harder, splashing onto his shoes and jeans although he was
pressed against the plate glass window. He thought about going

inside where it ought to at least be warmer, but the door was locked, no lights on, and the bookstore was too far, he'd drown before he reached it and his mother would definitely kill him then.

The rain, and steam rising off the street.

He sighed, and glanced behind him. In the window, a mannequin sat on a lawn chair, wearing bright colors and holding a martini glass as she oversaw her partner on the side, also brightly dressed and brandishing a tennis racquet over his head. They looked bored to death.

But at least you're dry, he told them silently.

Then the wind stopped.

And there was nothing but the rain.

Harder still, nearly solid.

His teeth chattered. He hugged himself and stamped his feet, winced, and stamped again.

Someone honked a horn.

The traffic wasn't moving.

On the other side of the street, neon smeared, was unreadable.

A man in a short raincoat trudged resolutely past, hatless, his speed no more than a stroll, his resigned expression suggesting he'd already given up running.

Harder still, and the awning's thunder sparked the beginning of a headache.

It can't last, he told himself; god, there isn't this much water in the whole world.

He eased to the right and looked across the mouth of a narrow gap between the buildings. The next store along was a luncheonette, and from the blurry light that greyed the rain, it appeared to be open. He sniffed. Wiped his nose.

"What do you think?" he asked the couple in the window.

Laughter directed his attention to the luncheonette's entrance, where two women stood beneath a rainbow umbrella. From their gestures they were trying to decide which direction to run, finally nudged each other and took off, away from him, toward the far corner.

The wind picked up again.

Spray tickled his face.

"Okay, guys," he told the display window couple. "Take it cool. I'll see you around."

The woman stared at him.

The man's hands were in his pockets; he only stared at the rain.

Scott braced himself, feeling as though he were about to plunge into a pool he knew would be freezing. In for a penny, he decided, and ran, gasping at the weights that dropped on his head and shoulders, clenching his teeth against the cold that sluiced down his neck and back.

The glass door was steamed over, ghosts and light inside, and he had his hand on the push bar when suddenly he froze. Looked to his right and tried to blink away the rain.

Staring at him?

How could she be staring at him?

The door was yanked from his hand and a voice said, "You taking a shower, kid, I'll give you some soap. Otherwise, would you mind moving aside?"

He didn't know what he said, some inane response to the sarcasm, and hurried back to the other store. Looked in the window. The woman was in her chair, holding her glass, watching her husband, whose racquet was still held high as he sighted on an invisible ball.

Scott sneezed.

He stared.

The mannequins didn't move.

FOUR

They laughed in the Starlite Diner that night, when Scott told them what had happened during the storm. No big deal. He didn't mind. As a matter of fact, he was glad. It was the first time since he'd walked in that they had stopped staring glumly out the windows, the first time they had shown a little life except to give the waitress a hard time—something they had never done when Eddie was alive.

"I mean, it really spooked the heck outta me, y'know?"

"Heck," said Barnaby Garing solemnly.

"Heck," Pancho Duncan echoed.

They sat opposite him in the booth, the self-proclaimed Dynamic Duo of Foxriver's high school football team. Star running backs of whom great things, magnificent things, miracles were expected next season, not to exclude the division state championship. Save for the hair and the jackets, they were clearly football players. And they were clearly amused.

"Heck," Barnaby said again, turned to Pancho and shook his head slowly. "Did you hear that, Supreme Halfback of the Universe? Heck."

"Disgusting, O Mighty Fullback of the Cosmos," Pancho agreed. "Man's practically a man, he can't even swear right.

Disgusting. His old lady ever heard this, she'd throw him in the slammer without a trial."

Despite his best efforts to prevent it, Scott felt a blush seditiously gathering somewhere around the base of his neck. If they didn't cut it out, it would soon enough merge into two glowing spots on his cheeks, at which point the guys would become unmerciful. Which would brighten the spots. Which would set them off again. And they knew it.

Pancho tried to look stern. "I think—"

"Hey, leave it, Duncan, all right?" Joey said. He sat on the aisle, hunched over a plate of french fries.

Barnaby ignored him, rose as far as the table would permit and called to the next booth, "Hey, Fern, you gotta do something here, Scottie's swearing again!"

There was no reaction from the girls.

"I said leave it," Joey snapped, looking up angrily without raising his head.

Barnaby sat, round face trying to decide what expression to wear, at last choosing his usual *sure why not* grin before picking up his hamburger, examining it, finally sighing and dropping it back onto the plate.

When no one said anything more, Scott turned to the window at his shoulder and watched the street, the sidewalk, wishing he were someplace else. This wasn't working. This was nuts. They were supposed to be talking about what had happened, about Eddie, about what they should do now; but all they did was pick at their food and bite each other's heads off.

Maybe they shouldn't have come here at all.

He watched a bus drift past, empty, the driver little more than a hunched fluorescent shadow.

At least, he thought glumly, there's some life out there, sort of.

The Starlite was on the corner of Summit Boulevard and Midhill Avenue, at just about the geographical center of town. Midhill began at the foot of Bank Road, on the river, and climbed to the boulevard where it faced the park entrance. It resumed on the park's eastern side and dropped, again, to the boundary of the next town. The diner, though occasionally refurbished, occasionally changing owners, had been on its corner for nearly four decades. Brushed aluminum on the outside, window booths and squared horseshoe counter on the inside, jukeboxes in the booths, ceiling fans, leather-topped stools, a recently added small dining room in back. Six-page menus in plastic. Tonight, cardboard turkeys and Pilgrims taped to the walls, paper pumpkins taped over the inside entrance. The owner, Nick Karacos, didn't mind the Pack taking up the space because they seldom bothered the other customers, spent a lot of money, and Eddie had talked the black-bearded man into bringing back malts and king-size banana splits which, despite Karacos's initial doubts, had grown into one of the diner's prime attractions. The counter had essentially reverted to an old-fashioned soda fountain.

Scott had once called it their clubhouse, and to his amazement the Pack had made it official.

Tonight, the clubhouse was more like a funeral parlor.

The girls, by custom in the next booth, were trying not to cry and doing a bad job of it, and the rest were sullen; Katie Ealton hadn't even shown up, no one had answered when Pancho had called from the pay phone in the men's room. It was, Scott supposed, almost as if they believed Eddie had left them on purpose. They didn't know what to say, they didn't know what to do, but however lousy it was, it was better, they had initially agreed, than staying home and listening to their parents tell them how sorry they were, how they knew how the kids felt, that they should do something, anything, to take the horrible affair off their minds.

"The cops came around to my place this morning," Pancho announced, fingering his upper lip out of habit. Last September the new principal had ordered him to shave off the mustache he'd been trying to grow. Pancho had done it in order to look older; all it had done, Scott believed, was make him look seedy.

"Me, too," Garing said. "Asking all kinds of stupidass questions about Eddie and his old man, drugs, hot cars, shit like that." He picked up his hamburger again and took a bite. "I told them they were nuts." He wiped his mouth with a fist. "You know they actually asked me where I was last night? Like I did it or something. Jesus."

"Yeah," Pancho agreed sourly. Lean to Barnaby's round, when he sat up he was taller than all of them by half a head. But he always sat hunched over, a terrified gambler hiding his cards, and a growing paunch Eddie had ragged him unmercifully about. "It ain't right."

"Well, somebody did it," Scott said without thinking.

They stared at him, almost shocked; quickly he looked away, back to the street and the tops of the heads of the pedestrians passing by along the Strip, which began with the Starlite—a half dozen blocks of restaurants, a pair of supper clubs, bars, shops, luncheonettes, and two duplex movie theaters, bright until well after midnight while the rest of the boulevard pulled away in streetlamp shadow. Someone looked up at him, folded newspaper in hand, but all he could see was a transparent reflection of his own face. It stared at him. He hated it. He looked like a girl. His hair was bad enough. He didn't have bristles like Pancho or sun-lines like Barnaby or even a distinctive complexion like Joey. They were flavors; he was vanilla. They were sports heroes and genius mechanics and sometime-rowdies; he was the one who knew the answers in chemistry. They were vulgar and braggarts; the only time he swore was inside his head, and even then not all that often. He never did understand why he had linked up with them, or why, in fact, he had been allowed to stay. There had been other members in the beginning when word got around, others who finally declared the whole idea stupid and broke away. Eddie hadn't tried to stop them. None of them had. They left, others came and stayed.

The Pack was always the Pack.

Then Pancho whispered, "Oh shit."

Their booth was in the front righthand corner so at least two of them could keep an eye on the entrance to check out who came in, who left, without having to turn around.

This time they did.

Joey moaned softly.

A tall man in an expensive dark suit and obviously cashmere

topcoat stood by the cashier's desk, leaning on the register and talking to a waitress. One finger stroked an enormous handle-bar mustache, too large for his mouth, though he somehow managed to get away with parting his thick hair in the middle.

Scott frowned when he saw the others studiously examining what food was left on their plates, but he didn't dare turn again. "What?" he said, keeping his voice low.

"Jorgen," Barnaby told him around a french fry. "Cop. Detective type."

Scott looked at Joey; Joey didn't look up. Jorgen. He almost laughed. "You kidding me? He looks like a stockbroker or something."

"He's rich," Pancho told him. "Lives in the Heights, almost right next to Tang. Word is, his folks left him a ton of money, he doesn't have to cop if he doesn't want to."

Scott shifted until he was pressed against the narrow sill, tried a casual glance toward the front, and looked away hastily when the cop met his gaze. And grinned. "He's looking."

"No kidding," said Pancho. "Bastard."

"Ignore him," Joey ordered. "He can't do anything, he's just trying to spook us."

Duncan, evidently stricken with inspiration, clapped and rubbed his hands, and launched into a spirited description of what he and Barnaby were going to do to Port Richmond during the Thanksgiving game Thursday morning. He predicted four touchdowns each. Barnaby told him not to be so greedy. Pancho declared it wasn't greed, just pure skill.

And for a moment it sounded as if they were back to normal, back to the way it used to be.

Until Barnaby said, "He's gone, dork," and Pancho instantly fell silent.

The diner filled the gap: cups rattling, forks and knives scraping, people talking not quite loud enough to be understood, not quite low enough to ignore, the girls inexplicably giggling, someone at the far end calling out for a waitress before he starved to death. A song on the jukebox, the booth's speaker too woven through with static for any of the words to be understood.

"Who?" Joey said. Quietly. To the table. "Who would do a thing like that?"

Scott knew he wasn't talking about Eddie just then; he was talking about a kid. Any kid. A high school junior. Hacked. It made him nervous. His left heel began to tap. He nudged Joey with an elbow. "Move."

Joey scowled at him.

"Move. I gotta go."

Pancho frowned. "Hey, it's not even nine yet."

"Leg," was all he said.

With a moan Joey slid out and back without a word when Scott moved into the aisle. As he buttoned his jacket, looked at them, looked at the girls, he had a feeling that somehow the Pack had died too. Or, at the least, was seriously ill. And the worst thing was, none of them seemed to know it yet.

The idea intimidated him, unnerved him. He turned sharply to leave before he blurted something he'd regret, and collided with Fern Bellard returning from the ladies' room. A second's embarrassed confusion, self-conscious grins, a muttered promise to see her at school tomorrow, and he hurried to the door, pushed into the glass-walled vestibule and waited a few moments before pushing outside and down the five brick steps to the pavement. The cold made him realize how overly warm the Starlite was, the shadows out here how bright it was inside.

He looked for the detective, didn't see him, and wondered how they could even begin to think one of Eddie's friends had done it. It didn't make sense.

"Scott!"

Eddie killed his father.

"Hey, Scottie!"

Somebody killed Eddie.

"Hey!"

That didn't make sense either; nothing did.

A hand on his arm, and he gasped, yanked it away, and promptly called himself thirty kinds of a jackass when Fern gave him a look between hurt and angry.

"Sorry. Thinking."

"Walk me home?"

He looked back. The others were outside too, hands in pockets, drifting away without moving.

"Sure."

She took his arm and they went on, not speaking, glancing now and then into a shop window, at the posters under the theater marquees—both of which extended, old-fashioned and garish, out to their curbs—moving quickly without hurrying until the Strip was left behind, replaced by businesses somewhat less elegant than those on the Strip's north side—clothing stores forever going out of business, a pawnshop, a storefront mission, a magazine store with an X-rated window, a handful of jewelry stores that featured rhinestones in their displays—all with apartments on the second and third floors. They in turn became duplexes with barely two feet between them, yards too tiny for trees but not too tiny for roses and stubborn grass and not quite sagging chain-link fences. Old houses and well-kept; if not freshly painted, then at least not falling down. A few shops on the other side of the street, including the market where Scott worked most afternoons, most weekends. The lights were still on; Relbeth stayed open late to catch the moviegoers who needed milk for breakfast, coffee, the little things they thought of when they left the house for the show.

"Did the cops talk to you?" she asked at last.

He shook his head. "Not yet."

"You see Jorgen come in?"

"Yeah."

"He's the one that came to my house. Nice guy."

"If he's so nice, why'd he follow us to the diner?"

A short man in an oversize threadbare topcoat looked up from a wire trashbin he was searching. Scott nodded to him as they passed, and the little man nodded back, whistled something, lifted his chin.

"How you doing, Leg?"

Scott paused, half-turned, and waggled a hand back and forth. "Could be better."

"I heard. It's a bitch."

"Yeah, tell me about it."

The man squinted against a gust. "I hear something, I'll let you know."

"Thanks. I appreciate it."

"No cops, though. Ain't talking to the cops."

Scott's expression told him not to worry.

The man smoothed a wool cap he wore close over his ears, peered at Fern, nodded politely, and returned to his foraging without a word.

"Friend of yours?" Fern asked in a low voice as they moved on.

"Not really. He comes around the store at closing a couple of times a week." Scott checked over his shoulder to make sure he couldn't be overheard, but the little man was already on his way across the street. "Him and a couple of others. They get the stuff Mr. Relbeth tosses out."

Fern made a face. "God, what a way to live."

He smiled. "His name is Blade."

"What?"

A quick laugh. "That's what he told me."

"Scott, you know the damnedest people, you know that?"

He lifted his free hand—*what can I say?*—knowing this would haunt him just like the time he'd brought them over to Mrs. Ferguson's toward the end of the summer. She was an old woman, probably older than God, who sat on a moth-eaten tartan blanket in the park on weekends and told fairy stories and folk tales to the little kids, or anyone who would listen. She lived a block down from Scott and his mother, and had once invited him over for tea. On a whim he had taken her up on it. The Pack had spent the whole afternoon, raining and filled with thunder, listening to tales of goblins and wee folk and monsters in lochs and beautiful fey women who lured lonely hunters to their deaths in the dead of winter.

Scott thought it was great, Eddie fell in love with her and was calling her "Gramma" by the time they had left, while the rest had voted unanimously that she was totally, absolutely, without fear of redemption out of her mind.

As far as Scott knew, none had ever gone back.

"You're like a magnet, y'know?" Fern said lightly. "A magnet for the weird."

When he looked at her, she crossed her eyes and stuck out her tongue.

As soon as they turned off the boulevard, the air changed, the smell and heft of it, age in charge here and food smells even at night with the windows closed and locked, cars parked along the curbs quite different from those up in the Manor, the neighborhood where most of the rest of the Pack lived. That place was obviously solidly middle-class, and a kind of buffer between the working-class South End and the money in Briarwood Heights, where Tang and Barnaby lived. Scott liked it here. It was like the chair in the living room, the one he used to read and watch TV in—it fit, it was comfortable.

It was, tonight, safe.

"Those dummies really got you, huh?"

He bridled, ordered himself to relax, she didn't mean anything by it, and finally smiled sheepishly. "Yeah." He glanced at the flame of her hair fluffed and curled, the freckles across her face, and stared intently into the distance. "They're weird, y'know? They look like something trying to pass for human."

She hugged his arm tightly, briefly, before laughing. "Bugs," she said.

"Huh?"

"Bugs. Big bugs. Beetles, actually. Actually, things that look like beetles that got all mixed up at birth."

He was lost. He squinted. "What?"

"Dummies spook you, big beetles spook me, the ones that have parts from all the other ones." A laugh. "Not for real, of course. I can kill a spider with my bare hands, stomp on zillions of centipedes with my bare feet, but a big beetle, one of those ugly black things, they made my skin crawl. I wouldn't touch one with a tank. Every time I look at one, I think of the other ones, the not-real ones and—"

She hugged his arm again.

He held his breath until she relaxed. "That's called a phobia, ma'am."

"Nope. Kid dream."

He waited.

"You know—critters under the bed, stuff like that. Kid dream. You grow out of it, you laugh about it when you get old and fat."

"You had dreams about bugs?"

"Laugh and you're history, Byrns."

He swallowed the laugh tickling the inside of his mouth.

"I saw that," she accused.

"I didn't do anything."

"Just in time, too," she said, and stopped suddenly.

"What?".

She jerked her thumb. "My house."

"Oh."

When her arm left his, he quickly stuffed his hand into his pocket, took a step down the street and nodded her a goodnight. She tilted her head just a little, smiled just a little, and waved before pushing open the iron gate that led to a stoop, to a rowhouse like all the others on this block, differentiated only by the trim, the postage-stamp gardens, the colors of the front doors.

"School," she called after him.

He turned around and waved, turned back and hadn't gone five steps before he wondered why she had picked him to walk home with. She never had before. She always went home alone. Always. He frowned over it, kicked a piece of blacktop while he considered it, reached home and decided it didn't matter why. It felt nice. Maybe, if he was lucky, she'd do it again.

"Let's not walk, okay?" Barnaby said. He looked down Midhill toward the river. "Let's take the bus. My treat."

"Big spender, Garing," Tang said, but he noticed that she beat him to the bus stop across the street, and was the first on when one finally stopped. He didn't blame her. He didn't much care for standing around with the park at his back. It was too big. Too damn dark. Funny how he'd never noticed it before. Funny too how he'd never noticed how pale people were, riding the bus at night. They looked like corpses on a trip from the undertakers to someplace only the dead knew about. It stank too, of fuel and smoke and spit and shit-all knew what else.

But Tang wanted to ride, and what the hell, it wouldn't kill him, right? Right. So what the hell. It wasn't like she was a dog or anything, that he'd have to think up some excuse why he was riding with her in case anybody saw him. She wasn't even dim, for that matter. Lots of people figured she was an airhead because she was so good-looking, and a long-haired blonde, but she was probably up near the top of the class, Ivy League material, shit like that. More like Byrns than like him.

They sat in the back on the benchseat.

"You meditating?" she asked once the bus left its stop.

"Nope."

"Running the tape of your glorious highlights on the field? A very short tape, I might add."

He sneered at her.

She shrugged.

"They're gonna think one of us did it," he said suddenly, but the horn blared at the same time, and when she seemed puzzled, he had to repeat it, not believing he'd actually said it aloud. But once it was out, he was positive that was the cause of his chest having been so tight all damn afternoon, of having the acid feeling he was going to heave every time he took a bite of that greasy burger.

They did.

They thought of one of the Pack had killed Roman.

The cops weren't checking on Eddie, not really; they were checking on him. The other guys. All those questions, not the ones about drugs and beer and shit like that; the other ones. The one Detective Jorgen kept asking with that not-real smile on his stupid face. Did you fellas fight a lot, Mr. Garing? Barnaby, Eddie ever try to steal your girl? Look, kid, I know how it is, okay? I'm not that old, I remember. You get a little wild once in a while, I mean look at the way you guys dress, and sometimes, before you know it, things get out of hand, right? No, I'm not accusing anyone, Barn, nobody. You know how it is—I just gotta ask the questions or the boss'll have my head.

You know how it is.

He did. He knew that nobody ever called him "Barn," and that included his parents, that any fights Eddie ever had lasted less than a couple of minutes, that nothing ever got out of hand because Eddie wouldn't let it.

That's how it was.

I understand that, Barn, but—

"Jesus," he whispered, and looked out the rear window, half expecting to see the cop in the fancy suit following in a fancy car.

"Barnaby, are you okay?"

He faced front and nodded, stiffly.

Of course he was okay. I mean, Eddie's dead and the cops are thinking I maybe did it so what the hell's the matter with you, bitch?, can't you see what's happening here, can't you under-stand anything but how your goddamn bra fits?

"Barnaby?"

"Our stop," he said, pushing away from the seat. "See you in class."

She called after him, wanting him to wait, she didn't want to walk alone. Pleaded with him. On the street she screamed after him until he finally did stop, did wait, and listened to her all the way to her house telling him what a total jerk he was, what a complete asshole, that he was making things up, that he watched too much TV, that this was real life, and there wasn't a cop in this town who actually believed one of the Pack would take an ax to Eddie Roman.

"No," Barnaby agreed. "But like Scott said, somebody did."

Pancho Duncan strolled up the boulevard, nimbly avoiding would-be tacklers, scoring record touchdowns, making impos-sible interceptions, bowing to the crowds, taking his pick of the chicks, until he couldn't take the empty shops, the empty offices, the empty street any longer. There was nothing inside in spite of all the light. And when he passed the place with the mannequins that had spooked Byrns-the-gimp, he decided that running would give him the best exercise, help get rid of the junk he'd eaten tonight. Hell; football season with only one game to go and he was already slacking off, getting fat. Lousy way to treat a beautiful body like his. If he kept it up, he'd be killing himself with the weights all spring, and he couldn't afford to blow it all now. Next year was the last; after that, it was college, the pros, endorsements, the works. Screw up now, he'd screw up his whole life.

Running would be good.

If only his boots didn't make so damned much noise.

"So," Laine said.

Joey leaned against a lamppost, arms folded over his chest. "Yeah. So."

He had to admit it—she was beautiful. She was the only one who could wear a ponytail, an oversize jacket, and those dumb saddle shoes, and not look like a total jerk. They made Tang look like a tramp, and Fern like some kind of orphan. Katie didn't even bear thinking about; she was a total mess. But Laine . . . hell, she looked good.

"So," she said, keeping her distance, her back to the boulevard, her gaze on the slope that led down to the river. "So, you still mad at me?"

He ought to be. The way she treated him, he ought to deck her, for god's sake, the hell with women's lib or whatever the fuck it was called these days.

"I don't know. No."

"I didn't mean it, you know." Dark eyes focused on him now, those wide lips darker because her back was to the light. "I was just teasing."

"Yeah," he said, "but Dale didn't know that, did he? He thought I was trying to hurt you, Laine. I mean, he's . . . he's . . . " Even now, after knowing the kid all this time, he couldn't say it.

Laine smiled. She knew. "Retarded," she said softly. "And he was just trying to protect me."

They stared at each other until an image of Laine's little brother beating on his chest and yelling made him smile, finally made him chuckle. "Little creep's strong."

She lifted an arm, made a muscle. "Of course. Takes after his sister."

"But I don't want him to think I was hurting you," he said sternly. "He doesn't know things like that, you know what I mean? And I like him."

She came closer, touched his chest with a finger that traced down to his stomach, back up to his neck before falling away. "I know. And I explained to him later we were only fooling around. Honest to god, Joey, I didn't think he'd take it seriously." She took his hand. "Sorry, okay?"

"Yeah, I guess."

He pushed away from the lamppost and they walked hand-in-hand to the rear of the diner where a municipal parking lot ran the width of the block. A fence and narrowly-spaced poplars blocked the houses behind. Any store could be reached from back here, but hardly anyone used the rear entrances. They walked through the alleys to the street. Habit, he figured.

"Take you home?" she said.

"Sure, why not?"

"You want to drive?"

"Right." He stood at the passenger door of a mile-long car and made a face at over the roof. "And your old man sees me, takes me to that clinic, does medical experiments on me, and I'm never heard of again."

"He's a doctor, not a scientist," she said. "Not a bad idea, though. It would keep you in line."

"Jesus, now you sound like my mother."

She laughed, and on the way to the South End, turned on the radio, trying to find an oldies station. There was too much static, for which Joey was grateful. He didn't think he could stand to hear that music now, not after last night, not for a while.

"Laine?"

She lifted her chin—*go ahead, I'm listening.*

Listen, Eddie was going nuts, y'know? Something was

bugging him the last couple of weeks, maybe it had something to do with what happened. Nuts, really nuts. I mean, you never saw the looks on his face, he never showed them to anyone but me. How the hell should I know why? He just did. But it was spooky, man, spooky as hell, worse than Byrns's store dummies. He was scared, Laine. The guy was scared shitless.

"Nothing," he said, and waved her attention back to the road. "Nothing."

Katie Ealton lay in her bed, blankets to her chin, hands clasped tightly across her stomach. She wanted to go to the Starlite, wanted it desperately, but her grandmother had insisted that she needed help tonight, her arthritis was acting up, she couldn't be left alone, couldn't climb the stairs or open a bottle, and besides it was only Wednesday, a school night, no time for a young girl to be out running around with killers on the loose. They had yelled. No. Katie had yelled, and her grandmother had just sat there, infinitely patient, until the tantrum was over.

Then Katie had gone to her room and watched a movie, but it scared her. Not fun scared. Really scared. For the first time in a long time, one of those giant animal movies scared her because she believed it could happen, so she went to bed and prayed for no nightmares and wondered if anyone else had heard the screaming last night.

FIVE

"Joey, I have told you a hundred times I am not going to do it."

"Why not?"

"I don't know, it's sacrilegious or something."

"Bull."

"Okay, so maybe it isn't, but it doesn't feel right, okay?"

He tossed a stone at one of the geese, missing it by ten feet, and she rolled her eyes, sighed without sound, shook her head in slow despair. She hated it when he got this way. Hated it. It made him look just like her kid brother, and that snotty little brat was the world's most complete total pain when he wasn't tearing her heart out.

Today, Joey Costello was running a close second.

Today was the third day the Pack had no leader.

Joey threw another stone and barely reached the water.

"C'mon, Joey, knock it off, huh? You're going to hit somebody."

"Yeah," he said disgustedly. "You wish."

They were on the east side of the pond, sitting on the grass above the benches. School had closed early, just before the first lunch period, the principal on the p.a. all solemn and squeaky telling them that if they needed counseling or just wanted to talk to someone about the recent tragedy—he never mentioned

Eddie's name, the geek, never mentioned him once—people would be available. Great. Three days after the fact, and on a Friday yet, they finally figured out that the students might have cared about someone like Eddie Roman. But that wouldn't bring Eddie back, and hardly anyone stuck around.

Joey met her and the others out front. Not one of them, however, could think of anything to do, didn't much care to do anything, and so had drifted away. One by one. Bloodshot eyes, hitching breath, muttering about maybe getting together tomorrow, see you around.

Joey had other ideas.

As soon as they were alone, he got this dumb grin on his face and asked again, for the millionth time, if she could borrow her mother's car so they could drive into New York, screw around in Times Square, maybe go up to Central Park. It was only a half-hour to the Lincoln Tunnel, for god's sake, what's the problem? He had been after her all morning, from practically the second she'd walked into homeroom, but she hadn't yet been able to make him understand that she wasn't up to it, not now. She had tried to prove it by wearing jeans that fit instead of strangling her legs and barely reaching her ankles, and a blouse she bought at the mall last month instead of the white shirt she had swiped from her father's closet. She had even left her leather jacket at home.

It didn't seem right, wearing that stuff, now that Eddie was gone.

Maybe the worst part was, there wasn't even going to be a funeral, or even some kind of memorial service. According to her father, who heard it from a cop friend, some Pennsylvania relatives were going to have the bodies flown to Pittsburgh as soon as the police were done. It was like, one day Eddie was there, and Mr. Roman was in his classroom, and the next day it was like they never existed. Except for the headlines. And the rumors.

Joey scooted down until he was in front of her, hands on his thighs. His motorcycle jacket was open, his T-shirt white and tight, his hair gleaming in the sunlight, ducktailed and slick. "Okay," he said, giving her a half-smile.

Here it comes, she thought.

"A deal."

I knew it. Every time.

"We go in, okay?, and I swear I'll do your trig for the rest of the year."

She giggled, covered her mouth, waved her free hand when he reared back with a scowl.

"What the hell's the matter with that?"

"Joey, Thanksgiving's next week, three weeks after that is Christmas vacation."

"So?"

"So with all the assemblies, half-days, stuff like that, how much work do you think we're going to have?"

"So I'll help you study. God, Laine, why are you making this so hard?"

She hugged her knees to her chest and rested her chin on them as she smiled her answer. A brat maybe, but he was her brat.

Making sure she could see how thoroughly disgusted he was, Joey rolled to his feet and stalked off down the slope, slapping one leg, looking around at everything, pointedly, but her. She watched him, but didn't get up, didn't follow. That would be a mistake, it's exactly what he hoped for; besides, she liked to look at his ass and that slight bowlegged walk he had when he was trying to be macho cool. Look out, you suckers, Joseph Costello is on the move. In time, every time, get in my way I'll blow you away.

The black leather was all wrong, she realized then; he should be in a duster, with six-guns, and riding a horse.

Joey the Kid, something like that.

What he was now, however, was Eddie's doing. But he and James Dean were dead.

A breeze ruffled her hair, and she swiped at it angrily.

If he really did get rid of those clothes, she thought, the first thing she would do is cut off her damn bangs. She hated them. They looked stupid. She hated the poodle skirts Fern Bellard had made for her and Tang; she hated saddle oxfords; she hated toreador pants and ratty clamdiggers; and she definitely hated popping bubble gum in class.

She looked down at an ant crawling over her foot, thought about squashing it, brushed it away with a finger.

Oh, and painted toenails too.

The weird part was—she hadn't hated any of it before. None of them had. The hate had begun when she had opened her closet this morning and automatically reached for that damn pleated skirt. When she touched it, her fingers had curled back as if they'd brushed something slimy. That was when she really cried. That was when she knew there was something terribly wrong.

But how could it be wrong?

Why was it so terrible?

It had begun as a goof and had ended up a way of life.

Now one life was over, and so were the Fifties.

She let her face slide until her forehead settled on her knees, pinched a small fold of skin until she shifted and the sting ended.

"Oh, lord!" her father had said that first night, when she'd pranced into the living room, hair redone, fluffy mohair sweater, Fern's skirt, the folded-down white socks, and saddle shoes. He stood in the kitchen doorway, glasses dangling from one hand, the other pinching his nose. "Please, God, don't make me go back, please don't make me go!"

She laughed.

He threw her a kiss and told her that she looked just like her mother when her mother was sixteen. That's when her mother had leaned over the banister and said, "Just as long as you don't wear penny loafers. You wear penny loafers, Laine, and I'm disowning you on the spot."

The penny loafers had arrived sometime in September, when Eddie, Joey, and Pancho found a place to buy their own loafers, with tassels and cleats.

"Don't tell me, let me guess," her father would say each time. "Eddie Roman's idea, right?"

Of course.

It was all Eddie's idea.

And oh Jesus, it was fun.

So why was it terrible, the clothes and the records and the picture of Fabian on her wall?

She stared at the grass, closed her eyes, and listened to the park—the little kids by the water, someone calling someone else, two guys down at the southern end playing acoustic guitars, cases open at their feet for donations; bicycle tires and skateboards rattling on the paths below and behind her, the squeak of a stroller, the squeak and bounce of a baby carriage; traffic on the surrounding streets; a jetliner overhead, coming down into Newark from someplace not here.

Joey thumping on the ground at her feet.

Indian summer, though the trees looked like death.

She raised her head just enough to peer at him over her knees.

"Okay," he said in resigned surrender. "Okay, so we don't go to New York. So what do you want to do?"

She was glad her legs hid the smile. "I don't know. What do you want to do?"

Growling, he showed her a mock fist and shifted until he was beside her, leaning back on his elbows. "Y'know, I been thinking about getting a haircut."

"Okay."

"Not a lot, you know, just a little." A look; a shrug. "I don't know, but it feels like I'm wearing a helmet, you know? It'll get Ma off my back, you know what I mean?" Then he sat up and pulled off his jacket, slammed it on the ground. "God!" He lay back. "God, that thing's hot!"

They watched a man and a woman arguing on the nearest bench; Joey laughed at a short black bum who wandered out of the trees across the way and plopped down above the path, began feeding the ducks that came right to him when he snapped his fingers. Laine recognized him, the one they called Blade, the one Scottie knew. A woman in a turban walked over to him, said something to him, walked away so stiff and formal Laine closed her eyes to keep from laughing. That was another one. The Queen of Foxriver, according to Fern.

A police siren startled them.

"I miss Eddie," she whispered.

"Yeah," he answered after almost too long. "They ought to fry the bastard who did it."

Blindly she reached out her hand. He took it, and squeezed.

"I tried to call Katie again today," she said.

Joey shrugged his indifference.

"Joey, come on, she hasn't been in school all week. I went over yesterday, I couldn't get in, her grandmother wouldn't let me. I swear that woman's crazy." She bit on her lower lip. "What if there's something the matter?"

"The matter is," Joey said, obviously not giving a damn, "is that she had the hots for Eddie, that's what the matter is."

She shook her head, hard.

"Christ, Laine, you don't know everything, y'know. Why do you think she stayed, huh? Didn't you ever notice that if Eddie wasn't around, she took off, or didn't even show?" He dug the ground again with a heel. "Jerk. She's probably crying herself to death."

The ducks fled when a spaniel charged into the water, returned on the other side and huddled, quacking softly.

The Queen of Foxriver slipped into the trees.

Laine tried to think of a way to tell him he was wrong, that she would have known something like that, you couldn't hide it from everyone. Just like you couldn't hide the other thing, the thing Joey knew and wouldn't talk about.

"Joey," she said, "what was wrong with Eddie?"

He didn't answer for the longest while; she had to look at him to be sure he hadn't fallen asleep.

"Joey, please."

"I don't know," he said at last, his free arm draped across his eyes. "He . . . I don't know."

"He what?"

"I told you I don't know."

"You're lying."

His arm slipped to the grass; he opened one eye. "Just leave it, Laine, okay?"

"Leave what?"

"Eddie. He was . . . crazy. Acting crazy."

"I know that," she snapped. "Damn, we all knew that. I want to know why."

He shook his head. "Crazy stuff," he muttered. "Kid stuff,

crazy." His chest rose and fell. "I don't know. He's gone, Laine, just leave it. It doesn't matter anymore."

The spaniel bounded up to them, sniffed at Laine's toes until she giggled and swiped playfully at its muzzle. It barked, wagged its tail, ran off to chase the ducks again.

"I had a nightmare last night."

He grunted.

"I was sleeping—in my dream, I mean—and I could hear somebody knocking on my window. Like with a stick or a pencil. It woke me up and I couldn't get out of bed."

"You were naked, that's why."

She dug a nail into his hand.

"Hey!" A moment later: "Sorry."

She let her gaze follow the gander circling the center of the pond, but she didn't really see it, just the white and its wake.

"At first I thought it was you doing a Romeo or something, but it couldn't be. My room's on the second floor and there's no roof or trellis, anything like that. So then I thought it was a tree branch, but there's no tree out there either. And it just kept on, all that tapping. Real quick, too, then real slow. Finally, I got up, I don't know why, I was so scared, and I went to the window and opened the curtains."

She held her breath.

The gander charged his mate, wings spread, neck straight, bill aiming for her side.

"Well?" He turned his head. "Well, what did you see?"

The goose dodged easily, and the gander settled down to preen as if nothing had happened.

"I didn't see anything. There wasn't anything out there."

"Ha."

"But there was something in my closet, and when it came out, I woke up."

Relbeth's Market wasn't large and didn't have to be. It catered primarily to the basics, and for last-minute shopping when people were too rushed to drive to the larger chain stores. What kept it most successful, however, was its butcher shop, and though Scott didn't mind working there most days, he could no longer stand to watch Mr. Relbeth work on the slabs of meat dragged out from the freezer. When the meat thawed, there was blood.

Because his leg was bothering him, his boss let him take the register as soon as he walked in directly from school, and he was glad for a chance to sit on the padded stool and watch the customers come and go. It was the first time he'd been back to work since Tuesday, and though many of the people knew him, knew Eddie had been his friend, they didn't ask many questions. He was grateful. He didn't think he'd know how to answer. Not that Mr. Relbeth would have let them take up his time anyway. He was in a mood today, complaining about the big chains trying to sabotage his store, complaining about the weather, complaining not very subtly about customers who always came in at the last minute, demanding they be able to reserve the best cuts, the fattest turkeys, when a sign had been in the window for weeks, warning that the last date for holiday meat reservations had been last Monday.

"They think they own you," the man said, dropping into a wobbly wicker chair he kept behind the counter for his frequent cigarette breaks. "Scott, you don't get into this business unless you want people to think they own you."

Scott rang up a purchase, bagged it, handed it over to a woman who glared at the owner and huffed out.

Relbeth pointed a bony finger at her back. "Worst one," he sneered none too quietly. "Husband wins the damn lottery, not even a million dollars, and she thinks she owns me. She should move to the Heights, she wants to own something."

Scott grinned. "She'll give her money to somebody else then."

"Bah! Let her, the old witch. Who needs it? Who needs the aggravation?"

Scott turned on the stool and batted away a cloud of the worst-smelling tobacco smoke he'd ever known. Thomas Relbeth smoked Turkish cigarettes, and if the stench was any indication, the man would be dead before he reached sixty. As it was, he looked damn near that age—his face and hands were spotted, his pate nearly bare, the flesh of a once-proud nose sagging into a hook. With dark pouches under his eyes, a slouch, and his slow speech, he seemed continually exhausted. But Scott had never seen him any other way, even when he threw parties for his employees, which he did every excuse he could find.

The pay was lousy, but the work was almost fun.

Relbeth scratched his skull with a long yellowed fingernail. "They never caught the guy, did they?"

"Not yet."

Relbeth snorted. "Cops can't find their ass with a road map." He blew smoke, shook his head, half closed one eye as he looked up. "Didn't see you on TV, son. Didn't the reporters come around?"

They had, but his mother wouldn't let him talk to them. Two of the New York stations had sent vans over, and the double killing had been on the six o'clock news Wednesday, a follow-up yesterday. He didn't think there'd be any more; there was nothing more to say. In fact, as he thought about it, none of the Pack had been on the air. A reporter and her crew had been at the school the day after, and a few kids in the yard had said what a great guy Roman was, lots of fun, always full of energy, stuff like that. Like they knew him. Like they really knew him.

"Your mother gonna get married soon?"

Scott blinked and sputtered. In two years he still hadn't gotten used to the way the man jumped from topic to topic without half taking a breath.

Relbeth cackled. "Don't look so surprised, son. She's a handsome lady, your mother is. It's going to happen, you know. One of these days it's going to happen."

Scott frowned. His mother? Good-looking? He tried to picture her the way a man might, one who didn't know her, and it made him blush. He felt the spots. He heard Relbeth chuckle. But he'd never thought of his mother that way before. She was . . . his mother, that's all.

The sun began to drift below the buildings across the street, drawing the color with it, taking the warmth.

The bell over the door jingled and Barnaby walked in, wearing a football jacket and sweater, regular jeans and high-tops. He reached into a shelf of candies and pulled out a handful of chocolate bars, dropped them on the counter and said, "What the hell you staring at, Byrns?"

Relbeth heaved himself to his feet and crushed the cigarette out in a coffee can he kept on a shelf behind him. "Keep the drawer closed, son," he muttered as he left. "Count the money later. I got chops to chop." He laughed, coughed, laughed again and swerved around the freezer.

"Bastard creep," Barnaby said, dropping a five-dollar bill into Scott's hand. "Son of a bitch ought to be stomped a few times, know what I mean?" He waited for his change, pocketed it, and peeled off one of the wrappers. "You're still staring, jackass." He stuffed half the candy bar into his mouth.

Scott shrugged. Smiled. Shrugged. Felt like an idiot and shrugged again. "Your clothes, I guess," he managed when Garing looked ready to leap the counter and grab his throat.

"What's the matter with them?" The boy examined himself with slow exaggeration, opening the jacket, zipping it closed, looking behind as though checking his hem. "They look okay to me."

"Well, sure they are," he said quickly. "But . . . I don't know, they're—"

"Normal?"

The tone was a dare.

"Yeah. I guess. Yeah."

"So I got tired of black, you want to make something of it?"

"Jesus, Barnaby," he said, "who yanked your chain?"

Barnaby ate the other half of the candy bar, stuffed the rest into his pockets. "Nobody," he said glumly. "They called off practice, I ain't got nothing to do."

"So you're going to hassle me, right?"

Barnaby grinned. "Why not?"

"Why didn't you just get a job, like normal guys do?"

"Normal? You're normal?"

Scott waited for the rest of the joke. It didn't come.

"Christ, Byrns, get a life why not. Why should I work when

I don't have to?" He headed for the door, paused to grab another handful of chocolate, and grinned over his shoulder. "Thanks for the treat, pal. See you around."

"Hey!"

The door closed.

Barnaby paused in the middle of the display window, laughed, and slowly, very slowly, lifted his middle finger before passing out of sight. Scott was halfway off the stool before he changed his mind. If Garing was that angry at something, or someone, there'd be no sense trying to catch him, talk to him, find out what was wrong. Even if he could. He'd only get pounded, and wouldn't his mother just love that. It was odd. Though he might be imagining it, that crack about being normal seemed awfully close to a crack about his leg, and Barnaby had never done anything like that before. That was Pancho's turf, seeing how close he could come to tasteless without getting the others literally on his back. Barnaby, on the other hand, had always seemed to realize how lucky he was that he had both his legs, that if he were like Scott, he'd have only his brains to carry him. More than once Scott had tutored him in one subject or another, for one test or another. Garing wasn't stupid, he wouldn't have failed, but there were just some things he couldn't find the handle to, chemistry being the worst.

So what was the crack all about then?

The streetlights came on, shadows molded into their night shapes.

Traffic increased and faded.

He made himself a sandwich for supper, and called home to tell his mother he'd be working a little late, that he'd already eaten.

The customers stopped coming.

Around seven, Relbeth let him go, telling him sourly that he wasn't going to pay for someone just to sit around and count his damn money. The floor had already been swept three times, the shelves dusted twice.

"It gets any cleaner in here, I'm going to be able to do operations on the side." He brandished a cleaver, then wiped it on his bloody apron. "Go home, son. Your mother's waiting."

It was cold outside.

Pulling up his collar, rolling his shoulders to settle his coat, Scott moved as quickly as his leg would allow, feeling a pinch and burn at the juncture of plastic and bone. He'd have to take it off when he got home, get out the crutches, maybe some rubbing alcohol. He laughed; he laughed again. Some guys, they get home from work, they take off their suits, their ties, put on their slippers, get out a pipe; he takes off his leg. It was no big deal. He'd been doing it since he was five.

Trouble was, though he hadn't told his mother, had managed to keep his discomfort from her, he needed a new leg already, this one only a couple of years old. He was growing, gaining weight, picking up height. But there was no money left, none to spare, and he'd been hoping to get along on the current prosthetic for a while. A long while.

Once she graduated law school and had her first job, things would be fine. She said so. So what the hell, he could last that long, it was only until next summer.

A bus hissed at him as he turned the corner and headed down his street. He started, chuckled at himself, and a few yards later glanced back and saw someone standing alone on the corner. The nearest boulevard lights were either out or in the wrong places, and it was too dark to make out face or sex. He shrugged without moving and moved on, thinking that maybe he would just stay home tonight. He didn't care that it was Friday, that the others would probably be at the Starlite. He was tired. He ached. And if Barnaby was still behaving like a jerk, he definitely didn't want to be within ten miles of the place.

On the other hand, Fern might show up, but he wasn't at all sure that was a good thing. They'd been friends until now, growing up together, hanging out in the neighborhood, some-times walking to school together, sometimes not. Nothing more. But the way she had talked to him the other night . . . no, the way she held his arm and smiled when they parted, that was different. How different, he couldn't say, but it was.

At the next corner he looked back again.

The figure was still there, dark and rigid.

Watching him.

Scott knew it was watching him.

He passed Fern's house and was tempted to ring the bell. Jerk, he told himself then, she's at the bookstore, went to work right after school just like he did. He sighed for relief, but didn't get it.

At the next block he turned right, glancing up toward the boulevard as he did.

The figure had moved; it was closer.

A gust snapped at his cheeks, and he realized he was hitching along, limping badly, the way it was whenever he grew too tall for his artificial leg. But this one was still fine. Sure. He was just moving too fast.

His home was midway to the next intersection, a detached shingle house set slightly back from those around it, thus giving it a slightly larger front yard. The grass was dead, the flowers gone until spring, and the single tree he had planted four years ago was not quite tall enough to reach the bottom of the second floor. Its branches were bare.

He swung into the walk and pulled himself up the stairs.

He hurt.

God, he hurt.

A hand on the doorknob, and he checked the sidewalk again.

The figure was there, just out of the corner light, moving toward him. Stiffly. Arms away from its body as if it were afraid to fall.

Watching him.

He couldn't see a face, but still it watched him.

Part of him was angry—it was Barnaby, mocking him, playing Frankenstein monster.

Into the dim spray of a streetlight, then, and it was still dark, still faceless, the sound of its footsteps softly hollow.

Part of him was scared—it was one of the mannequins come to get him, to take him with it back to the window with all the rest of the plastic human beings.

It slowed.

A car passed, headlights so bright he had to shade his eyes and squint, and in squinting realized his right hand was cramped from holding the doorknob so tightly, so long. He turned the knob. The car sped up the street. The figure had moved closer, back into the dark.

Barnaby; not Barnaby.

He pushed in and slammed the door behind him, hurried to the living room and looked out the window just as his mother came in from the kitchen.

"Honey, are you all right?"

The street was empty.

Sunset Books, the largest independent bookshop in the county, sat midway between the Strip and Town Hall. Just inside the entrance, on the left, was a high, blondwood horseshoe counter, and on the platform behind it, on a stool that permitted him to see the entire store without straining, sat a sandy-haired man in his early thirties, already prominently balding, wearing a sleeveless argyle sweater over a dull pin-stripe shirt. His severely-cut black beard couldn't hide the ridges and shallows of a face hacked from polished wood, nor could the sweater and baggy trousers disguise the man's impressive bulk. Fern thought Pen Tobin resembled an actor who thought he'd be playing a fullback and ended up as the absent-minded but ruggedly handsome professor.

She also thought he was a lech.

Though she was positive he was constantly fooling around with Arlette Bingham, the daytime clerk with a serious ego problem, he had never really made an actual pass at her, not in the year she had worked for him, but there was something about the way he looked at her these days that bothered her. It was, she thought, sort of like the way Pancho looked at her when he didn't think anyone else was watching. A quick strip of her clothes, a check of her figure, dressing her again and smiling so innocently she couldn't be positive she wasn't imagining it.

No; with Pancho she was sure. With Mr. Tobin she didn't quite know.

Tonight, even though it was Friday, supposedly a good night to buy, he had decided to close early, and she had spent the last hour patrolling the shelves, returning books to their proper places and straightening the sale tables. When she was done, she went immediately to her favorite spot in the store, what she had christened the Island—three badly upholstered armchairs dragged in from curbs during house-cleaning week, a couple of rickety tables with seashell ashtrays, and a fringed faded carpet that regular vacuuming would have destroyed. For walls there were four warped wood bookcases Tobin had discovered in his landlord's basement. Damaged books found their way here, some sale books, and the occasional magazine. No food or drink allowed. Voices down please, and if you're going to read, at least have the courtesy to buy the thing before you break the spine or dog-ear a page.

In the beginning, Mr. Tobin had been concerned that one group or another would co-opt the area as an impromptu, not to mention free, meeting place, or that people would use its relative privacy to swipe books and magazines, or the elderly would use it to rest their legs and feet. It hadn't happened. Teens could be found here as much as anyone else, gossiping, swapping lies, and even buying now and then.

Not long after its creation, she had gotten a raise.

A glance at the other chair, and she saw a faint image of Eddie sitting there, thumbing through a western. Of all things, the guy liked westerns. He really liked to read.

He chopped his father up.

A shudder was interrupted by a sudden yawn, and she winced when her jaw popped. As she massaged it, she sprawled in one of the chairs, skirt drawn to the middle of her thighs, shoes off and toes wiggling, and listened to the faint sounds of Tobin shutting things down at the counter. It had been a hell of a day. For some reason, nine hundred zillion people seemed to have been in the store at the same time, all at the last minute, all demanding instant service, all wanting titles the store didn't have and wouldn't have until Monday's afternoon deliveries.

She thought, she believed, she would sleep soundly until then.

Unfortunately for her feet, and the fact that she had to work all day tomorrow, it would be like this for the next several weeks, the between-holidays trade so necessary to get the establishment through until late spring. She had had no idea this was the way things worked. After all, you came in, you bought, you left, the books were always there. Cars had their seasons; who knew books did too?

The lights flickered, died, leaving only those around the perimeter still burning.

"Fern, I'm about ready.

She groaned loudly for an answer and looked at her watch— eight, and it felt like midnight. Maybe she'd stop off at the Starlite on the way home, grab something to eat to save her mother the trouble. It was always that way—she'd work late, and her mother would have full meal waiting when she got home, it didn't matter that Fern had already had something herself.

"You're a growing woman, Fern," she'd say solemnly. "You need your beauty rest, and you need to eat."

"Mom, if I ate any more I'd be a zillion pounds."

"I eat," her mother said, "and I'm not a zillion pounds."

True enough. She and her mother were the same slender size, the same height, wore each other's clothes often enough that sometimes they couldn't remember which belonged to who; her father thought they were nuts. Her mother said that's because he was too chicken to wear a dress.

Right, Fern thought, she could just see Arthur Bellard, actuary clerk and lay reader at the First Presbyterian Church, wearing a dress. He had a hard enough time when she wore slacks or jeans; wearing a skirt and blouse, like now, had been his condition in letting her get an after-school job. If she wore anything else, he'd lock her up for damn ever. She wondered if he was afraid she'd turn out like her mother.

Of course, if she went to the diner, Scott might be there.

So?

She grinned.

Or maybe that damn cop, Jorgen, the one who looked her over so many times when he interviewed her that she couldn't wait for him to leave so she could take a shower. He was good-looking, but he gave her the creeps.

The grin became a puzzled frown. There'd been nothing in

the papers or on TV about Eddie or his father, not since yesterday. She couldn't believe that someone who had done something like that in a town like this hadn't been caught yet. It was like the guy was a ghost or something.

Like Katie. Not a sign of her, not a word, calling the house and getting her grandmother, who acted as if Katie didn't know anyone except creeps and perverts.

"Closing," Tobin called.

A moment later, the perimeter lights went out, only the anti-theft spotlights left, crossing over her head.

Fern cursed him for not waiting and bent over to pick up her shoes.

And something long and hard and gleaming black crawled out of the one she first put her hand on. She yelped, jumped back, hit the chair and fell into it, pulling her legs up under her, pressing hard into the back.

"Fern, you okay?"

She couldn't answer.

The insect, too dark down there in the dark to identify, scuttled around the heel and moved toward the chair.

"Fern?"

Three inches, four; the biggest thing she'd ever seen.

"Fern!"

Her mouth opened to tell him, but the words became a bleating as the black beetle vanished beneath her. Under the chair. Looking, she just knew it, for a way to climb up. She knelt on the cushion, and brought fists to her chest when a second one crawled out of the other shoe. Larger. Blacker. Mandibles so long she could see them open and close.

She could hear them.

The lights flared on.

Her boss ran into the Island.

"There," she said, pointing to the floor.

"Christ," he muttered, and she closed her eyes when she heard him stride onto the rug, swallowed hard when she heard the prolonged papery crunch of his shoes crushing the bug. "God."

"There's one under the chair," she whispered.

Instead of looking for it, he picked her up easily and carried her away, set her down by the door and said, "What the hell was that thing?"

She leaned against him, hating herself for acting like such a helpless female, wishing her legs would stop trying to collapse. "I don't know."

"Wait here," he told her. "I'll set the alarms, we'll get my car, I'll drive you home."

Centipedes in the bathtub; spiders in the kitchen sink.

"Okay," she answered, and prayed her parents hadn't gone out to a movie.

Then Mr. Tobin said, from back around the Island, "Son of a bitch."

Her eyes widened. "What? What's the matter?"

"That thing I killed," he said, coming toward her, handing her her coat while slipping into his own. "I was going to scoop it up and dump it."

"So?"

"So I guess I didn't kill it. The damn thing's gone."

SIX

The clouds dragged themselves back over the sky not long after nine, stampeding the stars and moon, and a stiff wind from the northwest snapped at banners on the plaza, drove dust along the gutters, carried with it not the smell of rain but the crisp texture of impending snow. Thanksgiving decorations in the lighted shop windows seemed out of place, too cheerful, too bright, too false though the holiday was less than a week away. A malfunction of traffic signals along Summit Boulevard held cars bumper-to-bumper, drivers cursing the buses that didn't pull all the way in when they stopped at each corner. Intersections were blocked. Pedestrians nudged each other off the curb, in a hurry to get home.

It was a crime.

Calvin Nobbs glared at every car that refused to let him cross the street.

A crime they didn't see the signs, didn't see him, didn't see anything but a way out of this town.

He almost raised his cane to shake it at them, maybe even give them a whack or two just to let them know, but he remembered that the last time he'd done that, idiots had hustled him away to the police station and called Mazie to come take him home before he hurt somebody.

Hell, he wasn't going to hurt anyone.

He just wanted to get the hell across the street.

Before Christmas, if possible; definitely before midnight.

He coughed violently and grabbed his chest, clawed at it, pounded it until the cough and the pain finally went away. The wind tried to steal his hat; he grabbed the brim and yanked it down, then stepped off the curb when the WALK sign flashed, and dared the cars trying to beat the light to run him down. They honked. Someone yelled a curse. He ignored them. He didn't hurry. He was old, and he had a right, and if they didn't like it, they could lump it.

He had to get home.

He had to be there in case the screaming began.

Listening for it.

Straining so hard it gave her a headache.

Katie knew she was driving herself crazy, but she couldn't help it. She sat at her bedroom window on her hope chest, legs drawn up, chin on her knees. The lamp was out, the pane looked like black ice, felt like fire whenever she reached out to touch it to be sure it was still there. Her head tilted. A draft tickled her hair, slipped down the neck of the oversize T-shirt she used for a nightgown and tickled her breasts, made her shiver and hug her legs more tightly.

She stiffened her jaw against a yawn, rubbed an eye with a knuckle, then rubbed the other.

Time to sleep, but she didn't move.

She listened.

She stared, but there were nothing to see out there, not in the sky, and she was too low to be able to see the house behind without stretching. It didn't matter. It wasn't the sky or the house she cared about.

A muffled thump in the hall outside her door—Grandmother up again, using the bathroom as she did a dozen times between bed and dawn, the wheelchair lightly bumping over the threshold. She refused to turn on a light for fear, she said, of waking Katie. Katie's protests didn't do any good—*Grandmother, my door's always closed, for heaven's sake, you won't wake me up*—it was thump and roll all night long. And Katie's parents dead so long, she couldn't really remember it being any other way.

Star light, star bright, she thought as she stared at the clouds, their bellies reflecting the town below; if you're there, just tell me I'm not going nuts. Just give me a hint so I get back to the world.

A tear for Eddie slipped to her cheek and quivered there until an angry finger dashed it away, wiped it against her hip. That too was crazy. At least she could tell herself that the screams she had heard, that she thought she had heard, the night Eddie died were probably only her imagination, a loose fragment of nightmare, the connection made only when she'd heard about the murder. Eddie lived three blocks away; even with the windows open she couldn't have heard him. That was simple. The crying wasn't. He didn't love her; he liked her, she was part of the Pack. She loved him; she didn't always love him. He was too manic, too unnerving, once in a while too unintentionally cruel. But there was something about him, the way he laughed, the way his fingers were always snapping, the way he ran every place even when he was walking, that made her forget about Grandmother and the house and school and everything.

That was crazy.

The tears were crazy. She should be over it by now, or at least out with the kids, not locked away like some princess in a dark tower room waiting for a knight to rescue her from something she didn't even know what.

She should be gone.

But each night, after sunset, she remembered the screams and spent most of the time wandering the house, listening.

Crazy.

It was all crazy.

Another tear fell, and this one wasn't for Eddie.

SEVEN

They felt it in Foxriver, the sleepers and the dreamers, when midnight was done:

An unconscious divination of the transformation of the dark, a parting of the night, a funeral for the stars.

Sheets and blankets were tossed aside, pillows thumped and reset, legs moving slowly, arms drawing away from the sides of the bed; a faint whimper from the bed of a nightmare-plagued child, a sputtered moan from the bed of a man living alone, a giggle from a woman, a gasp from the dark where no one slept at all.

The Boulevard was empty, traffic lights changing now with no one to see them; streetlamps buzzing with no one to hear; a scrap of crumpled paper scuttling along the gutter with no one to see it, trying to climb the curbing, veering away from the drains, tumbling across the blacktop and bouncing onto the sidewalk, pausing, quivering, then slipping through the entrance of Foxriver Park.

There was no wind.

There was no breeze.

The paper kept moving.

So did the shadows.

• • •

The night watchman in the Rotunda kept moving as well, uncomfortable with the chill that had settled over the stone building. He didn't like walking, there were too many echoes, he cast too many shadows, but standing still was worse. Standing still meant listening to the elevators talking when the elevators had been long since shut down; standing still meant listening to the whispers behind the police station's inner door though he knew full well all the night shift stayed on the floor a level down; standing still meant listening to the stone creak and doors slam and hinges squeal and his uniform rustle and his breath come too loud.

As he passed the model of Foxriver Then And Now he paused, checked his watch, took out a handkerchief and lightly dusted the glass that covered the miniature town. He did it every night. There never was any dust, but he did it just the same, then looked down through the light no brighter than a dying candle to make sure no one had stolen his town.

He did it tonight.

There was no dust.

The town was safe.

Though straight down the center the glass had been cracked.

PART TWO

WHEN WE
GREW UP

EIGHT

Nobody died until Slap Zubronsky heard the cats.

NINE

Blade Murtaugh stiffened when he heard the rat slip under the plastic of his garbage-bag blanket. He knew it was a rat; it was always a rat, they never left him alone, they were always after him, nibbling at him, warning him that one night they'd stop playing with him and feast. It was wearisome. Bothersome. He almost decided to go back to sleep, let the critter do what it wanted, he was too tired anymore.

It nipped him on the calf.

He yelled, kicked, flung back the plastic and scrambled backward on his buttocks until his head struck the brick wall that formed the back of his bedroom alley.

"God damn!" he shouted, reaching for, grabbing, throwing a tin can at the rodent.

The can missed.

The rat didn't move.

"Son of a bitch," Murtaugh said, and pulled up his trouser leg, examined the skin and praised God it wasn't broken. No rabies this morning; just a raging rabid thirst.

He threw another can.

The rat backed away slowly.

Grime-crusted knuckles massaged his eyes, pressed against his chapped lips. Then his palms flattened against the walls on either side and pushed him up as his knees popped, his ankles creaked, his vision blurred and doubled for a second and made his eyes water.

The rat didn't move.

At the mouth of the alley some fifty feet away he could see shadows passing through glaring light, Friday people on their way to start their Christmas shopping, a few late to work, all wishing the weekend would hurry up and get here. Probably one in eight glancing in and none of them seeing a thing. That was the beauty of it, these places he'd discovered. Four of them on this side of the boulevard alone. There were others, but none so deep, none so narrow, none blocked to the second story. He slept in this one, napped in two others, had a cardboard living room in one not half a step from the police station entrance in the town hall.

Keep moving and they won't get you.

A moving target is harder to hit.

The rat didn't move, but its tail slapped the ground.

"Ah, go on, you bastard," he told it, and slapped the night's dirt from his tweed overcoat.

It didn't move.

"Cheeky little shit, aren't you?"

There was nothing left to throw. All the garbage—in bags, cans, bags shoved into cans whose lids wouldn't stay on—was up near the mouth where the trucks could get at it easily. Back here things were forgotten.

Murtaugh; and the rat.

Improbably his thirst increased, and his stomach began to demand solace soon.

Shaking himself to adjust the coat's padded shoulders, he took a step toward the chubby rodent, growling and shaking a fist.

It backed away, tail thumping.

Murtaugh grinned. "Little prick." He kicked, missed, fell against the wall and kicked again.

The rat sat back on its haunches and opened its mouth to show him all its teeth.

"Jesus."

He coughed, and spat phlegm to one side, then ran as fast as he could, striking out as he passed the little vermin and whooping when he felt the side of his tape-lashed shoe hit the beast's rump. He didn't look back, and didn't slow down until he reached the sidewalk. Once there, blinded and blinking, he sagged against the wall's corner until he could catch his breath, a hand splayed across his chest, the other pinching his cheeks, wiping his chin. When he was ready, he adjusted himself again, spat on his palms and slicked his hair into place, checking his appearance in a clothing store window.

Not too bad, he decided after examining front and profile, straightening one lapel, flicking a piece of unidentifiable something from the tip of his thrice-broken nose. The overcoat hadn't yet seen a winter, he'd shaved yesterday at the Methodist Mission over on January Street—had to, they wouldn't give him Thanksgiving dinner unless he had—and there was still something about the face, the cheery flush that made his dark skin less menacing, the eyes that rejected pity, that kept people from shying away whenever he asked for a dime, a quarter, a chance to do some work.

Not too bad at all.

Given time, he might even look handsome again.

Unless the rats got to him first.

Oh hell, he thought, let's not start that, Blade, let's not look for trouble.

A test smile, then, a wink that all was well, and he considered stopping in at the bookstore. The bitch behind the counter always wrinkled her nose when he went in, and he always gave her his best *how-do* smile. Arlette. Snooty black bitch sees a black man down and out, figures she's got it made. Time was, she would have died to crawl into his bed. Time was. Now, all tits and tight skirts, probably laying Tobin in his office, she just wrinkled her nose and turned away. Once, only once, she had tried to stop him, the first time, but Tobin had let him in, hung around, and bless him had said nothing when Murtaugh took a chair and a book and spent a fair hour reading. Once a week, after that. Just to keep his brain in shape.

Pen Tobin hadn't recognized him.

Murtaugh didn't expect it, but he knew that someday it would happen. And since it might be today, what with the goddamn rat waking him up and all, he changed his mind and headed for the park. A day like this, it was the best place to be, not inside. Comfortable there and a chance for the night to get out of his bones. Besides, maybe Slap would be around. He grinned and wiped his nose with a finger. Him and Slap Zubronsky—the Hat Trick Boys. Part of a two-bit high school hockey team that for two years suddenly became glorious, became champs, the Hat Trick Boys setting all kinds of records, senior year even going to the regionals. What the hell. Stand this town on its ear the way they used to, make them take notice. Maybe. Maybe not. Didn't matter. He hadn't seen Slap in over a week, the man busy working pastel pictures on some paper he'd found behind a supply shop last month.

"My way up and out, man," Zubronsky had said from the dark of his own alley when Blade had found him. "Some guy, he's gonna see this stuff, he's gonna let me do a mural." A toothless smile a hundred miles wide. He'd snapped a finger against his gums. "Get me some choppers, bite a few ladies."

Right, Blade thought; right.

Trouble was, Slap was good. Very good. And from his spot by the park wall, he'd actually begun to sell a few things. A buck here, a few bucks there. Even some shit for Tobin's bookstore.

Up.

Out.

Didn't matter.

Slap was there, wasn't there, it didn't make any difference because Murtaugh's stomach was playing tuba like a fiend, and across from the park entrance was a bar, a new Chinese restaurant, and the Starlite Diner, which he hadn't gone to since he'd graduated from junior high God alone knew how long ago. One of them would have breakfast in the dumpsters in the parking lot behind them, and some stale bread he could feed to the birds at the pond.

And if they didn't have it, he could move on down the street, checking out all the other restaurants and sandwich shops, lounges and bars, maybe even the movie theaters. It was like a personal smorgasbord once you learned how to work it, once you let the cooks and chefs and busboys know you would even take a job if you couldn't take their garbage, or there was no garbage to take.

All in the working.

It was all in the working.

Of course, it helped that he was short, not quite the national average from the papers he had read. Hard to be a terror when you looked like a starving kid gone old before his time.

Also, the cops wouldn't hassle him, there in the park, sitting under a tree or down by the pond, not bothering anyone, not getting in anyone's way. He was known to them, most of them to him, and as long as he didn't pester the mothers and children, reserved his panhandling for the streets, they left him pretty much to himself.

Although it was warm again today, Indian summer refusing to let go, last night's taste of cold proved that autumn was at last giving way to the next season. Which meant he'd sleep better than usual in his private bedroom alley. Until it got cold, real cold, and he had to worry about freezing.

Goddamn rat.

Yet the alley was certainly better than going to the Mission. He only did that when he had to swallow his pride. Pious college kids and middle-age women, clucking and fussing over him, promising him a future and giving him soup. Making him pray, for god's sake, before he dropped onto a cot ten times harder than the mattress he'd made for himself.

Fat lot of good prayer had done for him lately.

Yesterday they had prayed more than usual, and louder, figuring the holiday was probably something special, had some special pipeline right to God from the pumpkin pie. Didn't help the Indians when the Pilgrims slaughtered them, did it, hell no. Didn't help him when it all went to hell, hell no.

Free turkey, though, free pie.

Lots of loud praying.

Goddamn rat.

As he passed a hardware store, he reminded himself to check

out one of the downtown construction sites, find a board or something, a two-by-four tossed aside. Clean the alley out. Bash the rat's goddamn brains in and have them for supper.

It wouldn't be the first time.

And it definitely wouldn't be the worst thing he'd ever eaten.

He nodded.

Something to look forward to—the perfect end to a perfect day, which he knew was ahead when the first woman he approached gave him a dollar . . . and didn't caution him not to spend it on liquor.

Perfect day.

Even the goddamn rat.

Even the food he found in the cans, some of it fresh, that filled him as he ate it on the slope above the pond, letting the sun try to warm him. He was careful to keep his mouth clean. Folks didn't give when you looked like a cannibal. Not that he was bothering anyone today. He had decided that today was for sitting and sunning and watching the girls.

Which reminded him of Bonita, made him wonder where she was and roll his eyes because he knew damn well where she was. At the train station. Almost always. Counting the windows of the cars that passed her. She had a number, she once told him back behind the movies, that when she reached it would take her away to someplace like Arizona where it was always warm and people always smiled and she could get rid of her disguise and show the world what she really was.

He grinned, hid the grin when an old woman scowled at him, walking her old dog.

What she really was was nuts.

Even Slap knew that.

And Slap's elevator didn't exactly always leave the first floor on time.

Murtaugh asked her, "Bonita your real name?"

"My secret name," she had answered, finger to her lips he was surprised to see still looked good to kiss. "You're the only one who knows it. You tell it, I'll die." Her face had hardened, become stone, scared the piss out of him. "I'll kill you if you tell it."

He hadn't. Not to anyone. Not even the kids who talked to him now and then, like the gimp kid he called "Leg" and talked sports with now and then, and the redhead in the bookstore and the jock a hundred feet tall who didn't believe Blade had ever played hockey but kept asking him how it was all that time, to be famous.

Famous is, Murtaugh had told him, as famous does.

Meaning, famous is a load they dump on your back and forget to tell you it's too big for you to carry when you're too young to get laid.

The kid had frowned, dropped him a buck, and walked away.

Murtaugh hadn't been able to resist: "And high school famous ain't worth a shit!" he'd yelled.

The kid had laughed, and kept coming back every once in a while. He made Murtaugh nervous, but what the hell, talking to him was better than a sharp stick in the eye.

They were all right, those kids; at least they didn't treat him as if he were nuts.

He snorted and slipped a handful of crumbs onto the ground a few inches from his left foot. A young duck, one of two that had waddled out of the water when he'd clucked an invitation to the family, approached the pile in a hurry, talked to it, stabbed at it, scattered it, and wheeled when its brother tried to get in on the meal.

He smiled and slowly drew up his right leg.

Every year he had to retrain them; every year the stupid birds forgot who he was.

What the hell, the world had forgotten who he was, most of it. Sometimes he wasn't even sure himself.

A nurse strolled by, arm-in-arm with a man in a perfectly pressed pale suit, She waved; the man only nodded, so obviously puzzled by the woman's greeting a bum that Murtaugh could do no less than wave back and salute.

Nice lady, that one. Twice sewed him up when punks had tossed him around, just for the hell of it. Good hands. Soft hands. He remembered her smell being not like a hospital but like talc and sweet candy. He never saw the guy before, he must be new in her life.

Lucky lady.

The ducks were called back by their parents.

"Go on," he urged them quietly. His hands opened. "Nothing left today."

They did, tails swinging so hard one lost its balance and skidded on his beak when it reached the bank.

Then Murtaugh lifted the other leg and hugged his shins. His coat was open, shirt unbuttoned to the center of his chest. He hadn't worn the sport jacket he'd found a week ago because he knew it'd be too much padding too soon. It was too warm now, sweat pooling under his armpits and around his waist, but you couldn't panhandle unless you really looked like a loser.

God, he thought, wasn't that the irony of it.

Son of a bitch Blade Murtaugh has to *work* at looking like he has no money, no job, no goal in life but survive from dawn to dawn.

Something crawled around the back of his neck. He slapped at it, rubbed at it, wiped his hand on the grass without learning what he'd killed.

Of course, in the old days he didn't hardly have to work at all. Everything he wanted had come his way, no sweat, goddamn, like he was King Midas in the flesh. He had even had a decent house out there on Long Island. No mansion, but what the hell. Mowed his lawn. Paid his taxes. Went to parties his bosses threw. Saw women who actually looked back at him and didn't flinch. Not like now. Not like Arlette the bitch Bingham. Hell, no, not like now. And it hadn't taken much. One damn lousy investment, one sliver ever so carefully shaved off his tax form, and some cretin down in Washington catches him. First time; last time. The contacts dried up, more taxes came due, more contacts slipped away like jackals in the sun, more taxes . . . the panic.

White man gets caught, he gets a slap on the wrist, naughty boy, shame shame, pay the fine and take it off your taxes; black man slips away.

Trouble was, he'd long since lost the bitterness. It had helped keep him angry until the day he admitted he was the one who had screwed up, no one else. Got caught. Caught hell and went there to live.

He wiped his nose on a sleeve, burrowed his chin against his thigh.

Hadn't been for the panic he might've gotten through.

Hadn't been, however, had been, and he hadn't.

One day he has this gorgeous car right off the boat from Italy, paid for in cash; the next day he wakes up in some dive in some town in New England, no money, no food, god knows how many days' growth on his face, stinking like vomit and feeling twice as bad.

Goddamn.

Hanging around until winter, getting the hang of it, living on the streets, getting a grip on self-pity, then drifting south when he damn near froze his ass off. It had taken him a month walking and stumbling, not really realizing where he was heading until he ended up in his hometown.

Nobody had recognized him; he told no one his name.

Hat Trick Boy, prodigal son, goddamn, goddamn.

He wondered what Tobin would say if he walked right up and said, "Hey, Pen, you remember me? Blade? Fastest skater in North Jersey? Umpteen zillion goals senior year, remember? How you been, man?"

Tobin would shit.

What the hell.

Pay for your sins.

He touched the board beside him.

Goddamn rat gonna get his tonight, for damn sure.

Unless he heard the screaming.

He heard the screaming, shit, he just might keep that rat around, train him like a watchdog, keep him safe.

He shivered, hugged himself more tightly.

Never. Never in what was left of his life did he ever want to hear that sound again.

Going for his evening constitutional last week, checking out the trash, hunting less for food than something to add to his living room alley, and this shriek, this high-pitched, brain-busting, soul-sucking shriek comes out of the night like a bat bent for hell. Never ran so hard in his whole damn life. Kept him in bed for a day, shaking like fever had taken over his muscles.

Stopped him from walking around the neighborhoods during the afternoon, watching the gardens bed down for the season, stopping now and then to talk to an old woman who knew that he knew what he was talking about when he suggested mulch over there and cedar chips over here.

Sometimes they even tried to hire him.

He always declined with a smile and a polite salute.

Though the thought of putting his hands in dirt, killing weeds, smelling flowers . . . sometimes it was a thought.

Yeah.

And maybe he'd teach the rat like he taught the ducks.

Why the hell not? A rat's got more brains.

He picked up the board and laid it across his knees, hung his wrists over the ends and stared at the water.

Got more brains than he does, that's for damn sure. He had the brains, he could've made something of himself, come back from adversity, cleared his name, started over. Instead, everybody's back turned on him, all doors closed and locked, he took the slide, and found it good, and besides he was too damn tired, even a mule knows when to balk and when to move before the whip gets used again.

He dozed.

He didn't dream.

TEN

The station at Foxriver was little more than a raised wood platform fifty yards long between the north- and southbound tracks. Above it was a gleaming peaked roof held up by squared metal posts, the recessed lighting just bright enough for people to see where they were going on cloudy days. There was no stationmaster, no ticket office, no place to buy coffee or soda, and only three newspaper dispensers that were, without fail, empty by the time the last evening commuter train passed through. The tracks crossed the river just above North Bridge, made a right turn behind the forbidding VA convalescent home, and followed the park until they slipped down the hill and headed for Hoboken and the Hudson River. Opposite the station to the east was a row of closely-placed, determined fir which hid the houses behind; between the platform and the park wall a parking lot forever scheduled to be widened.

In the middle of the day it was generally deserted.

Bonita Logan liked it that way. It was the only place she had been able to find where the monsters couldn't find her, the monsters they kept caged in the schools every day, teaching them how to tease her, make her cry, make her say bad words, make her break down and give them her real name, make her forget who she really was. Dancing around her, calling her names, laughing, pointing, gesturing to make her blush until someone bigger chased them away, then chased her away. She never chased the monsters herself. That would be wrong. A queen had knights who did that work for her.

Like Blade, and Slap, and the knight with one leg, and the knight so big he could crush boulders with his bare hands and kept telling her how pretty she looked, like a movie star he used to see on TV, and sometimes handing her a dollar or two and waving when he left her to be with the other knights who always wore black armor.

Sometimes, of course, her knights were on a quest and she had to deal with the monsters all by herself. That was okay. She was strong. She always had been. Had to be to keep the monsters from stealing her name, her soul, her eyes that everyone had always said was her best feature. Huge. Round. The color of the sky in the middle of May.

"Bonita," they would say, though of course they used her real name, "someday you're going to break hearts with those eyes."

Something flapped between the rails. A piece of colorless paper that looked like the wing of something small trying desperately to climb out of the way of the train.

She watched it until it settled.

Then she settled herself, passing smooth hands over her thighs, smoothing the wrinkles from the too-large jeans she'd been nursing along since last August; drawing her lamb's wool coat over her legs, smoothing out the rough spots; patting her hair near the color of Blade's skin, smoothing out the curls she hated, wished she could banish because they made her stand out, just like her eyes; adjusting the cloth she'd folded into a convoluted turban around her head, touching the silver diamond in the center, smoothing the bow whose tails trailed down her back; folding her hands carefully, ladylike, in her lap, squeezing her fingers together so the veins that bulged along the backs of her hands would smooth out, go away.

When everything was ready, she waited.

For the train.

She had a feeling about the next one. It would be the one that gave her the number that would take her away. It had to be. Foxriver was making her nervous. Usually she liked it here. Not too many little monsters bothered her these days, they were too busy thinking about Christmas, not too many cops tried to hustle her into a cell, not too many men tried to hustle her out of her pants and leave without paying.

She tapped her foot.

She felt the air begin to move.

She felt the rush of the train before it even reached town.

Number, she prayed; please give me the number so I can go away.

Usually, Foxriver was fine.

It wasn't anymore.

One of her knights was dead, killed by the invisible dragon that had left its den in the night country, and the other knights hardly noticed her at all anymore. At first she had been angry, wondering who they thought they were, deserting her in time of war; then she had been sad that the teachers who taught the monsters seemed to have poisoned her knights as well; then she had resigned herself to fighting the fight alone. It was what all good queens did in the end. Fight the fight themselves. The knights, after all, were only human, and being human, they were scared.

Being a queen, she wasn't human.

So it bothered her that she was nervous, because that meant there was another secret somewhere in town, one she didn't know, one she had to find out, one she didn't want to find out before she reached her magic number and was taken away to someplace warm.

The tracks hummed.

She straightened her back, pursed her lips, tried to clear her mind so she could begin the count.

And in clearing her mind, she heard the scream again.

The scream of her knight.

Like the scream of the train's brakes when it stopped at the station and the people got off in a rush and swirl of dark colors, not talking, breath steaming like horses back from a run, and she stared at them with her beautiful wide eyes and nodded

politely when one smiled at her and scowled when one sneered
and gasped when the train pulled away without warning and
she hadn't been able to count a single window.

Oh Lord, she thought; oh Lord, I'm gonna die.

Gonna get out, Slap sang gaily to himself as he touched up a
bit of the sky over a sagging barn in a barren field; gonna get
out, gonna get rich, gonna take Blade to the best restaurant in
town, gonna get laid, maybe Bonita, gonna get new clothes,
gonna get warm, gonna stay dry, gonna get out.

Protected from the wind by screens he'd fashioned from
scraps of metal, fifteen sheets of stiff paper were propped
against the alley wall. The private alley. So private, not even the
cops knew about it, and Blade didn't always remember.

Slap's hands, stubby fingers and flesh sagging, stained with
pastel chalk.

He tipped back his golfer's cap and glared up at the sky.

Not enough light. Never enough light. Can't see what I'm
doing, gonna mess it up, never gonna get out.

A tear broke across his cheek, and he swiped it away angrily,
leaving behind smears of chalk dust.

Too many shadows.

Cloud-shadows.

Wall-shadows.

Cat-shadows. Creeping around him all the time, creeping
around the house, tripping him, making his mother mad
because he kept stepping on them and she kept telling him why
couldn't he act like a man, grow up, stay out her way or she'd
use her magic powers to call the magic cats to take care of him
if he didn't stop being a baby. Cat-shadows sneaking up on him
in the night, wanting to tear his eyes out, his tongue out.
Cat-shadows he stalked in the park with the club he'd made
from a dead branch. Cat-shadows died. Cat-shadows bled.
Cat-shadows didn't bother him ever, ever again.

He laughed without a sound, wondering how the damn hell
he'd lived through his mother's craziness. It hadn't been easy.
And after graduation, the jobs he had hadn't been easy either.

Nobody cared that he'd scored more goals than even Blade. The jobs weren't easy, and sometimes they weren't there. Say goodbye to his mother, the old bitch, say goodbye to the damn cats, put the world on his finger and spin it, pick a spot, go find the jobs and all the money he could spend. Not easy. Not here and not there, New York and Delaware and Pennsylvania and once even down in South Carolina. Not easy. Easier to come home, live in the park, forget the days.

A cloud brief and thin chilled the alley.

He'd have to quit for today.

He couldn't.

Not since Pen Tobin was going to put his mural in the bookshop window, all the people looking on, buying things, just because of him.

And not since the man had come that morning, come to the wall on the south side of the park and saw what Slap had done and had stood there while Slap worked, touching up, never satisfied, shaking from the cold though the sun was white and hot, nearly weeping when he almost messed up a dog trying to catch a duck down by the pond. The man watched without speaking. Slap knew he was there, had seen him before, had sold him one flower-piece for nearly five bucks.

Then the man had said, "Do you have any training? Formal training in art, I mean?"

Slap looked over his shoulder, cringing. No one spoke to him. They watched him. They dropped coins, once a dollar, in the coffee can. They walked away. They never spoke.

"I played hockey," Slap said, voice harsh with disuse.

The man nodded.

Slap touched up a gravestone.

Never satisfied; ever.

The man tapped his shoulder.

Slap nearly screamed.

"The man who has that bookstore, he said you did that display he's putting up in his window. That right?"

"Three days. Three days in the alley."

A pause.

"Take this," the man finally said, and dropped a business card on the sidewalk. "Come and see me Monday morning. No. Monday I have to be in the city. Tuesday. Come on Tuesday. Bring a couple of things. That cemetery over there, a few more. You've never had any training?"

Slap shook his head. "Hockey," he said. "I'm a Hat Trick Boy. Slapshot. Hat Trick."

The man smiled and walked away.

Slap sat on the ground heavily, swallowed, grabbed the coffee can and clutched it to his chest. Stared at the park wall bricks. Breathed as evenly as he could. And knew that he was frightened. Hell, he was terrified. It was a joke. Bastard kidding around, making him think things he thought only in his alley dreams, making him go to some office, some gallery, some shop, and laughing at him with his friends, tearing up his pictures, throwing him back into the gutter.

He looked up at the sky again, remembering that morning, how he'd grabbed his pictures and chalks and had run a million miles along the river, along the sidewalks, until he figured the man hadn't followed him to laugh at him with his friends. Then he decided to believe it. Why not? Believe this, believe that, what was there left to lose for Christ's sake?

Now there was no light left.

Tuesday morning.

He had to wait all weekend until Tuesday morning.

It scared him to death.

Bonita adjusted her turban, lifted her chin, marched off the platform, and headed for home. She hadn't counted windows. After missing that train, the whole day had been wasted and she had only sat there, trying to decide if that meant she needn't bother with the weekend trains too. She didn't know. It was confusing. This had never happened before. She decided to take a walk through the park to clear her mind, have a look at her subjects and make sure they were well, then return to her bedchamber and study the diary she had been keeping for years. It had all the answers. She would find the one she needed and know if she had to return here tomorrow.

If she did, that would be fine, she would be ready.

If she did not, that would be upsetting, but she had been upset before and she was strong and she would handle it just as she always had.

As she passed through a gap in the wall flanked by stone pillars pigeon-stained and crumbling and made her way slowly down the path toward the pond, she wondered if perhaps Erma might be of some assistance. A good handmaiden she was, never complaining, always smiling, always willing to share her food. It was shame Calvin wasn't noble born. Had he been, Bonita would have given him a title and permitted Erma to marry him. As it was, Calvin wouldn't even make a good squire. He yelled too much. He called her names. He called Erma names. He called the fat serving woman names, who always yelled back like the gutter servant she was. He would never make a proper duke, nor even a decent baron. Once a commoner, always a commoner, she always believed, and Calvin Nobbs was about as common as common got.

The ducks and geese were fine.

A young couple raced across the grass, but Bonita didn't scold them. It was, after all, coming on winter, soon enough to be cooped up in their huts, huddled around their meager fires, sipping broth and salted meat and waiting for spring. Let them have their fun. She was young once; she remembered.

"Bonita!"

She stopped, held her breath.

"Hey, Bonita!"

A slow turn to her right, frowning slightly when she didn't see anyone until she looked up the slope, and he came toward her, topcoat casually draped over his shoulder, hair tossed by the breeze, teeth showing in a smile that made her wonder. He stopped when he reached her, so tall she had to look up.

"I haven't seen you around," he said quietly.

She said nothing; she could say nothing.

"You're all right, aren't you?"

She managed a nod, and swore under her breath when she felt the turban slide over her brow.

He looked beyond her, scanning the park. "I've missed you."

She breathed again. And smiled stiffly.

His hand gently floated to her shoulder; he leaned down; his breath ghosted past her ear. "I'm going to be open late tonight, Friday and all. If you've nothing to do . . ." He shrugged. The hand didn't move.

In her stomach something lurched, became cold, became warm, became so hot she stepped away and nearly stumbled.

He didn't help her.

"I may drop in," she said at last, her voice small and crystal. "I have other things to do first."

"Of course," he agreed quickly. "I understand." The coat snaked from his shoulder into his hands, flipped around like a cape and his arms pierced it, his hands reappeared and he unfolded a lapel. Then, before she could stop him, he checked the park again, leaned over and kissed her cheek.

"Until later" was the whisper that made her shiver as he left, not looking back, fading into the shrubs and the protection of the trees; "Until later" was the echo that followed her as she walked twice and three times around the pond, staring at the water, seeing darts of light that stung her eyes; "Until later" was the promise that made her frown and mutter and forget what she was and who she was until she remembered that she hadn't counted the windows.

She would tell him, she decided; tonight, this night, she would tell him everything. Perhaps then he would help her.

Her lips almost betrayed the smile she felt.

He was a nice man, was the gallant Lord Tobin, but he didn't know it all even if he believed he did; and when he did, it would be too late, he'd be deeper in her spell and nothing would save him from becoming her king.

She was, after all, not like the others.

She was, after all, not as crazy as he thought.

On the Boulevard she lifted a hand and the magic light turned to let her pass, the carriages stopped with groans and grumblings, and she crossed, nodding imperiously to those drivers whose faces she could see. On the other side she paused, suddenly uncertain, feeling the cold that slipped down the sides of the buildings, feeling the wind pull at her turban, feeling something made of ice slide up one leg and stab at her thigh. She gasped. She grabbed a lamppost and lowered her head, humiliated that her subjects should see her this way, hating the tears that smeared her makeup, tasted salty on her lips, fell to the sidewalk and shattered like glass.

A hand touched her shoulder. "Are you all right, lady?"

She nodded without looking up.

"You want me to call a doctor?"

She shook her head.

Go away, she thought; please go away.

The speaker did.

The pain left with him.

She pushed away and began to hurry, not caring now how she looked, only knowing that something terrible had just happened, some magic had struck her helpless, made her vulnerable, made her common; it had attacked her in the open, and she hadn't even heard the scream.

ELEVEN

First thing Saturday morning Slap stood on the other side of the Boulevard, skipping left, skipping right, trying to see through the traffic as Pen Tobin stood in the display window of Sunset Books. The girl who worked with him was on the sidewalk, dancing in place with only a sweater tossed over her shoulders to keep herself warm. He could see her breath from all the way over here and felt sorry for her, wished he could help her; she was the one of them, one of the kids who kept the other kids from kicking his pictures away when he displayed them at the wall. He didn't know her name. He didn't really care. She was a kid. She had plenty of time to learn his.

C'mon, c'mon, c'mon, he urged; hurry up, all the people gone, done their shopping, no one left to see, c'mon, c'mon, c'mon, hurry up.

He stepped anxiously toward the curb, pulled back, and snarled when someone bumped into him, hard, shoved him away and called him a name.

No, he told himself; no time for mad. Watch the girl and Tobin, make sure they get it right.

The girl raised a palm, gesturing the man higher, lower, higher again and to the left as he held a roll of tape in his mouth and a clumsy cardboard cutout of a reindeer in his right hand.

Doing it, Slap thought gleefully; god damn, they're really doing it.

A little to the left, the girl signaled once more, *not so far, back, the other way, that's good, that's perfect.*

Tobin set the tape.

Slap mopped his forehead with a sleeve, rested his free hand against his chest where his heart was trying to get out in a hurry. They keep this up, they won't be done until Easter, what good will it do?

Tobin picked up a wreath-bedecked snowman with a jaunty top hat and they did it again. And with a horse-drawn sleigh, a robin wearing a too-large muffler, a decorated Christmas tree with a silver angel on top, two little kids having a snowball fight, finally fourteen flattened book covers pinned to a large, colorful, and detailed drawing of Foxriver Park after a gentle fall of snow. Slap had been paid twenty dollars for the scene; the cut-outs had been thrown in extra. *Give Your Imagination Something For Christmas* letters proclaimed across the top. Slap's letters.

It looked wonderful.

It looked . . . perfect.

He couldn't help it; he applauded his delight, set his cap backward, then sprinted across the street as soon as he spotted the room, and hid between two parked cars, rubbing his hands, wishing Bonita and Blade were here, they'd see how soon he was getting out, oh boy.

"Looks nice, Fern."

He looked around just as a girl with a ponytail passed behind, a tall kid with tons of hair at her side. He knew them too. The boy didn't like him, once called him a nigger even though he wasn't, he was just dirty, but the kid didn't care. Slap didn't either; Blade was the nigger, what the hell. Blade didn't care.

"Thanks, Laine. Slap—you know Slap? he has the pictures up at the park?—he did them."

"He the black guy?" Laine asked.

"No, that's Blade."

"Right," Joey said, clearly not giving a damn. "Scott's old gimping buddy."

"Jesus, Costello," Fern said, "lay off, okay?"

The boy muttered something else and the girl with him yanked his arm hard, making him yelp. Slap grinned, covered his mouth with both hands, and ducked in case they heard him.

The crowds thickened, thinned, packages and bags and boxes and ribbons and the sound of a bell being rung on the corner and from somewhere up the street near the plaza the smell of roasting chestnuts.

"You going to the show tonight?" Laine said.

An impatient rap on the window; Fern shrugged at Tobin, who was glaring at her, shaking a book cover in one hand.

"I don't know. I guess so." She pointed, and her boss taped. "Actually, I think maybe Scott just wants to go to the diner."

Joey groaned and smacked his forehead. "Again? You two guys practically live there, for god's sake. What's the big deal all of a sudden? You afraid to go home or what?"

"Ask Scott," Fern told him, and directed another cover to its place before hugging herself, then before blowing into her hands and pressing them to her cheeks. "The guy that followed—"

"Oh my god." Joey shook his head, half in anger, half in disgust. "Look, Bellard, ain't you two gonna get it through your heads nothing's going on?" He put an arm around Laine's shoulders and leaned forward, grinning. "No disappearing monster bugs, no Jack the Ripper, no whatever the hell it is you two numbnuts thought you saw."

"Joey—"

"Why don't you just go to whatshername, the"—he waved his free hand, nearly struck a passerby—"the frigging *Queen* of Foxriver." He laughed unpleasantly. "Tell her to look in her crystal ball, maybe she can tell you something."

"Joey, stop it."

"Well, c'mon, Fern, you guys are acting nuts. That fucking Tobin just made a pass at you, that's all."

Slap frowned, checked the traffic, and moved up a car, keeping low, gotta keep low, wondering what that bigmouth son of a bitch has to do with Bonita, why he's making fun of her like that.

"I didn't imagine it," Fern said stiffly, and turned her back to the street.

"Great," Laine said to the boy. "Just great."

Joey kicked at the sidewalk. "Christ." He kicked again, scratched his head vigorously. "It's just that you guys are acting just like Eddie did y'know? I mean—"

"I know what you mean," Laine interrupted curtly. "And you know that isn't fair. Eddie's—"

"Oh Jesus, spare me," he said, looking up at the sky.

Slap didn't get it. First he argues with the one girl, then the other, then talks like he's arguing with himself. What a jerk. He'd have to remember all this, tell it to Blade, give his friend a laugh.

"God, it's freezing out here!" Fern declared loudly.

Tobin held up a hand—*hang on, we're almost done.*

"He just wants to see you freeze your nipples," Joey said, and laughed.

Slap watched both girls roll their eyes, heard the girls say they'd call before tonight, before Fern started for the bookstore entrance.

"Nice pigeon," Joey called, pointing to the robin. Laine giggled and they merged with the crowd.

Pigeon, Slap thought angrily, watching them leave, looking at the window, tilting his head one way, the other, standing on his toes and staring again; that ain't no pigeon, you stupid shit, don't they teach you nothing no more in school?

Bonita lay in her bed.

The basement ceiling was cracked and sagging, flakes of paint and plaster peeling away, poised, just waiting to fall on the bare floor, on her.

Her hands were clasped loosely across her stomach.

Beside her, the furnace coughed and grumbled; above her, she could hear someone stomping hard toward the front door.

It sounded like Calvin. He never just walked, he always had to stomp.

On another day long ago she would have climbed the stairs, cornered him, yelled at him, ordered him to be more respectful in the presence of his queen; today she only smiled and closed her eyes.

Last night she had done things to Pen Tobin he had only read about in books. Breasts and lips and hands and legs, and all the time him wanting to know where she lived, why couldn't he meet her there, how could she be like she was when she lived on the goddamn street for god's sake, where did she learn all this stuff, and she had only smothered his common questions with her breasts and lips and hands and legs.

Tonight she was seeing him again. Twice in a row. Something they had never done before. Once a month, maybe, sometimes twice when it was summer, that's all. Not two times in a row, never, ever two times in a row.

By the time she was done with him, he had begged her not to leave. But of course she had to. No queen was ever found in the bed of a lord. It wasn't done. She had her reputation to think of, and her kingdom.

The smile widened to a grin.

But she had him.

The hell with sitting in the cold and counting train windows.

The secret number wasn't in glass after all, it was in the Sunset Books cash register, and for the longest time since waking she had scolded herself for not thinking of it before. She must have been crazy to be so stupid, or deliberately led astray by the fat serving women who called her names no real woman would call another, or deluded by a spell cast by the old woman who lived alone on the next block.

It didn't matter.

She knew now, she knew it all, and she licked her lips in anticipation, shifting, wriggling her hips, feeling for a moment the protective sword she kept under her pillow, the sword she'd taken from the kitchen upstairs. That had been when Calvin the Commoner had threatened to beat her.

Maybe she would use it before she left the castle, nip, so to speak, the rebellious conspiracy in the bud.

Maybe not.

Not tonight.

Tonight she would grace Lord Tobin right in his shop, tomorrow she would visit the village shops and find out how much gold it would take to take her to the warm place, and the day after that, or the day after that, she would bid her knights farewell and head into the setting sun.

She giggled.

The furnace sighed.

There was no doubt in her mind—unless the magic got her again, today she would be queen, and tomorrow she would be making plans to be gone.

Cap pulled low, Slap sat against the park wall, his wall, and grinned at the traffic, grinned at the pedestrians, grinned at the cat he heard in the brush behind him. Rustling the leaves. Probably stalking a bird. Survival, Blade, he thought; cat's gotta do it, Hat Trick Boy gonna do it for sure.

His grin widened.

No cat bothered him now, slanty eyes and all that fur. Sneak around all it wants, it don't bother him anymore.

Gonna get out, man. Gonna get out.

Hat Trick Boy done scored himself a goal.

He closed his eyes to the sun.

Didn't matter that he hadn't been able to find Blade, tell him about the boy, what the boy said, what the girl said. It wasn't important now. His mural was up, he was gonna see the man with the card on Tuesday, he was gonna have new teeth, he was gonna have new clothes, Blade could wait until tomorrow to hear what he had to say.

Tomorrow was Sunday.

The Lord's day.

The perfect day to tell Blade how it was all gonna turn out.

He shifted.

He might even go to see Bonita, tell her about all his money, maybe she'd do to him like she was doing to Pen Tobin, who didn't think anybody knew about it. He giggled. Shit, everybody knew it, everybody on the street.

Eyes closed, sun still warm on his face, he clapped his hands softly and sighed.

My, he thought, ain't it all just damn fine.

TWELVE

The Boulevard was empty, all the lights and noise and pedestrians farther down, on the Strip. Even the shops had minimal illumination, and what traffic there was sped past without slowing because there was nothing to see. Tires crackled as the temperature dropped; steam rose silently in ropes and pyres from manhole covers and vents in the sides of buildings; a crisp tough to the air, the promise of snow.

Slap, his cap pulled down as far as it would go, ragged collar turned up, extra newspaper stuffed into his sneakers to cover the holes, stood alone on the sidewalk outside Sunset Books, hopping excitedly from foot to foot, hands tucked into his armpits and grabbing at his ribs. The blast from a bus passing behind him made him squint, watered his eyes, but he shook his head to clear them and grinned.

It was still there.

The snowy park was still there, just as he'd drawn it.

Gonna get out. Jesus God, hallelujah, I'm gonna get out.

Blade, Bonita, you gotta see this, you gotta know.

He'd awakened from his nap in the dark, suddenly frightened, not knowing where he was. And once his senses returned, he'd nearly been flattened by a truck as he ran across the street to find something to eat behind the diner. Nothing. And nothing anyplace else he could get to before the anxiety finally grabbed him by the shoulders and swung him around and kicked him all the way up to the store.

Just to be sure.

Just to be sure it hadn't been a dream.

A glance up and down the sidewalk, not liking what he saw, faint lights and shadows, like ghosts were out shopping tonight just beyond the corner of his vision. It was no way to think. Next thing he knew, he'd be spooking himself over cats and that wouldn't do. This afternoon the cat in the park hadn't bothered him, and he was proud of himself, damn proud, for not finding his club and beating in its head.

No cats bothered him anymore.

No damn ghosts either.

A deep breath, a sniff, a knuckle across one eye, and he moved closer to the window and giggled, moved back to the curb and shook his head at the robin. Damn thing looked like a mummified pigeon, it sucked, he wished Tobin hadn't used it, it ruined the whole thing. But since he couldn't do anything about it, he could only hope the man whose card he now had tucked safely into his cap wouldn't see it, or think maybe it really was a masked pigeon. Out Christmas shopping, like the sign said. Imagination. Christmas. Vacation. Something he couldn't remember what it was, though as soon as he got out, got rich, he was gonna take a zillion of them every year.

With thumbs hooked into his suspenders, he stepped down off the curb and cocked his head side to side, stepped up again and licked his lips. He was awfully thirsty and his mouth felt filled with grit. He ought to head down to the Starlite, try to cadge a drink, or hit one of the bars, cadge a real damn drink. Celebrate is what he should do. Celebrate until his brains ran out of his ears. What the hell, why not?

A car passed, horn screaming.

He jumped back onto the sidewalk and swallowed, leaned forward and stared at the juncture of store and pavement. It was dark there, dark there all along the street, and he thought he saw something moving. Creeping. Sneaking. Like a rat. Or a cat.

He swallowed again.

Look at the snow, jackass, look at the snow, no cats there, look at the snow and the trees and the kids having fun.

He did.

A hand gripped his arm and he whimpered, cringed, planted his feet, didn't want no cop moving him along.

"Damn," said Blade Murtaugh, "you're worse than a rabbit, I swear to god."

Slap twisted his arm free. "Just looking," he said sullenly, and sniffed. "Just looking." Sniffed again.

Murtaugh peered closely at him. "When was the last time you ate, you idiot?"

Slap shrugged. What did it matter? He was on his way, all them people looking at his snow.

Murtaugh shoved a roll into his pocket. "Damnit, you gotta eat, man. You don't eat, you don't get energy; you don't get energy, you don't work." He snorted. "Shit, you ain't never getting out of the streets, you look like a zombie. Idiot."

Yes I am, Slap told him, no words, just a look; I'm getting out and you're still here.

Blade grunted, and rubbed the back of his neck. "You gonna stay here all night?"

"Might."

"Idiot."

Slap grinned and winked.

Murtaugh shoved something else in after the roll and wandered off, muttering to himself, turned around suddenly and came back, put his hand on Slap's shoulder. "You watch yourself tonight, man, you hear?"

Slap frowned. "What for?"

Blade scratched his neck fiercely. "Don't know, Mr. Hat Trick. Just got a feeling." He chuckled. "Somebody let all the electricity loose."

"Zap," Slap said, poking Blade's stomach with a thumb.

"Right. Zap." And he walked away again, muttering again, once in a while punching out at the air.

Slap didn't watch him go. Murtaugh was gone. Slap was still here. Working on it, working on getting out. Murtaugh was history.

Would be better, though, if he wasn't so scared.

A cruiser floated toward him, a spotlight exploding, pinning him like a moth, turning his head. He held up a hand to protect his eyes and, with a wave to the horse-and-sleigh, the stupid robin, all that beautiful snow, he walked south. Hunched. Tugging his cap low. And when the light snapped off and the cruiser sped up, he managed a two-step and a quiet "Hot damn." Last time those fuckers mess with him, that's for sure. Last time. Next time they'll be saying yessir and nosir and can I wipe your nose sir. Next time they see him, he'll be out, up and out.

He nibbled on the roll. Stale, but what the hell.

He crossed the Boulevard and walked along the park's stone wall, dragging his left hand lightly over the bumps and tiny holes, knowing every one. Ahead, a bunch of kids ran through the entrance. Deep inside he could hear music, figured a jam session, didn't want to go. They were there sometimes, especially in summer; guys with guitars and saxophones and trumpets and stuff, just playing down by the pond where they didn't bother nobody. Made a few bucks and moved on. In winter they didn't stay so long, but they were still in there until their lips and fingers froze.

When he reached the entrance himself, he hesitated. All the lights were on the other side, and he could see heads and faces in the Starlite windows. Licked his lips. Rubbed his stomach. Snapped his suspenders and decided that he had enough liquor at home to last him until Tuesday.

That was the important thing.

He had to last until Tuesday.

All right, then.

As he stepped into the dark, he looked over his shoulder and saw Blade fussing around the florist shop that even this late had a booth outside the door. Blade and his damn flowers; Blade and his damn grass; Blade and his damn ducks and trees.

Hat Trick Boy and his god damn weeds.

Slap laughed and gave Murtaugh a friendly flip of his finger, and ducked quickly, silently, into the brush.

Unlike the alley where he did all his work, his real home was cramped. Several large cardboard boxes torn apart and reassembled into a monk's cell jammed under a pine tree's heavy lower boughs and tucked hard into the southwest corner of the park wall. Laurel and boxwood took care of the other sides, cut it off, and the ground was thick with years of needles and leaves falling, settling, and forever smelling damp. It was barely large enough to stand up in, just long enough for him to lie down in, on several layers of blankets stolen from the January Street mission. A tiny window had been cut in one wall, but not for light—for air, and to make sure the cats didn't sneak up on him without him seeing. He had no candles, no lantern. He didn't want them. Everything he required was within reach—can opener, cans, a small apple crate in which he kept his other clothes, taped on one wall a wrinkled photograph of him and Blade after the last game of the last year when anyone knew his real name. He could only see it in daylight; at night he didn't have to.

He sat on the bed and hugged his knees to his chest.

Tomorrow he would spend the whole day in his private place, making sure his pictures were safe, fixing those that needed fixing, deciding which ones he would take to the man who gave him the card. He smiled. That part would drive him nuts. That part would make him crazy.

But it would keep him from remembering how scared he was.

The breeze crept down the pine, ticked the needles together.

What would he do with all that money?

Cool air slipped in through the window.

New clothes? A real meal?

A branch scratched against the roof.

He rocked and grinned and hugged his knees more tightly. Nope, no way. A place to live. An apartment. Three rooms, maybe four, a real bathroom and not the bushes outside, a refrigerator, a stove, a real bed, a chair, his pictures on all the walls or maybe he'd paint a mural, good god clothes in the closets and his name on the mail slot and he'd probably go nuts filling all that great *space*.

The breeze gusted and the walls trembled.

Blade would come over for dinner.

Bonita would come over and take off all her clothes.

Pebbles fell from the top of the wall and rattled on the roof.

The grin snapped off. His head lowered until it pressed against his knees. His arms began to ache from grabbing his legs so hard.

Hat Trick Boy don't know if he can do it. Nothing has changed for years, and now all of it changed.

Oh shit.

Something landed on the roof. Something heavy. Something hard.

He looked up, reached up, felt the cardboard sagging. He thought it might be a rock until the sagging moved, and he heard something walking up there. Slowly. Quietly. Stopping at the edge just over the window.

Settling down.

Pine needles ticked.

Slap closed his eyes and prayed it was only some drunk, some kid.

Gonna get out, he prayed, hunched over, slowly falling to his side.

Go away.

He opened one eye and looked toward the window, only the window wasn't there. Black was there. Blacker than the night. Blacker, and colder, and moving swift when he screamed.

PART THREE

WHAT WE
LEARNED

THIRTEEN

Nobody dreamed.
Nobody screamed.
Nobody died until the giants came.

FOURTEEN

Snow in large flakes late Saturday night when most beds were filled, most dreamers trying to seek small comfort in the dark; wet flakes that melted as soon as they touched the ground, soon turning streets and sidewalks and windshields to ice, ice gathering on dead branches, in gutters, on grass; small flakes by false dawn that gathered and spread and fell so thickly the air seemed thick with fog and those who went to church went with heads already bowed.

No sound.

Snow swallowed it.

No wind.

The storm had its own breath and the snow traveled along it in slow spirals and whorls, sharp nails ticking against window panes, gathering on sills, porches losing their first step by Sunday afternoon, their second by night, plows scraping and sanders spitting, an automobile waltzing in slow motion through an empty intersection until it struck, in slow motion, a telephone pole.

By midnight the large flakes had arrived, and those who claimed to know how to tell the weather by a look claimed the storm would soon be over, large flakes didn't last, the clouds weren't that thick.

Monday noon was dark; the air was white and still falling.

Schools closed, businesses didn't bother, only one train stopped at the station, but not for long.

The silence continued except for chains on old tires and the grate of shovels on walks and the blast of a snowblower that couldn't quite force its revolving teeth to the ground; Briarwood Heights lost its telephones when ice split a wire, and the South End, for a while, lost its water when a pipe nearly a century old cracked beneath the street and the blacktop collapsed and a geyser erupted, steaming, bellowing, the water freezing immediately as it came down.

Monday night the storm passed.

Tuesday morning had the sun, distant and pale and not a threat to the snow, and by nightfall the plows had gone, the sanders were empty, the shovels put away, the blowers back in the garage.

No sound.

No wind.

The light on Summit Boulevard was sharp and had sharp edges, not cut from the night by razored blades but the blades themselves, colors too garish, too loud, like the sound of frozen heels cracking on the frozen pavement. During the afternoon, city crews had been working, fixing Christmas tree–and star-shaped frames to every other lamppost, winding them with colored bulbs, hoisting a fifteen-foot natural wreath over the entrance to the Rotunda. Strings of lights framed shop and office windows as well, and all the windows of the Starlite, some of them blinking, some of them dull, most of them framing elaborate or simple scenes of the season.

The Salvation Army in front of the theaters—two horns and a drum, tambourine and soprano; a Santa Claus on the corner—a bell and gleaming pot; more pedestrians than usual on a weekday evening, to see the lights and the snow and to catch the sales in the shops now open late every night. Christmas carols. A stray flake or two. No one paying attention

to a small headline in the day's paper, the discovery of a
vagrant's body in Foxriver Park.

From the warmth of the Starlite, Race Jorgen watched them
pass the curbside dispensers. He sipped his coffee. He put out
his cigarette. He checked his watch and wondered if the Pack
was going to show up tonight. He had a feeling they would; it
was only seven-thirty. And a second cup later he saw Barnaby
Garing come around the corner with Pancho and Tang, start for
the diner's steps and stop when Barnaby saw him and said
something to them.

Jorgen smiled.

Within five minutes they were all there, intercepted by
Garing, standing on the sidewalk, stomping their feet, making
a great show of not wanting to come in. A small herd of horses,
breath steaming, streaming, unsure in which direction they
should be ready to flee from danger. Pressed close to the diner's
wall, out of the way of the crowds.

He smiled again and slid out of the booth.

They intrigued him, those kids. Anachronisms for the fun of
it. But now that their fearless punk leader was gone, it was
beyond him why they stayed together. A couple of jocks, a
hood, and a one-legged brain; a dumb blonde, an almost
overweight redhead, a doctor's kid, and a frizz-haired orphan
living with her dotty grandmother. They lived all over town,
families made all levels of income, and the only thing they really
had in common was being in the same high school class.

And the murder of Eddie Roman.

Maybe, too, the death of a poor slob named Slap Zubronsky.

Silently he sighed against the anger that had lodged with him
most of the day, an anger born of helplessness and a feeling that
he ought to know, ought to *know* what was going on in his
town. He had known Slap for several years. A harmless
grinning idiot who had once been a sports hero around here
when he was much younger. Why the jerk had lived on the
street was something the detective didn't know, and didn't
much care about knowing. But the guy clearly had some kind
of talent, and after seeing that Slap wasn't going to do anything
himself, Race had sent one of his friends around to have a look

at Slap's artwork. No obligations, no promises; but the friend had liked what he had seen. Honestly liked it. A chance then for the dope to get back on his feet. A little late, maybe, but what the hell, it was better than the alternative.

Race winced at the thought as he paid his bill and pocketed the change, felt the anger again.

It made no sense that Slap should be dead. A chance like that—a little money, his own place, an honest-to-god bed to sleep in every night—he wouldn't do anything to lose it. And though Race thought the guy was several thick slices short of a full loaf, he also knew Slap wasn't stupid. In fact, "nervous" could have been his goddamn middle name, he was always so jumpy. So why, now of all times, had he decided to sleep in the park instead of an alley, freeze to death, and be eaten by the dogs and cats, and probably a few rats?

It didn't make sense.

Not to him.

Not after he had seen the condition of the body, and had seen the claw marks, the gouges, the frozen blood, the open mouth.

Put him in a bedroom and he could have been Eddie Roman.

He had pressed for an autopsy, more than the usual casual examination, but he'd been overruled. Shit, he'd been told, the guy was a bum, why waste the money? Froze, snacked on, dump him in potter's field. What the hell.

Swallowing against his temper, he stepped outside, pulling on his gloves, buttoning his topcoat, adjusting his muffler. The Pack began to drift away as soon as they noticed him, heads down, behaving so patently unsuspicious that he had to grin.

"Hey," he called, pausing on the bottom step and leaning on the railing.

They stopped.

"Hey, kids, hang on a minute, okay?"

They didn't all turn around, and none turned completely, but he noted that the boys managed to put themselves between him and the girls. It happened so slowly, so imperceptibly, he didn't realize it until it had happened. A pack, he decided, in more ways than one.

"Christmas shopping already?"

Joey Costello, hands defiantly in his jacket pockets, lifted his chin. "Maybe. So what? You figure we robbed a store or something?"

Jorgen lifted an apologetic hand. "Nope."

"So?"

"So nothing. I just wondered if you heard about the body. The one in the park, I mean."

There was no answer, but he could see that they had. He could see as well that the gimp and the one called Katie were nervous, fearful. He frowned. Afraid? Of what?

"You knew the guy, Scott, right?" He kept his voice low, and the gimp moved closer.

People stared as they passed; no one stopped.

A bus hissed and chugged at the corner.

"You knew him?" he asked again.

"Yeah. Yes, sir, I did. He's Blade's buddy."

Jorgen nodded. He knew that too. Two idiots who didn't really belong on the streets. Only one of them left now. "Have you seen Blade lately?"

Byrns shrugged, shook his head. "But he didn't do it, if that's what you're asking."

"Neither did we," Joey muttered sullenly.

Jorgen stroked his mustache, took the final step to the pavement, and smiled. "Do what? He fell asleep and froze to death." He looked straight at Scott. "Right?"

He should have been echoed; it was what he expected. Scott, however, backed away toward the others, Fern taking one arm, Katie holding the other. They turned together and walked away, the rest falling in behind. Like a shield. A wall. Instinct hinted he ought to press after them, keep talking; caution suggested he had plenty of time.

He rolled his shoulders, jutted his chin, started up the street with every intention of going home. A final glance over his shoulder, however, showed him one of the jocks, the tall one, Pancho, trotting after him. They were the same height, close to the same weight, but Jorgen tensed when he stopped and saw the way the boy's skin had tightened around his eyes.

"Listen, man," the kid said, keeping his voice low, a thumb

snapped over his shoulder, "you got something to say to us, you say it right, okay? You bring us in, you talk, we talk, but stop the hell following us around."

Race walked.

The kid walked with him.

"Hey, Pancho, look—"

The boy's hand came up, stopping just short of jabbing a finger in his chest. "You leave us alone, you find out who killed Eddie. Next time, we get lawyers."

Well, well, Race thought, the kid's been watching his TV.

"Okay," he answered as if it didn't matter. "No sweat, kid. No problem."

"Damn right," Pancho told him.

At the corner he turned down the street, toward his car parked at the curb. Pancho didn't follow.

"Anything else?" he asked, walking a step backward.

"Nope."

He waved, winked, turned his back and turned again, waved again, without knowing why and knowing the kid would be royally pissed.

"Take it easy," he said.

"Right," Pancho said, and stared at the cop's face, taking in the mustache, the eyes squinting against a sudden brief breeze, nodded sharply and walked away, nearly marching. He could feel the asshole staring after him, and it was all he could do not to grin. That wouldn't be cool. But he'd had enough of Jorgen's sneaking around all the time, showing up where he wasn't wanted, asking questions that made it seem as if he still thought one of the Pack had done Eddie. His own father was beginning to wonder, for Christ's sake, and when Pancho had seen the cop in the diner, he'd almost gone in and punched out his lights.

Joey had stopped him.

But the way the freak had stood there, like they were just shooting the shit, old friends and crap, it made him mad.

He did grin then.

He had told off a cop and had gotten away with it, and only wished he could look back to see the look on the asshole's face.

Barnaby tapped his arm when he caught up. "Nice."

"Damn right."

"You're gonna tick him off," Joey complained softly, his arm around Laine's shoulders. "He'll bug us forever."

"Never happen," Pancho said. "I put the fear into him. Lawyer fear. He bugs us again, we'll sue his ass off."

Tang giggled, Fern laughed, and at the next corner they argued without rancor over where to park it and rest. It was cold, much colder than early December had a right to be, and Joey was all for packing it in and going home. Pancho said nothing beyond a grunt or two. Joey bothered him. The guy wasn't right, jumping around like he was walking on wires, snapping at Laine, snarling at everyone else. Maybe it was a good idea to leave. What the hell, all they'd do is talk about . . .

He huddled against himself, shoulders hunched and arms tight to his sides.

"Well, I don't give a damn where we go as long as we for god's sake get there," Barnaby said.

Tang rose on her toes and looked back the way they'd come. "He's still gone. Why didn't we just go back to the Starlite?"

Pancho wiggled his eyebrows. "Why not my place?"

"Walk?" she said, slapping her arms across her chest.

"I'll carry you."

"In another life," she said, not quite grinning.

Oh sure, he thought glumly; everybody gets a crack at you but me. He turned away, just as Katie pushed through to his side.

"You heard it, didn't you," she said.

She looked like a mouse. Pale skin, pink nose, tiny eyes, the shortest of them all, the highest voice. He called her Eddie's pet, though never to her face, and though she was pretty enough in a sisterly kind of way, he'd never been able to connect with her. He couldn't figure her out, all her bug movies and bug posters and talk about mutations and permutations and computer computations; it as like she actually believed all that crap she watched in those old films.

"Heard what?"

Her head tilted to one side as if she were trying to look through a hole under his jaw. "You know."

He did.

Jesus, he did.

"Aw, Christ," Joey said in disgust. "Can't you just leave it alone, bozo?"

"Hey," Pancho warned. "C'mon, Joey."

"Well, she's freaked, for god's sake."

Katie didn't look away.

Pancho checked Barnaby for moral support, but Garing was jogging in place, puffing louder than he had to, inching closer to Tang and blowing at her cheek. She batted the air between them. He moved in. She yanked his wool cap down over his eyes.

"Hey," Scott said, and Pancho immediately grabbed Katie's shoulder and turned her to him. Anything to get those eyes off his face. It was spooky. Worse, because she knew, and he didn't think Barnaby did.

"Hey what?" he said.

"I'm freezing my leg off here, do you mind? Are we going back or what?"

"You heard it too," Katie told him.

"Oh, that's it, that's it," Joey declared in disgust. He grabbed Laine's hand. "I ain't freezing my ass off just to listen to this bullshit." He leaned close to Katie. "We're going to the diner. You want to come, come, but you don't say shit about this, okay? Not one goddamn word."

He practically pulled Laine off her feet as he stomped away, and Pancho didn't know what to do. Tang had nudged Barnaby into moving after them, Scott clearly wasn't going, he was already off the curb with Fern just behind and heading for the other side, and he was left with the mouse.

Who took his arm.

"Pancho, I'm scared."

Mouse-voice; little-girl voice.

"I'm so scared."

"Look, I don't know what you're talking about."

He started to back off; she wouldn't let go.

screaming

"Pancho, please!"

in the middle of the night

Her arm was outstretched. If he took another step, she'd fall. Little eyes big now, lips almost black against a skin snow-pale.

"It—it was a nightmare," he said at last, brushing at her hand. "I had a goddamn nightmare, okay?"

She shook her head.

"It was a nightmare," he insisted.

The hand lost its grip.

in the middle of the night

"Pancho!" Scott called from the opposite curb.

He waved, shook his head, called to Barnaby to wait up, his ass was freezing, then grinned and bowed to a woman who glared at his language. But he didn't stop moving. No way he was going to get into this bull. He had a nightmare. Katie had a nightmare. Lots of people have nightmares on the same night. It's not like everyone has their own time for bad dreams. That was nuts.

"Pancho, please, come with us."

She was nuts.

"Where? I'm cold."

Katie's mittened hands gestured weakly. "I don't know. Someplace. C'mon, don't go. Please?"

Ten feet away, people between them, ignoring them. Santa ringing his bell. She moved toward the curb and bumped into a wire trash bin.

"Pancho, just a couple of minutes," Scott called.

Right. A couple of minutes with a bunch of loons, I'll be a squirrel by morning.

He shook his head, whirled and leapt as though slamming a basket home.

"Panch!"

"Later," he called to Scott.

Scott rolled his eyes and watched Duncan sprint after Barnaby and Tang, dancing among the pedestrians, making two more phantom baskets on phantom hoops fixed to the lampposts. When he dropped the second time, the crowds swallowed him. He was gone.

What a jerk, he thought.

So you're a jerk, he answered, because he hadn't believed it when Katie claimed they had all heard the screaming the night Eddie had died, and the night Slap had been killed. Even if they didn't remember it, they had heard it. Joey was right, that was crazy talk, but he didn't have the nerve to tell her that to her face. And when she said they had to do something about it, talk about it, figure out what it meant, he just couldn't ignore her the way Pancho had.

But Pancho had heard.

He knew it.

He had seen it in Duncan's face.

And that made him nervous, because he hadn't heard a thing.

"You all right?"

Fern rapped his shoulder until he looked at her, hair squashed by a ski cap, face darkened by the cold.

"No," he said. "My leg is frozen to my leg. I'm going to have to take a scalding shower just to get it off."

She hit him again, a little harder, and he couldn't stop a laugh. She was embarrassed a little. They usually were whenever he made a joke about his leg. It was like he was supposed to pretend it was real until he got home, away from everyone else. As soon as he had figured that out, he seldom passed up a chance to make at least one of them squirm.

"All right," Katie said angrily, wedging herself between them, grabbing an arm, marching them forward. "Screw him. He wants to be a jerk, let him. We'll do this ourselves."

Scott let himself be pulled along.

"The way I see it," Katie told them, looking up at first one, then the other, "is that it's some kind of mind thing, you know? Like a link with Eddie and that dead bum."

"Slap," Scott said. "His name is Slap."

"Okay, but it doesn't make any difference what his name is. I mean, it's the mind thing we're looking at. It's like . . . maybe somehow we're turned into people who are going to die. We can hear them doing it—dying, I mean—no matter where we are, see, but that doesn't do us any good because by then it's too late, right? Sure it is. So what we have to do is figure out how we can do this mind thing to people *before* they get killed. That way we can warn them and they won't die."

Scott opened his mouth, closed it when she said, "Of course, they won't believe us. They never do. They'll think we're nuts. What we'll have to do, I guess, is talk to that cop, Jorgen, tell him about this, and then, when it happens again, he'll believe us and help us figure out a way to . . ." She frowned. "No, that won't work. The cops never believe anything until the very end. It'll have to be someone else. Like a scientist."

"We don't know any scientists, Katie," Fern said.

"Sure we do. Dr. Freelin."

"He's a doctor."

"Practically the same thing. The point is that the cops will listen to him. If we can get Laine to get him to believe us, then we'll . . ."

Scott waited.

Katie lowered her head. "I sound like a jerk." She stopped, turned them around, started walking north again. "I sound like I ought to be locked up."

Scott agreed, but he didn't say it aloud. Instead, as gently as he could: "You know, maybe Panch was right. It could have been a nightmare."

"Twice? Both times when people died? All of us?"

They stopped under a theater marquee, the Apollo, the running lights from its border talking away shade and shadow from their faces. Scott nudged them toward the ticket window then, away from the crowds. Katie stood on her own, back to the street, hands in and out of her pockets, squinting at the posters, at the woman in the glass cage taking someone's money, at him. At him.

"I didn't hear anything," he said at last, softly.

"You did," she argued just as softly.

He shook his head. "No."

Fern tugged at her gloves. "Katie, for crying out loud, there's no connection between Eddie and Slap."

Katie's expression said there was.

"And even if there is," Fern continued, "it has nothing to do with anybody's nightmares."

"That's right," Scott agreed. "It just means there's a nut out there, that's all." His voice deepened. "And it means that Eddie didn't kill himself. He was murdered too."

As soon as he said it, he blinked rapidly and looked up the street toward the diner. Is that, he wondered, what Jorgen thought too?

"I heard it," Katie insisted quietly, a diamond tear in one eye. "I . . . " A long sigh that lifted her shoulders. ". . . did."

"Katie."

And he looked at her with such sorrow, such pity, that suddenly she couldn't take it anymore. She ran. Ignored Fern's cry. Ignored Scott's calling. She ran up the street through the crowds, hearing the bells and the carols deafeningly loud and harsh, dodging a woman laden with wrapped presents, brushing the arm of a man trying to fish something from his topcoat pocket, finally passing the diner and swerving around the corner.

A mitten brushed over her eyes, but she wasn't crying yet. She wouldn't cry. She wouldn't let them make her. Maybe that would come later, but right now she was too angry. They were all lying; she knew it; she had seen it in all their eyes. And maybe they'd admit it to each other, but they wouldn't admit it to her. Oh no, not her. She was only Katie. Eddie's pet. She knew that's how they thought of her. Don't take her seriously because she's not worth the trouble. Just a pet. Pat her on the head, tell her she's a good girl, and push her gently on her way. Give her a bone. Give her a treat. Poor little orphan girl. Poor little nut.

She ran.

She slowed.

Ice formed in her lungs and made breathing sharp.

A foot slipped on a small patch of dark ice and she nearly tumbled into a snowdrift shoved up by the plows.

She walked.

Into the Manor, it wasn't very far now, she didn't live as far north as Laine or Pancho.

On the edge.

She lived on the edge, just like being on the edge of the Pack. Eddie's pet.

But not anymore.

The sidewalk narrowed between drifts high on her right and lawns on her left, in some places only as wide as the shovel that had cleared it. Her shadow crawled over the lumps and freezing hillocks of white and grainy slush, dipping and climbing like a shadow-cloud over a rolling meadow. Her ears began to sting. Her lips began to chap. Her shoulders began to stiffen from being hunched so long against the cold.

All right, she thought, kicking a chunk of ice out of the way; all right, they don't believe me, or they won't admit it. All right. That's okay. I won't say anything else, I'll let them figure it out on their own. They'll come to me. They will. Eddie's pet's got a brain. She knows things. It won't be long. Somebody else'll die and they'll come to me, no sweat.

Snow dropped from a branch.

She reached her block and quickened her step, anxious now to get home and have some cocoa. Gram would have it ready. She always did. Somehow she always knew when her Katie would get home.

A gleam of silver ahead.

She tried to snap her fingers at her good luck, and laughed when her mittens wouldn't cooperate.

Closer, and the cold lifted tears in her eyes; she couldn't tell if it was a quarter or a crushed bottle cap.

If it's a quarter, she told herself, I'll live forever, or at least long enough to see Barnaby so damn old he won't be able to grope Tang anymore.

Giggling.

Stopping a yard short and closing her eyes. Heads, I'll pick it up; tails, I'll still be broke. A shake of her head, and a memory of the time she had passed on a five-dollar bill because Lincoln's face was to the ground. Bad luck to grab a president by the back of his head. It was dumb to be superstitous, Scott teased her about it all the time, but it hadn't failed her yet.

Her eyes opened.

"Right!" she said.

It was a quarter; it was heads.

She pulled off a mitten, leaned over and watched her shadow slip ahead of her.

And keep growing.

Slowly. Taller, and wider; she spun around to see who had snuck up on her, who was trying to dump her into the snow, and stumbled back with a silent cry when she saw something down at the end of the block, something huge, immense, rising from what seemed to be a hole in the street. Too black to make distinctions, but too big to be natural.

She didn't wait until she could see it clearly.

She ran.

The shadow grew; she could hear it—slow footfalls slowly crushing the snow as it followed, branches whipping and snapping, a hollow drumlike echo every time it took a step.

The shadow grew no matter how fast she moved.

A high-pitched whirring.

The lights before her darkening.

The tortured twist of a lamppost bent over at its base.

"Help!"

Shadow growing.

"Somebody, help!"

The rattle and crack of a tree toppling into the street.

She screamed, and slipped, and ordered herself not to fall the way they always did in the movies.

The shadow grew, sweeping across every yard, along the street, smothering the houses, taking away the stars, taking its time because it knew she couldn't win.

Whirring climbing higher up the scale.

Hollow echoes.

Snow falling in clumps and showers in a new storm from eaves and branches.

Ice tripping her as she leapt onto her front walk and streaked toward the porch, glancing left now and nearly stopping when she saw something towering over the trees, over the roofs, no shape or design, no eyes, no mouth. In darkness it was darker, and reaching out to grab her head.

Up the steps two at a time, throwing herself at the door and falling inside, yelping at the pain in her knees, twisting onto her back and kicking the door closed.

"Katie?" A deep voice, weak and trembling with age.

Katie gaped at the door, waiting for it to shatter. She couldn't move, could scarcely breathe.

Waiting.

"Katie, child, for heaven's sake, are you all right?"

Waiting.

Dark blotting out the tiny window in the center of the door.

"Gram, run!" she cried, finally turning over to her hands and knees, kicking herself to her feet and dashing down the hall toward the kitchen. "Gram, run!"

Her grandmother, a white-haired gnome half buried in a robe that dragged on the floor, looked away from the milk simmering in a saucepan on the stove. "Katie, dear, you're tracking snow."

Katie slid on the linoleum, grabbed the door frame to stop her. Momentum spun her around, faced her to the front where she saw the streetlight through the door window, glittering harshly.

She couldn't find a breath. "Gram."

"Take off your boots and coat, dear. You'll catch your death dressed like that in here."

"Gram."

"Don't argue, just sit. Drink your cocoa and go to bed. It's late. I don't know why you stay out so late on a school night. You'll never get to college this way. Never. Now sit down, child, my Lord, you're trembling."

Katie sat as she peeled off her mittens, her coat, yanked off her boots and felt the floor beneath her stockinged feet. The smell of warming milk. The smell of her grandmother as she fussed around the kitchen.

Watching the door.

Watching the light.

"Gram," she said, finally looking at the old woman. "Gram, something chased me."

FIFTEEN

An old-fashioned room, more suited to the house than the people who lived there: carpet fringed and darkly floral, wallpaper a trellis of rose vines with large leaves, small chandelier teardrop crystal with a brass globe in its center, oval mirror, china closet, sideboard, dining room table large enough to seat four, or would be if half hadn't been covered by textbooks, notebooks, legal pads, a mug with pens and pencils, a portable electric typewriter.

Scott leaned over his history book, not at all enthralled by the economic background of the Civil War, grunting silently as he tried to wedge charts and maps and the facts they represented into memory for tomorrow's test. He'd been trying to study since getting home and couldn't hold his concentration. Opposite him, his mother, chewing on a pencil eraser, the pencil itself flopping side to side, flipped pages of a much larger text, swearing and grunting herself. He watched without raising his head, his hair a veil he didn't bother to lift. Blowing up only fluttered it; swiping at it was futile.

"Sheepdog," she said.

"Huh?"

She smiled and leaned back, stretched her arms over her head. "Get a haircut. You look like a sheepdog."

A draft fluttered across the back of his neck. He didn't bother to check for an open window. It was the house. Every inch of it could have been sealed, the house itself buried under tons of mud and rock, and the draft would be there, summer and winter. But only for those who sat in this chair.

"When I was your age, boys had to prove they had ears."

He curled a lip—*ha ha very funny*—and closed his book, rubbed his eyes, yawned so widely his jaw popped twice. "I quit."

"Do you know it?"

"If I don't know it now, I never will."

"You want me to quiz you?"

As he shoved the book aside he shook his head and reached for the newspaper.

"Scott," she said, "you're read that a hundred times tonight."

His knuckle lightly rapped the story of Slap's death. "I just can't believe it, that's all." He scanned the three short paragraphs; there was, again, nothing new. "I didn't think he was that dumb." Another rap, harder. "He knew better, Mom."

"Maybe he was drunk."

Wearily: "No. He didn't hardly drink. He wasn't a wino, Mom. He just . . . I don't know . . . he just lived on the streets."

There was no evidence of belief in her expression, nor was there inclination to argue. Just a tolerant half-smile that told him not to bother trying to convince her. Suddenly he remembered Mr. Relbeth's remark, and stared more closely at her—hair as fair as his and longer, a rounded face with heavy lips and eyes a spring sky; when she stretched again, letting the pencil fall to the table, he had to look away to avoid noticing her figure. It embarrassed him. She was almost sexy.

"Mom, how come you never married again?"

He gasped and sat back. God, he hadn't meant to say that. Hadn't even known he'd been thinking it.

She didn't seem fazed. "Too busy, Scott. You, school, work—who has time for a social life?"

"You should make time. Really."

Her smiled made him feel like a little kid. "Are you worried about my old age?"

He shrugged. "I don't know. It just doesn't seem right, that's all."

"And what brought this on?"

He shrugged again. "I don't know. Nothing, I guess. Just wondering."

She slammed her book shut, dropped a legal pad atop it, and shoved it all into the mess at the end of the table. "Well, wonder no more, Scottie dear. When I'm ready, I'll be ready, not before." She pushed away from the table and stood. "Thirsty. You want something?"

"Nope."

He watched her walk into the kitchen, snug jeans and loose white shirt, and looked away quickly. Jesus, Byrns, she's your *mother*, for god's sake. Looked into the living room and decided to watch some TV. He didn't know what was on and didn't care. His brain felt like oatmeal, and he didn't want to have to think. Reaching behind him, he grabbed the crutches propped against the china closet and manhandled himself up. His leg was off, upstairs in his room, and he could have hopped in, which is what he usually did despite his mother's fear that he'd take a fall and split open his skull. After all these years he was damn good at it; and after all these years she still wasn't used to seeing him sweep through the house on a single leg. It drove her nuts.

He dropped onto the couch, dropped the crutches to the floor, and stretched out, grabbing the remote control from the table behind his head. Across the room, the drapes had been pulled over the front windows, but he could feel the cold pressing against the panes. Not as cold as yesterday or the day before, but cold enough. Cold enough.

Slap died out there.

Slap was killed.

Katie thinks we somehow all knew it.

He was halfway through the channels when his mother wandered in, a glass of diet soda in one hand, a cigarette in the other. She sat in a wing-back chair near the window, which, he knew, meant she wanted to talk, not watch television. He turned it off. She grinned at him for reading her mind.

"I've been thinking about this Slap," she said, curling one leg up under her.

He waited.

"And Eddie."

Her hair was held back by a stiff plastic headband, a few strands escaping to fall over her brow. Incongrously, he thought she looked too young to be a mother.

"And I'm thinking," she continued, "that you're thinking there's probably some kind of connection."

He shifted uncomfortably.

"Now." She sipped, put the glass down, put her other leg up and twisted into the chair's corner. "Joey told you in school that the body was pretty much torn up."

"His brother, Al, is a cop. That's what he told Joey."

She nodded. "But the paper said some animals probably got to him. He'd been dead, they figured, since Saturday night, Sunday morning."

"Yeah, but—"

"And the paper also said that the police are ready to conclude that the Romans were a murder-suicide."

"What?" He sat up abruptly. "But—"

"I know, I know." She waved him silent. "It's their way of saying they haven't a clue to what happened. Just as you don't have a clue, a hint, a suspicion of how this Slap could in any way be connected with Eddie Roman."

"Slap's dead."

"He froze to death."

"He was cut up, Mom!"

"Animals."

"Mom—"

"Animals, Scottie. Animals."

Maybe, he thought; maybe not. What he didn't understand was why his mother was making such a big deal of it. It wasn't like he was mooning around the house all day, or going out to play Hardy Boys or something. It was just that Slap, though maybe not running on all cylinders, wasn't so nuts that he didn't know enough to get in out of the cold. Which made him think about Blade Murtaugh and how he was handling the death of his best friend. Probably not good. He scratched at his good leg absently. Maybe he should go out, try to find him. Maybe he could buy the guy something to eat. Maybe he should knock it off before his mother locked him up in the funny farm.

He felt her watching him. "I'm okay," he muttered.

"I'm just concerned you're making more of this than you should." She unfolded her legs. "Like that business the other night."

Damn, he thought.

"It was Barnaby, Mom, that's all. He was trying to scare me."

The son of a bitch.

"And I'm concerned about Katie."

"Mom," he said, patience clear, "she watches old movies, okay? That stuff about the mind thing she got from one of them. Nobody believes her."

"Are you sure?"

"God, Mom, you think I'm nuts?"

She leaned forward, pushed her hair behind her ears. "I think, Scott, you're still not over the shock of Eddie's death. None of you are. It's only natural that you start looking for answers where, in some cases, there are none but those you already know." The headband came off; she dropped it beside her feet. "It isn't always satisfactory, hon, but then life isn't either. It's—"

The telephone rang.

Automatically, he reached for the receiver and said, "Hello?"

"Scott, it was after me."

Katie, he mouthed to his mother.

"What are you talking about? What was after you?"

"I'm not sure. But I think it was whatever killed Eddie and that bum." A muffled panicked sob. "Oh God, Scott, what the hell are we going to do?"

Laine knelt on the living room couch, elbows on the back, palms cupping her cheeks, breath fogging the pane as she stared out at the street. She was miserable. She was furious. She had snapped at her father the moment she'd walked in the house, snapped at her mother for defending him. And it was all Joey's fault. After they'd returned to the Starlite, complaining about the cold, Katie, and the cops, Joey kept staring at some woman seated at the counter. He couldn't take his eyes off her. When she called him on it, only half joking, he insisted she was somebody he thought he knew, someone who came to his father's firm once in a while.

She called him a liar without really knowing why.

He left, and left her alone to walk home in the cold.

The bastard.

One foot kicked lazily, braked abruptly when an automobile sped past, and she could hear even through the closed window its radio playing "Eddie My Love" so loud the lyrics blurred with the music.

Eddie.

She started kicking again.

Damn, she hadn't thought of him in days, not really, and in remembering, she wondered why. It wasn't as if she didn't miss him, because she still did. Maybe she would for the rest of her life.

But not to think about him?

Even the newspapers hadn't mentioned him, or his father, for the past few days, except to say that the remains had been transferred to Pennsylvania for burial. In last Sunday's paper, the chief of police, who looked like a starving turkey, said the case was still open, though it appeared increasingly likely the determination was as they'd originally thought: murder-suicide. Which, her father had translated sarcastically at the breakfast table, meant they were putting the Romans aside while they covered other, more current things. Just over two weeks, and Eddie Roman was no longer current.

"Laine?"

She looked heavenward and didn't answer.

"Laine?"

Not now, Dale, she prayed; please, not now.

He came into the living room from the front hall, barefoot and no shirt, a towel draped around his neck.

She didn't move.

He waved both arms. "Laine?"

Towheaded, blond, little-boy skinny. He hopped from one foot to the other, hugging himself.

Her parents were in the kitchen; she could hear them talking, laughing quietly.

"Dale, I'm busy."

"Doing what?"

"Thinking, okay? I'm thinking."

It wouldn't do any good. She recognized all too well the expression on his face, the way his eyes slipped side to side and wouldn't focus on her. Ten years old, and now he looked five.

He would never be much older.

"Jesus, Dale, it's only a bath, for god's sake."

When his lower lip began to quiver, and he started sniffing hard and fast, she hated herself for wanting to smile. Smiled. Kicked off the couch and walked over to take his hand.

"Okay," she said, "but just this once, all right? I've got things to do."

He didn't say anything.

And said nothing until, after turning on the tub faucets, she had poked his plastic baseball bat into the linen closet, into the hamper, behind the toilet, in the cabinet under the sink. By the time she had finished, he was undressed and in the water, laughing.

"No dragons, okay?" Laine told him.

"No dragons," he echoed.

"No witches."

"No witches."

She almost cried when she said, "No bad guys," and he nodded so hard the bathwater sloshed. But there had been bad guys. Five years ago. Her mother and Dale walking through the park, and four kids not even from Foxriver had jumped out of the bushes and knocked them both to the ground, stole her mother's purse and, as an afterthought, kicked Dale several times in the head and chest. Three operations saved his life, mended his ribs, but not one had saved his mind.

He didn't remember. At least, she thought, not like the rest of us would.

"No bad guys," he said, grinning, his canine teeth still missing. He slapped his hands on the water. "I'm swimming."

"And I'm thinking," she told him mock sternly.

He splashed her lightly and giggled.

She growled and splashed him back, made sure he had soap and a face cloth before returning downstairs to stare out the window again.

The mad was gone, though.

Concern took its place.

Something was wrong with Joey. He was worse than Dale these days, ever since Eddie had died, jumping at shadows, biting people's heads off, and making her generally crazy. She knew he hadn't really been trying to make time with that woman; she knew her loved her and wouldn't deliberately hurt her; she knew that he knew something about Eddie before the killing and it was driving him nuts and he wouldn't say a word.

She flopped around and stared at the wall.

Maybe she should call him, apologize, make it right again.

Maybe she should call Scott or Fern to see what they thought. Pancho and Barnaby were hopeless; every passing day they seemed less interested in the Pack, and never even hung out with them at school unless Tang was around.

Something thumped under the floor.

She sighed without a sound. Dad again, fussing around in his basement workshop. He couldn't drive a nail, saw wood in a straight line, and had once made a bookcase for her bedroom— the shelves had collapsed two days later. He claimed it helped him practice surgical techniques. She had come to believe it was a way to torture his family.

The thump, a little louder, and she pulled her feet onto the couch.

She hated the basement. Despite all the improvements he had made, it was still too dark, too damp, too smelly. A perfect place for spiders and centipedes and things you never saw to breed and plan and come after her while she slept. She shuddered, scowled when the thump seemed to come from under the couch, and called, "Mom, Dad's trying to tear down the house again!"

"I'm what?" he said, walking into the room, drying his hands on a towel.

She looked at the floor, looked at her father.

"Stan, what's all the shouting about?" her mother asked, walking from the dining room, carrying a tray piled with doughnuts.

Laine heard Dale whooping upstairs.

"Honey?" Stan said.

"There's someone in the cellar," she said quietly, pushing against the couch's back.

"Oh, I don't think so, dear," her mother said, putting the tray down.

"I *heard* him."

Stan tossed the towel aside. "No problem." He walked back to the kitchen, and Laine ignored her mother, listening instead to the cellar door open, squealing on its hinges as usual, listening to the footsteps fade to nothing, and return.

"Nothing," he announced, sat beside her, rubbed her shoulder. "Maybe you ought to get to bed early. You have a history test tomorrow, right?"

She nodded.

Her mother turned on the television.

Dale cried out that he was ready for sleeping.

"I'll do it," Laine told him, quickly uncoiling, nearly running for the stairs, shouting, "I'll get it," when the kitchen telephone rang. It would be Joey. Gruff and embarrassed and wanting to tell her he was sorry.

"Hey, Laine?"

It was Scott.

"Laine, I think something's wrong with Katie. I mean, seriously wrong."

No sound.
No wind.

• • •

No wind at all, but Katie could hear things moving out there nonetheless.

In the yard.

Sounds like branches scraping across glass.

Sounds like huge feet crunching through the snow.

Sounds like monster horses snorting in the cold.

But she wouldn't look.

She sat at her vanity, wrapped in a terry bathrobe, brushing her hair. Ignoring the sounds because they weren't really there. They couldn't be. The bedroom window was closed. A bomb could go off in the backyard and she wouldn't be able to hear a thing.

Imagination is what it was. Hearing them talk about that bum who'd died in the park, thinking about the nightmare that had made her think she had heard the screams.

Both of them—the bum and Eddie Roman.

Working herself into what her grandmother called a state; it was crazy. Letting herself be chased by phantoms; it was nuts. Calling Scott like that, babbling like a jerk, swearing him to secrecy when she heard herself and realized that if word got around, she'd never be able to show her face in school again.

She brushed her hair.

It didn't matter. Scott didn't believe her.

Downstairs, in the living room, she could hear the television murmuring. Her grandmother would be in her favorite chair, rocking almost in time to the background music of whatever show she was watching, repeating the dialogue to make sure she understood it. Reaching out every so often to pluck a cookie from the plate beside her. Using a handkerchief to brush the crumbs from her quilted robe. Adjusting her glasses ten times a minute.

The furnace rumbling, deep in the cellar.

She brushed her hair.

The warmth from the air vent behind the vanity glided over her bare feet; the smells of her room, from the cedar hope chest to the perfumes to the talc that clung to the flat of her chest; the smells of the house, from the old wood to the new carpeting to the lingering aroma of dough and chocolate drifting up from the kitchen.

Familiar.

Comfortable.

She brushed her hair and didn't listen to the outside.

SIXTEEN

Joey stood at the end of the walk and threw up his hands. "What the hell'd I do now?"

Laine kept her back to him. She took the porch steps one at a slow time, opened the front door deliberately slowly, and went inside without even a wave.

"What'd I *do*?"

She didn't come out.

He stood there for five minutes and she didn't come out.

Take the hint, Costello, he told himself at last, and he walked off, kicking at stones and shadow, punching the air, picking up a hunk of rock salt and heaving it at a cat crouched in the middle of the empty street. He missed. The cat just looked at him. "Bastard." He shook his head and moved on, around the corner, where he broke into a run that soon had him sweating, panting a little.

It was Katie Ealton's fault, not his.

Last period, study hall, she comes up to him in the cafeteria with Scott and Fern, plunks herself down and starts talking crazy again. Walking scarecrows, invisible bugs, giants in the streets. Laine is there, getting nervous, and says something about someone hiding in her cellar. Her cellar! Jesus H.! So what can a guy do, right? He had laughed. He had looked down the table at Panch and Tang, and he had laughed. They laughed. Scott tells him to shut up and without thinking, he reaches over and grabs the gimp by the shirtfront, practically pulls him out of his seat.

That's when Katie slapped him.

That's when he let go of Byrns and took a backhand swipe at the mouse. Hell, he didn't want to hit her, didn't hit her, didn't even come close. But she's the one who started it, and she's the one who claimed he knew something Eddie knew, something that would kill them all if he didn't tell them now.

Crazy. Out of her goddamn mind.

He picked up a stick and belted a fence with it, lifting a *go-to-hell* hand when someone yelled a scolding.

God, Eddie had been right—women were a total pain in the ass. They made you say things you didn't mean, and when you said things you did mean, they took it all wrong. Then they made you apologize whether you were wrong or not, and made you feel like a shit doing it.

He grabbed another stick and heaved it across a yard, listening to it cut the air like helicopter blades before clattering against a trunk.

Well, this time he didn't give a damn, he wasn't going to call just to have someone to be with. He could have a lot of girls. Fern, for one, was always looking at him over the top of her notebook, he was sure of it; and Tang had been dumped again, she'd probably go out with him in a minute. He didn't need Laine and her stupid temper, that's for damn sure.

Eddie was right.

Women were a pain.

Eddie was . . .

He stopped in the middle of the block and looked around, suddenly aware that he didn't know where he was. This wasn't his neighborhood, that's for damn sure. The houses were huge, set well back from a narrow road hidden from the sky by trees he figured were older than God. Stone fences, brick posts, white chains across curving driveways to keep the slobs from coming in and leaving their fingerprints on the grass.

Christ, where the hell was he?

He allowed himself several deep breaths, watched the steam rise and vanish, let his mind put Laine aside for the moment so it could catch up with him and give him a clue.

The block was long, and sloped down away from him.

He hated things like this—wandering around your own town, waking up and thinking you've suddenly gone into another state, maybe even another country.

He hated it.

It was spooky.

And he stared at the houses, the snow-topped walls, the leafless trees, trying to snap things back in focus, bring him back to Foxriver.

As he walked, a brilliant white limousine came at him up the low hill, windows tinted, reflecting the empty branches, the fences, and finally him as he turned to watch it slip away. A few backward steps, and his inner compass kicked in, and though he still didn't know the specific name of the street, he knew, finally, exactly where he was.

"Oh shit," he said, and turned back around.

There it was.

The river.

Not much of one, but sufficient to require a bridge at either end of town if you wanted to head west without going out of your way, and wide enough to stop all but the best swimmers from making it to the other side. Not deep, but strong, and the spring and autumn rains made it stronger, higher, which was why there were no homes on this bank. A few had been built there once, but the river had taken them a chunk at a time. Now it was all grass and trees, a long skinny park for people who wanted to do nothing but watch water move.

By the time he came to a full halt, the road ending in a T-intersection, he knew that he wouldn't get home by supper if he went back up the hill. He'd have to walk along Bank Road and hope to catch a ride.

Shit.

So he swung left and began a slow trot, keeping his gaze on the narrow verge, wishing there were sidewalks, glad the night and the trees on the other side hid the river.

He heard it, though.

Between the crunch of his footsteps, the rasp of his breath, he could hear it.

Not everybody could.

Most people remarked on how peaceful it was here, the city above and traffic smothered by distance, the woodland on the other side keeping the next town out of sight.

They couldn't hear it. The water. Slapping at the bank in the shallows. Hissing around the bridges' pilings. Grumbling to itself as it plowed southward toward the Atlantic. Whispering. Always whispering. But only if you could hear it.

Half a mile later he had to stop. A needle in his side, sweat in his eyes, a pebble in his sneaker that took forever to get out.

The hell with it.

He'd take a left at the next street.

He didn't know why he hadn't done it in the first place anyway, just turned around and gone back up. This was stupid. He was going to be late no matter what he did, his mother would lecture him all through dessert, and then he'd have to practically promise on his damn knees to clean his room for the rest of his life before she let him out again. But only after he'd taken a shower. It was a thing with her—you go out at night, you take a clean body and clean underwear.

Eddie was right.

He started running again, and did take the next left, and did climb the hill, and was late for supper.

He didn't care if his mother yelled.

At least he couldn't hear the river.

And he wasn't surprised when, the second he walked through the front door, his mother, standing in the kitchen at the end of the hall, took one look at him and said, "Pah, you smell like a pig! You go up and take a shower before you come down into my house!"

She was at the stove, polka-dot apron around her waist, greying hair in a net to keep it out of the pots steaming and simmering as she wielded spoon and spices while jutting her chin at the ceiling.

"Now, before you stink the place up!"

"Ma!"

"Go!" she commanded, and he shook his head dismally as he trudged up the stairs, muttering at the unfairness of it all the way to his room. His father was on the living room couch, suspenders down off his shoulders, evening newspaper in front of his face. But there was no appeal there; the old man ran the world outside, but the old lady was in charge once you came through that door.

Maybe he ought to just go to bed.

And thought it again, several times, when the house proceeded to conspire against him: there was hardly any hot water and he could barely raise any suds, the faucet in the sink sprayed him from a leak, he tripped over the throw rug in his bedroom and slammed his shoulder against the wall, and, on his way back down in fresh clothes, a splinter on the banister lanced into the heel of his right hand.

"Shit," he said, sucking on the wound.

"Joseph!"

Shit, he thought.

They were already at the kitchen table—the tiny dining room was for Sundays and guests—and his father glowered at him over the top of his glasses.

"Language, boy," he warned, voice sounding like glass poured over sand.

"Sorry, Poppa," Joey said, and took his seat.

"You shower?"

"Yes, Ma."

"You don't smell like it."

"I did, already! God."

His father picked up a knife and used it for a pointer. "You don't talk like that in my house, you hear me, Joseph? I get enough of that at the company. Now you apologize to your mother for your tone."

On an ordinary evening he would have done so gladly and eloquently, just to keep the peace. An acceptance, a kiss on the head from his mother and a gentle warning not to do it again, and within minutes they'd begin teasing him about his girlfriends, his hair, the music he played too loudly in his room.

But Laine had defied him today, treated him like dirt, practically accused him of wanting to get into that woman's pants right there in the Starlite. How the hell was a man supposed to take something like that? Why the hell wasn't she more like his mother?

"Joseph," his father said. Quietly.

"Right. Sorry."

A crowded plate of meat and vegetables was dropped in front of him, and gravy slopped onto his lap.

It was scalding.

"Christ!" he yelled, shoving back his chair and swiping at the spreading stain with his napkin. "Jesus fucking Christ!"

His father lunged to his feet, beefy face angrily dark. "Joseph!"

Joey looked from him to his mother, who hadn't made up her mind yet whether to be sorry for the accident or furious at his language. Then he said, "Aw, the hell with it," and, leaving the man bellowing after him in Italian, he stormed out of the room, grabbed his coat and stormed out of the house.

By the time he reached the street, the old man was on the porch, screaming, and Joey spinning about to walk backward, yelled, "Why the fuck don't you speak English!" turned again and ran.

God, he hated them.

All the time they were embarrassing him, the whole damn neighborhood embarrassed him. It was like living on some kind of old movie lot—old men on porch steps smoking cigars at night, old women in rocking chairs or lawn chairs, flabby arms crossed over their flabby breasts, yelling at the kids playing in the street, the air constantly filled with the aroma of spices and pasta and cheap perfume and car polish.

He hated it.

One more year, though; one year and he was eighteen and out of here before anyone remembered what the hell he looked like.

Three blocks away there was a drugstore with a pay phone, and he stood in the booth for five minutes, flipping a quarter in one hand, willing himself to call Laine.

He couldn't do it.

It wasn't his fault.

When his stomach began to grumble, he stopped at a luncheonette and ate a tasteless hamburger, playing conversations in his head—first, telling off his parents and having them tearfully accept him back, then settling Laine into the woman she ought to be. It always worked in his head. It never worked when he had to do it.

Some little kids were having a snowball war in an empty lot not far from the river. They asked him to be umpire, make sure no one put rocks in their missiles. It lasted ten minutes before they asked him to leave. At the tops of their voices.

Christ, he thought, ready to rage, ready to cry, what the hell am I gonna do now?

The first thing he thought of was to go get himself some beer.

The evening turned warm, warmer than it had been for almost a week, and mist rose from the snowbanks, the lawns, nudged by a light breeze to run in coils across the street. Scott thought it all too much like early autumn, and he was glad when he finally reached the bookstore. Fern wasn't working tonight, Mr. Tobin and Arlette Bingham talking alone behind the counter. He nodded to them and headed for the Island, changed his mind and made a slow tour of the aisles, not really interested in anything in particular, not really caring if he left without buying. All he had wanted was to get out of the house, away from his mother, who wouldn't let things alone.

Katie this, Fern that, shadow scarecrows and dead bums—she insisted he was making too much of nothing and was, in the process, ruining his health. But she hadn't heard the terror in Katie's voice or seen her ghostlike complexion in school today. And she definitely hadn't heard Laine's story of invisible prowlers in Dr. Freelin's cellar. He didn't tell her that. If he had, she would have called out the psychiatric brigade and locked them all up.

For their own good.

"Looking for anything special?"

He jumped as he came around the head of the aisle. Miss Bingham smiled politely at him from behind the register. Mr. Tobin was gone.

"No, thanks. Just looking around."

Miss Bingham shrugged, said something about being available if needed, and turned her back.

He wandered on, hovered around the children's section and thumbed through fairy tales, stared at the young adult section and examined mysteries and thrillers, looked at his watch and decided he was wasting his time. What he really wanted to do was find a quiet place to think, and perhaps talk with the Pack. Being jumpy on his own was one thing; having everyone seeing monsters around every corner was something else again.

And whether it was grief, as his mother insisted, or something else he couldn't name, it all had to do with Eddie.

He left, paused in the recessed doorway to zip up his jacket, flip up his collar, then turned right toward the Strip. Carols in the distance sounded tinny and too loud. The Santa Claus competed with the Salvation Army. As he passed a string of clothing shops, he reminded himself not to wait too much longer to get a gift for his mother.

Maybe for Fern, too.

Nothing spectacular, of course. Nothing that would break him and give her the wrong idea. But she was all right, all things considered, so why not? A bottle of perfume or something. Bath oil. Scented powders. Whatever girls liked these days. But if he did, he had to be prepared for some world-class kidding. Pancho would be unmerciful, Barnaby would be downright nasty, and his mother would probably worry about him and Fern eloping and moving to California.

Maybe it wasn't worth it.

The store with the mannequins.

He stopped, looked in the window. There were customers inside, a clerk leaning against a glass counter and blowing on her nails, and the mannequins still in their winter vacation poses.

You didn't move, did you? he asked them. You couldn't have.

You couldn't.

• • •

Murtaugh hovered at the mouth of the alley. There was money to be made down at the movies, tonight was Date Night, especially if the customers had had a good time; but there was also that damn rat he knew was waiting for him back there.

Of course, if he went to the theaters he might be able to get himself something to drink at the Stag or one of the other bars. Then he wouldn't give a damn about the rat, or the cold, maybe even forget about Slap all chewed up to hell and never drawing again.

No. Damn, goddamn, no damn good.

If he did that, he wouldn't be alert enough tomorrow to hustle some work from people cleaning their driveways. Maybe find something permanent for the spring working yards and gardens. Alleys weren't safe no more, park filled with killers, he didn't think it would come to this, but it might be time to get out.

Gonna get out, Slap, he thought tearfully; shit, I don't want to die.

There was even a guy up at the Heights, a cop, who had offered him a steady job last week, just to take care of the grounds. The same guy who used to talk to Slap about his drawing. That would get him out. That would keep him safe and away.

That scared him.

Because right now, tonight, there were only the alleys and himself.

And the goddamn rat and all its cousins.

He looked down the street toward the Strip, wiped his mouth, puffed his cheeks and blew.

If he took that job, hotshot Hot Trick Boy, his life would have to start over.

That scared him too.

The board he'd been carrying around all day was lead in his hand, and his shoulder ached, and his feet.

If he went in, the battle would be short.

Rat brains.

He grinned.

And heard something moving, a gliding, a whispering, far enough back to be part of the black.

He shifted the board to his other hand.

The rat had called his buddies.

But this here was his bedroom.

Goddamn rat.

A trash can rattled.

An eighteen-wheeler blasted past him, pushed him closer to the dark.

Money, or rat?

He stood on the sidewalk, shifting from foot to foot, crooning to himself, trying to make up his mind, knowing this was no good, knowing this wasn't the way to do something for Slap, his memory, no good at all. Kill the rat? Get a job? Jesus, he hated this; Jesus Lord, he was scared.

Then a hand touched his shoulder, and he whirled, board high, teeth bared, eyes so wide they instantly began to tear.

Scott held up his hands and backpedaled quickly. "Hey, Blade, Jesus, man, it's me. Scott Byrns, remember? Relbeth's Market?" He swallowed as he watched recognition scrub the fear and tension from Murtaugh's face, but he kept his eye on the two-by-four until it dropped to the man's side. "Hey, I'm sorry, I didn't mean anything. Really."

"It's all right," Blade muttered, shifting away from the alley's mouth. "Can't be too careful these days. Can't be too careful."

Scott glanced at the traffic, looked down the boulevard toward the diner. A police car stopped at the traffic signal, motor idling, its passenger window down to release the crackle and static of its radio. "Hey, I'm sorry about Slap, y'know?" His hands moved, circled, found their way back into his jacket pockets. "Bad news."

Blade, his face nearly hidden by his topcoat's wide collar, shuffled a few steps north, a few more south. "Yeah. Bitch."

Scott agreed with a nod.

"Was gonna get out, y'know. Little bastard was gonna get out." He pointed at the alley with the board. "Rat wants to kill me."

Scott didn't know what to say. This, he thought, was a big mistake. He should have just walked on by, said "hi" and kept on walking. The little man was obviously not working on all fronts, and for the first time he began to feel apprehensive. He took a step downtown.

"Rats," Blade said, sidling in the same direction.

"I know. I read the papers." He thought the man was talking about Blade, how he died.

Blade looked straight at him then. "You hear it, Leg?"

Scott frowned. "Excuse me?"

"You hear it, I said."

You heard it, Katie said.

"Hear . . . hear what?"

Blade sniffed, wiped his nose with a sleeve, checked the sidewalk in both directions, looked around Scott to the street. "What killed my Slap," he said quietly, so softly Scott had to lean closer to understand. "They said he fell asleep." He shook his head. "Slap don't sleep like that. Never did. Bounced around too much. Had him a place up there"—pointing north with the board—"for cold times. Not in the park. That was his warm times and day times, maybe take a nap, you know what I mean?" The board tapped the concrete. "I heard it."

You heard it, you all did.

Leave, Scott thought; the old guy's flipped, so leave, go home, listen to your mother drive you nuts, it's safer.

"Heard what, Blade?"

"The screaming," said Blade Murtaugh. "All the screaming that night."

A high-pitched moan; Joey raised his fists to the stars and spun in a slow erratic circle, tried to see past them to the Truth that lay beyond. The can in his left hand spilled cold beer on his head.

"Oops." He giggled. Lowered his arms. Spread his legs and sniffed, wiped his nose with a sleeve.

He was in the jungle. He had to be. Who cared if it had snow? Monster trees all around, bushes with thorns, things that crept around behind him and in front of him, scared shitless to show themselves because he was Joey Costello and he was going to tear their asses out and wear their hides for gloves.

He emptied the can and threw it over his shoulder.

Tear their asses.

Why did his mother hate him so much?

He lashed out at a bush and was fascinated at the way the shriveled leaves scattered, drifted, took the color of the moon and slipped away, into black.

Black panther.

Squatting in the middle of the path just ahead. Eyes watching him, not blinking, the gleam of a claw, the hint of a fang.

Joey sneered at it, curled his lip at it, dropped heavily to his knees and felt around until his hands closed over a large stick. He shook it clean of dead leaves and used it to push himself back to his feet.

"Come here, fucker," he said to the big cat.

When the panther didn't move, he yelled and charged and ran the beast through and watched it thrash in agony on the point of his sword. When it died, he crushed its head with a heel, laughed, hiccuped, and moved on.

Damn, it was cold.

Not bad cold, but cold enough.

Laine should be here now. She should see him. She should know how he could take care of himself. Care of her. Care of the whole goddamn world if only they'd give him the chance.

A lion.

Mane of fire, roar of thunder.

A tightness in his throat, but he knew this was a challenge he couldn't pass up.

It was a fierce battle. A heroic battle. Twice he was thrown to the ground, twice he stumbled to his feet and battled on; twice more he was thrust by a giant paw into a tree, and twice after that he pinwheeled into bushes he couldn't even see because the lion lived in the dark, and Joey Costello fought in the dark, and he didn't need no goddamn light to show him how to shove that sword right down that lion's throat and out its frigging gut.

He was thirsty.

Jesus, Mary, and Joseph, but he was so goddamn thirsty.

Then he came to the river, where a crocodile lounged on the muddy bank, its tail languidly fanning through the water.

This one was too easy; it was over in a minute.

Exhausted, chilled through by the night breeze, he ignored the snow and fell onto his back to stare at the sky, counted four hundred and thirty-four stars before he rolled onto his side and threw up.

The river talked to him.

Staggering to his hands and knees was the best he could do when he heard it through his sobbing.

Whispered to him.

He had never understood what it was saying, not since the day he and the others—Eddie Roman is dead, but he was there too—had defied a summer swimming ban and had had a party under South Bridge. They dove off the prow-shaped concrete skirts around the pilings, pushed each other off, used tires ten times bigger than they were that his father had gotten from the trucking company warehouse. Eddie was nine; Joey was nine-and-a-half; the river was low, and as long as they stayed by the shore there was no danger of the current taking them under. The river was shallow there, not quite as high as the top of their heads. They shouted, they shot the hell out of each other, and they scattered with laughter when a cop came down to chase them. That's when Joey slipped and fell off the skirt. On the way he grazed his head, and in the water he heard the whispers until the cop pulled him out and his father carried him home.

He grinned, and threw up again.

The river whispered.

That night, when his mother stopped her bawling, he got the worse spanking he had ever had in his life.

Water splashed.

But no one believed him when he told them about the voice, about the things that lived down there below the oil slicks and the floating debris and the once-a-year body because someone jumped in and couldn't swim. Or didn't want to.

Eddie did, though. Or said he did. Just a few weeks ago, they were on the bridge throwing water bombs at the boats, Pancho ahead because his arm was stronger, and Eddie said, "I heard them, Joey."

At first Joey hadn't known what Eddie was talking about; and when he figured it out, he almost hit him because he thought Eddie was yanking his chain. Then he saw Eddie's face—almost pale, almost sweating, like he was scared and didn't dare tell.

Pancho laughed.

Eddie didn't say anything else.

But, for a while, it made Joey feel good.

The trouble was, he thought as he finally lurched to standing, he knew damn well it was all in his head. It didn't matter that it scared the shit out of him sometimes, because sometimes what was in his head was scarier than anything anyone else could imagine.

Water splashed.

Then Pancho called night before last and said, "Eddie was right."

That's all: "Eddie was right."

He gagged.

Thirsty; he was thirsty.

Pancho was an asshole. He never knew what the hell he was talking about except when it was football or something dumb, like math. What a jerk. He could add numbers in his head Joey couldn't even imagine, but Eddie had somehow convinced him that Joey really heard voices.

Christ.

A bird flew out of the trees and sailed low over the water.

The moon rode the river's center.

He sat on the bank, the water three feet below him. "I stink," he told it, rocked forward, rocked back. "I stink, I stink, I stink, ain't that right?"

His head began to throb.

His stomach rolled over in acid.

Between him and the moon the water began to bubble.

"Goddamn," he said, squinted, shaded his eyes with one hand. "Goddamn." He tapped his shoulder, crooked a finger. "Hey, Laine, you bitch, come take a look at this. You ever see anything like it? What is it, gas or something? You got gas or something in this fucking river?"

Laine, the bitch, was of course too good to talk to him just because he knew the difference between a girl and a real woman.

Well, the hell with her.

He kicked the bank with his heels.

Yeah.

The hell with her.

He smiled. He laughed. He shook his head carefully and decided to go home and forgive his parents for treating him like shit. What the hell. They deserved it.

The water boiled.

Call Pancho in the morning, tell him what the hell, let's get our hairs cut.

His mouth tasted sour, and he spat.

A bird screamed behind him, in the dark.

The water opened.

The moon dimmed, dimmed again, and was gone.

"Jesus, Laine," he said, "what the hell is that?"

SEVENTEEN

Without warning, Blade doubled over with a loud grunt, his hands clasped across his stomach, his feet taking him in a backward stumble until he collided with the building wall. His knees sagged. He nearly fell. Scott took a step toward him, thinking the man was having a heart attack, a seizure.

Blade moaned and said, "God!" The board dropped to the sidewalk and, without thinking, Scott picked it up.

"Blade?"

The little man dropped to his knees and clamped his hands over his ears. "Oh, God!"

There was no one on the street within hailing distance. Scott stepped closer, and jumped back when Murtaugh leapt to his feet and screamed, "God!" before launching into a run that took him around the corner before Scott could react.

"Blade!"

He couldn't run. The best he could do was an awkward trot that made his thigh ache almost instantly. By the time he reached the corner, Murtaugh was already halfway down the block, reeling from side to side, topcoat flapping, falling once into a snowbank and flailing about as if he'd been wrapped in a flimsy web.

"Blade, wait up!"

The police car at the traffic signal suddenly burst into light and siren and squealed around the corner and down the hill toward the river, followed seconds later by another, and an ambulance that came from the other direction.

Sirens then from other parts of town, and he couldn't help scanning the sky for signs of fire.

Murtaugh scrambled and crawled and pushed to his feet, slapped at his coat, and ran.

Scott knew it then, and his throat dried instantly—the man had heard something.

Someone else was dying.

He punched his thigh angrily, demanding it work, demanding he not be slowed, and hurried on, gulping for air, feeling sweat gather and slide down the middle of his back. Watching Blade slip into the hazy twilight between streetlamps and appear again under the light's fall. Virtually walking now. Sporadic spurts of running more like tripping. But not close enough or slow enough for Scott to catch him.

"Blade, hey, wait up!"

Murtaugh turned like a lost drunk.

Scott waved the two-by-four.

Down by the river there was gunfire.

"Laine?"

She looked up from the book Dale had asked her to read to him—goofy, chubby, cartoon monsters living in a little boy's attic, lots of teeth but they were his friends. She frowned. For some reason, he was scared, but she knew it wasn't because of the story, this was his favorite, she had to read it to him practically every night. He had left his place beside her and had twisted around until he was kneeling, peering out the window.

"What is it, Dale?"

"Somebody hurt."

Her frowned deepened. "What do you mean?"

He looked over his shoulder, puzzled. "I hear him crying. Real loud."

She closed the book and half closed her eyes as she strained, trying to filter out the normal sounds of the house. "I don't hear anything."

Dale looked back into the night. "Real loud, Laine. Real hurt."

Pancho sat up abruptly.

"What is it?"

He stared through the car's rear window and down the slope to the river. Despite the moon it was black, and North Bridge blacker still.

Tang eased away from him as she pulled down her T-shirt, adjusted her skirt. "Panch, is something the matter?"

Lips dry, he said, "Didn't you hear it?"

"Hear what?"

Oh shit, he thought; oh shit.

The Queen of Foxriver screamed in her bed, and upstairs, in the living room, Calvin Nobbs banged on the floor with his cane. Trying to get her to shut up. It was bad enough, the other noise, but this was too much.

He hit the floor again.

The cane broke.

Erma didn't turn around at his cursing, at the screaming down in the basement apartment. She stood at the window with Mazie and watched a police car streak down toward the river.

She hugged herself despite the heavy sweater she wore.

"Again," Mazie said, voice small.

Erma nodded.

Calvin took hold of a ladder-back chair and thumped it on the carpet.

The Queen kept on screaming.

"We're moving," Mazie said.

Erma nodded.

Calvin kicked the chair aside and stomped to the door under

the staircase. "I'm going to kill her!" he yelled. "I'm going to tear her heart out!"

"Shut up, Calvin," Mazie said, just loud enough for him to hear. "Go upstairs and pack."

"We can't, Mazie, you know that," Erma said, turning away from the window, still hugging herself.

A siren made her jump.

Mazie took one of her hands.

The Queen stopped her screaming, and Calvin marched into the living room. "I'm tired," he announced. "I'm going to sleep."

Erma didn't say a word. She only watched him climb the stairs, painfully slowly.

"Old bastard," Mazie muttered flatly, almost with affection.

Yes, Erma thought; yes.

And hunched her shoulders when she felt the night move.

"Pen," the woman gasped.

Tobin looked down at her, at the beads of sweat shimmering down between her breasts, at the perspiration masking her face, at the hair plastered to her skin. He wanted to say something, but he was afraid. Not of the words, but of a passerby hearing.

They were on the platform behind the counter, not quite out of reach of the dim lights in each ceiling corner, and all someone had to do was look through the window at just the right angle, around the reindeer and the sleigh, and the rest of Slap's pictures, and they'd learn damn quick what a bookseller did once his shop had been closed.

Yet he hadn't resisted when she'd made the suggestion. Demand. He had been too far gone already. He hadn't seen Bonita in several days, he couldn't even get the high school girl to smile anymore, and Arlette was available. Nothing more. She had kissed him passionately the moment he had stepped out of his office and announced they were closing, touched him in a hundred places at once before he could react, a fevered frenzy that stopped his lungs and damn near scared him; and when she undressed by shrugs and kicks and a guiding of his unsure hand, she could have asked him to do it in the middle of the duck pond at high noon and he would have said yes.

She gasped again, eyes open but nearly rolled into her head.

A heel kicked his buttocks, spurring him, commanding.

He gulped for air and tried to move faster, but it was beyond him. He could only do so much, and somehow, despite her protests, it never seemed enough.

He stretched his neck then and almost lost it—a large beetle had crawled onto the raised platform, just like the one he thought he had squashed the other night for Fern. Its antennae scooped the air. A hooked front leg touched the flooring.

"Jesus, Pen!"

A hand gripped his shoulder and pushed, yanked, pushed again, and dug in.

"God!"

He looked down and nearly exploded when he saw her head twisting side to side, flushed, sweat running, tongue slipping over her dry lips, swallowing air and gasping again.

He looked up quickly, knowing he had to think of something else—lyrics of a dull song, counting by fives, the capitals of the fifty states, anything, for god's sake, anything at all.

The beetle moved closer.

Its single eye caught the dim light and made it seem blind, its legs now seemed much larger than they should have been. Lifting, curling, falling again. Hairy. Clawed.

"Hey," he whispered breathlessly.

"A minute," she begged. "Please, Pen, just a minute."

He couldn't help it—his stomach jumped with the birth of a laugh he tried to keep down.

She bucked.

The beetle stopped, waved at the air, turned its back, and walked away. For all the world, he thought, like some bored voyeur who hadn't found the excitement it demanded.

Then he saw the second one, on the counter above his head.

"Christ!" he yelled, and rocked back onto his heels.

Arlette swung at him, saw the beetle, and shrieked.

He threw a book at it.

It vanished.

But he couldn't help wondering how many more of them there were.

Laine exploded out of the house, battling into her leather jacket, one hand trying to swipe at her eyes though the tears hadn't yet started. Katie had just called, hysterical, babbling and sobbing even though Laine had tried to calm her down. But she did hear "Joey" and "the river" enough times to send her flying from the house before her parents could stop her. She paused on the porch to catch her breath, to tell herself that panic now would do her no good, would send her into a tree before she reached the river.

Something thumped loudly underfoot. She looked down. It thumped again, hard enough now to send vibrations through her legs. Inside, she heard Dale begin to cry, heard her mother comfort him.

It thumped again, and this time the boards rose a little.

She leapt off the porch, clearing the steps, veering across the snow toward the car parked in the drive. Into it, blessing the engine when it started right away, cursing when she backed out so swiftly she hit the curb across the street.

Slow, she ordered; slow, damnit, slow.

But she still heard Joey's name, an echo with tears, while she wrenched the car into a right turn that skidded her onto French Street and forced her to cry out and swerve to avoid running down someone jogging in the road.

He wouldn't, she told herself; please, God, don't let him.

The road dipped, the incline not as steep or as long as it was farther north. She slowed. Tears suddenly drenched her cheeks. She stopped and pulled over, climbed shakily out.

No, God, please.

There were lights at the bottom as she hugged herself, saw people crowding onto the sidewalk, breath smoking in the streetlight, voices sharp in the night air. She used the street instead. Two cruisers down there at least, and an ambulance van with its blunt nose pointing toward the water. Cops were all over the place, flashlights streaking across the snow and through the bare black branches, walkie-talkies hissing, two of them setting up sawhorse barriers on Bank Road; one white-jacketed attendant was opening the van's rear doors.

From well off to her left a crackling of gunfire that stopped as quickly as it had begun.

One of the spectators cried out.

She didn't dare think. She didn't dare want to know why Dale had heard something and she hadn't heard a thing.

She kept to the center, praying, sniffing hard, and didn't know when Katie came up beside her and grabbed her arm and hung on. Crying. Unable to talk.

Twenty feet up from the intersection another barrier was set in place just as the girls reached it. People moved in from the sidewalks. The police refused to answer their questions. One of them, however, kept his hand on the butt of his holstered revolver.

Laine gnawed on her lower lip. "How do you know?" she finally managed to ask.

Katie sniffed and looked up at the sky, down at the blacktop, blinking rapidly. "I was walking, y'know?, I couldn't stay in the house, Gram was being a pain, and suddenly all this starts coming down. Some guy was there, the little guy Scott knows? The black guy? Anyway, the cops chased him away, I heard them talking after he left."

Laine grabbed her shoulders. "You sure . . . Joey?"

"God, I think so."

Laine gripped the sawhorse as hard as she could, staring at the activity below, stoking the courage to slip under and run down there. She couldn't just stay here. She couldn't stand around and not know.

People came up behind them, beside them, some with cameras, most asking questions no one could answer.

And then it was quiet.

Katie sobbed once and grabbed Laine's hand.

Attendants hurried a stretcher out of the trees, a cop walking behind, a walkie-talkie to his lips and a shotgun braced against his hip. Someone lay on the stretcher, but she couldn't see who it was because the face had been covered; all she could see was the blood.

"I'm going to throw up," she whispered. "Please, God, don't let me throw up."

Katie gripped her hand harder. Her tears had stopped, a packet of tissues in her other hand.

The ambulance doors closed.

"Look!" Katie said, leaning close, tugging her arm. "Hey there's Scott. He's coming this way."

The police made no move to leave.

Katie tugged again, and Laine didn't resist as her friend led her toward the sidewalk. Her legs had become rubber, her throat sandpaper, her eyes nearly blind—all she could see was Scott Byrns moving through the crowd, ignoring those who spoke to him, one hand jammed into a hip pocket, the other hand at his side, gripping a long piece of wood.

Katie waved.

"No," Laine pleaded.

Katie stood her by a tree and told her not to move. That was all right. She couldn't move if she wanted to. She knew. By the look on Scottie's face, she knew. He'd been crying. Or was about to.

When Katie stopped him, spoke urgently to him, and he swung his face in her direction, Laine didn't care that the strength left her legs, didn't care when they rushed over and propped her up under the arms. She said something about her mother's car, and didn't care when they brought her to it and put her in the back seat. Katie slid in beside her.

"The keys, Laine," he said tonelessly after sliding in behind the wheel.

"Can you drive?" Katie asked.

"No," he said, "I'm going to push it all the way home."

Dale heard, she thought in the midst of a black fog; oh my god, did Dale really hear and I let Joey die?

"Laine, the keys?"

Katie found them in her pocket and handed them over, and he backed all the way to the end of the street, as she told him how she'd come to be out tonight.

She couldn't look at his face.

Katie said, "Was it . . . I heard it was Joey."

No, Laine thought, and closed her eyes tightly; don't answer, please don't answer.

He didn't, but a long year later, Katie grunted as if someone had punched her in the stomach and her lungs wouldn't work and her voice wouldn't work and she barely heard him say they'd have to talk later, probably tomorrow, something about the street people, something about . . . but no . . . Jesus, no, it wasn't suicide.

After that, he said nothing.

After that, Laine heard nothing but the sound of her own razor-edge sobbing, the ambulance crying away into the night, the sudden memory of gunfire that made her eyes snap open.

"Scott, I heard guns—"

"He wasn't shot."

"Oh god."

Then who was? she thought; who were they shooting at?

She wanted to scream; all she could do was whimper.

Scott let the two girls weep, feed on each other's grief, while he drove to the Freelin house as fast as he dared, as fast as he was able. He checked the streets in case he spotted Blade, but Murtaugh was gone. Had been since Scott had stumbled onto Bank Road and there had been all the activity. There was no one now. Not even another car.

Once at Laine's house, he explained to her folks what had happened and walked away, declining the offer of a lift home. When Dr. Freelin came after him, coatless, shivering, insisting he couldn't walk all the way to South End tonight, not after what happened, Scott told him it was all right. Really. He needed time. Time alone.

Dr. Freelin, pale even in the dark, glanced back at the house. "She's going to be hysterical all night."

"Maybe you should take her to the hospital."

"No." He took off his glasses and rubbed his eyes. "No, I can take care of her." A squint at Scott. "I don't like this, you know. Walking home alone. Maybe I should call your mother."

Scott turned away and did his best not to limp. "You'd better get back to Laine," he said over his shoulder.

He wanted to walk.

He had to walk.

He hadn't seen the body, but after searching futilely for Blade, he had seen Detective Jorgen stumbling out of the trees, shaking his head and coughing into a soiled handkerchief pressed against his mouth. He didn't move, only waited, until the policeman spotted him and walked over as yet another cruiser shrieked to a halt and its occupants piled out with revolvers and shotguns drawn.

A weary frown: "What the hell are you doing here?"

"I heard a scream."

"Yeah." Jorgen rubbed his face with both hands, dusted clots of snow flecked with grass from his coat. "Yeah." Someone called from the riverbank. "Go home, son. There's nothing you can do here."

Scott reached for his arm. "Who was it?"

Jorgen stared at him for so long, Scott almost lost his temper.

Until: "Your buddy. Joey. Joey Costello."

The scream was there, the denial, the rage, but the detective defused it by walking away.

Just walking away.

Scott felt the burning in his leg, the throbbing at his temples, but he didn't turn around, didn't go back. The night had turned colder, and the cold felt good, it kept him moving, kept him from thinking too much about the body on the stretcher and all that blood staining the sheet, kept him from thinking too much about the ambulance lights staining the snow, the faces, the houses that faced the river, kept him from noticing the car pacing him at the curb until it honked, and he started to run. Couldn't run. Knowing he was going to die. Knowing that the monster who had killed two of his best friends was here . . . now . . . and he was alone in the dark.

"Scott!"

He began to cry.

Not for Joey, not for Eddie, not Slap.

He cried because he couldn't run, not really; he cried because he wasn't like the rest of the world and it just wasn't goddamn fair; he cried because his mother practically in the middle of the street finally snagged him in her arms and held him to her breast, caressing his hair, rocking him, cooing to him, and finally leading him to the car. He cried because she didn't say she was sorry, that it was a terrible tragedy, that if there was anything she could do, all he had to do was ask.

He cried because she said, "Scott, what's going on?"

EIGHTEEN

In all his dreams he had both legs, and both legs were strong, and since they were strong he could run.

But not fast enough.

NINETEEN

It was the sedative, he supposed, that had dragged him into unwilling sleep. His mother had called a doctor, and the doctor had called the all-night drugstore, and she had picked up the prescription—with him in the car because he wasn't about to be left alone—and he had taken the two pills, sitting at the kitchen table, his mother leaning against the sink and watching him.

Watching him.

Watching him when he woke up, sweating, drying his face with a sweet-smelling towel.

Watching him as she massaged his leg down to the stump, shaking her head whenever he winced at the pain that had burrowed deep into his muscles and wouldn't go away, not even after he'd taken a long hot bath.

Watching him when he came downstairs, using only one crutch, and dropped into his chair at the kitchen table. Groggy, feeling not quite lined up with the rest of the world.

"I'm not going to start fall apart, Mom," he said at last, lips twitching in a sort of a grin.

"I'm concerned."

"I know. But I'm okay. Really."

Her expression told him she thought he was lying through his teeth, that he couldn't possibly be okay, not after last night.

She didn't argue, however. She made brunch—it was almost noon—and left the room on a feigned and sudden errand when he stared at her—*jeez, mom, i'm not going to cut my throat on the butter knife, either*—until she couldn't watch him anymore.

He ate toast and cereal, drank milk and wished for coffee, looked down in astonishment when his spoon scraped across the bottom of the bowl and he realized he was done. He hadn't tasted a thing. He yawned, stretched, shook his head in a vain attempt to clear it of the cobwebs left behind by the medication. Yawned again. When the telephone rang, he started, sat back, tried to make sense of his mother's conversation in the living room, but she spoke too softly and he scowled, thumped the chair around and looked through the window in the back door.

Greylight.

Snowlight.

There must be clouds, maybe another storm on the way.

Swell. Great.

Joey's dead.

He felt as if he'd been clubbed across the back of the head, the cobwebs abruptly gone, clear memory restored. He grunted, quickly covered his mouth with a hand and closed his eyes, leaning over, gripping the table, forcing himself to breathe slowly and deeply until his stomach decided it wouldn't empty itself. He coughed, choked, coughed, and leaned back heavily, head back, gaze on the ceiling and not seeing a thing.

"Oh god."

Tracing a line in the plaster until it reminded him of the river.

Sitting up, pushing bowl and glass aside and settling his elbows on the table, clasped hands across his brow.

"Man."

The questions refused to line up in any rational order. They just came as he stared at the tabletop and shook his head: What did Murtaugh hear? Who were the cops shooting at? Why was Joey down by the river? Why did Katie lie about being out last night? What were the cops shooting at? Why did Joey die? How did Laine—

She heard.

No.

Katie heard.

No.

He looked around the kitchen, seeing it all, seeing nothing.

Blade heard.

No.

It's the medicine, he thought; the medicine is making me nuts. You can't hear somebody dying when you're blocks away. You can't hear it. You can't.

They had.

A sudden need to do something made him grab the crutch from the floor beside him. Once up, he started for the living room, stopped, and went to the back door. The snow in the tiny back yard was broken here and there by bird tracks, cat tracks, a scuffed line of footprints where his mother had gone to the back fence to shake the heavy snow off the branches of a sapling before they snapped. A haze distorted the air just enough to be discomforting. Preview of a storm. If he were outside, he knew he'd be able to feel it, almost taste it.

He turned when his mother came back, raised an eyebrow with a question he didn't answer.

"It's been ringing all morning," she said, tossing the dish towel onto the counter. "That detective wants to talk to you, Katie has called three times, and some damn reporters." She shook her head in disgust, then lifted her hands. "They're talking about drugs, Scott. They're talking about the Pack's enemies, gang wars—"

He laughed.

It wasn't the least bit funny, but he couldn't help the laughing, and couldn't stop it, not even when she hurried over and brought him back to his chair. Tears. Hiccups. Drinking a glass of water so fast he began to choke, and waved off her attempt to pound him on the back. And when he had calmed down, he assured her, almost resentfully, that no, there were no drugs, and no, there were no rival gangs, and no, he didn't think some maniac had it in for the Pack because Slap Zubronsky was dead too and all he did was draw pictures.

"There's no connection," she said, dismissing Slap by turning her back.

Yes, there is, he thought.

"There is," he said. "I don't know how, Mom, but there is."

And then: "Mom, how did Joey die?"

She grabbed up the towel and twisted it in her hands.

"Mom? Was it like Eddie?"

She nodded. "Maybe worse."

Swallowing didn't rid his mouth of the acid.

"Detective Jorgen didn't give me the details." She turned around. "But he did tell me you were there last night. Why?"

Because, he wanted to tell her, Blade Murtaugh heard the screaming.

Because, he did tell her, he'd been at the bookstore, heard the sirens, and followed them. He told her about Katie and Laine, and she told him that Dr. Freelin had called, which is why she had been there with the car.

The telephone rang.

"I'm going to take that damn thing off the hook," she said, striding out of the room, the towel once more thrown aside. Less than a minute later, he heard the receiver slam into its cradle, heard a string of curses that amazed him, and heard something that sounded remarkably like his mother kicking a chair.

"Mom?" He hurried into the hall, stood at the living room entrance and saw her in the middle of the floor, fists at her sides, cheeks flushed. "Mom?"

"That," she said, barely moving her lips, "was Mr. Thomas Relbeth. He wanted to know . . . he had the nerve to ask if you were okay and if you were going to come to work today." A deep breath. It didn't seem to help. "He said it was important. Fridays are always important."

Scott almost laughed again. "He's just hyper, Mom, don't worry about it. He's got some chain guys trying to buy the store, that's all. Don't sweat it." His smile didn't crack her glare. "So what did you tell him?"

"I told him where he could put his goddamn overpriced store, that's what I told him!"

Oh, nice, he thought; get me fired, why not, Mom.

He saw her distress then, and realized that she was frightened.

For him. Maybe even for the other kids, but especially for him. It made him soften his expression, shrug an apology for the unspoken scolding. When she suggested he lie down again, he took it without dissent. He needed to think, and that would be impossible as long as she kept hovering over him, mother bird, and asking him how he felt.

The telephone rang, and he said, "My turn," with a grin.

"Scott?" It was Fern. "Jesus, Scott, what are we going to do?"

They talked for nearly an hour, dissecting the previous night step by step, crying openly, crying inside, talking about the murder as though there was, truly, a homicidal lunatic running around Foxriver. The police seemed to think so. Fern said that Tang had told her there were more cops on the road than it seemed the town had. Tang herself was holed up in her room, vowing not to come out until the century was over. Neither of them had heard from Laine, though, and repeated attempts to call Katie had met with her grandmother, who didn't, Fern said bitterly, want to admit Katie even lived there. Barnaby had hung up on her, and Pancho wasn't answering.

"It's not a psycho," he said at the end.

"Then who is it, Scott?" She sounded weary, not hysterical.

"I don't know."

"Great. Then who does?"

"I don't know that either."

A pause, and he could hear his mother in the kitchen.

"Okay." She didn't sound convinced. "So, do me a favor?"

"Sure."

"Don't go out today?"

He shrugged. An easy promise to keep; he wasn't feeling good enough to face the world anyway. "No problem." He sensed a relieved smile then when she hung up, and after he put the receiver back he pushed himself to the center of the couch and stared out the window. The street was quiet. A few cars now and then. A passing cruiser that made him shiver. A gang of little kids sweeping down the sidewalk on the other side, pelting each other with snowballs, shrieking, disappearing, their voices hanging, and quickly gone. The cruiser again.

He dozed.

He answered the telephone despite his mother's objections: talking briefly to reporters who wanted to know how he felt, telling them all it was a pretty stupid question, how did they think he felt, and grinning at the street for his boldness; talking to Detective Jorgen, who wanted to know why he'd been in the area, listening to his answer with an occasional grunt, and not responding when Scott found the nerve to ask if the man thought Slap was part of all this; talking to Mr. Relbeth, who begged him to come in; talking to Fern again, to Barnaby, who wanted to know, angrily, who the hell Fern Bellard thought she was, trying to get everybody scared shitless like that.

Talking until his ear ached, and his mother took over, less tolerant, snapping, finally unplugging the phone and shaking a fist at it before she went to the store to get something for supper.

They ate in front of the television.

They saw the story of Joey's murder.

Scott couldn't bring himself to cry again.

He was, at the last, trapped in the toy department, the mannequins gathering in front of the elevators, whispering among themselves, pointing awkwardly in the directions each of them would take in order to search him out, drag him out, make sure he understood that their legs came off too. Both of them. One of them had brought a lawn mower up from the gardening department, it didn't matter that it was winter, and he saw himself suddenly in the yard, little, very little, napping lightly in the sun, listening to the mower buzz, listening to his father yelling at his mother about something or other, it was probably money, listening to the grass, not feeling anything but a hard thump against his side, the screaming pain delayed because he didn't know what had happened. Watching the mannequins prepare to take his other leg off. Faces in shadow.

Gesticulating. Separating. The mower buzzing across the polished floor. Calling his name softly. While he hid in the tent pegged on artificial grass and prayed that he wouldn't be caught, that it wouldn't happen again. Huddling. Eyes closed. A hand tapping his shoulder and a wooden voice saying, very softly, "Boo."

Saturday he went to work. He had to. Staying in the house was driving him up the wall, his mother's hovering wasn't helping, and he knew that if he didn't talk to someone face-to-face soon, he would probably tear off his clothes and run naked down the street. For a change, his mother didn't argue. But the only people who came to the grocery store were the usual customers, not his friends. They gossiped with Relbeth, clucked over the way the town was going to hell, turning into another New York City, and giving him such looks of pity that by the time the sun began to set, he wished he had stayed home.

Besides, his boss was in a mood.

"They" were out to get him. The big supermarket chains again. His refusal to sell, he had become convinced, had turned their tactics to sabotage more insidious than they'd ever used before.

"Oh come on, that's crazy," Scott said, counting the register money for the fifth time in an hour.

"I shit you not, boy, they're going to fire my house or something, you watch." The stench of the Turkish cigarette close to his face. "Bricks through the window, garbage turned over, you watch, they'll do it. Force me." The cleaver dropped onto the counter. "Sons of bitches are greedy, you know. Too damn greedy. Don't care about the little guy. Don't give a flying, if you know what I mean.

Scott's smiled was strained. "So what have they done?"

Relbeth laughed. "Done? Nothing. Not yet." A finger shook over the register. "But you watch, boy, you watch. I know them. I see them at work. Any day now they're going to trash this place, just to let me know I ain't getting away."

Scott looked to the ceiling for help.

"You going to the funeral?"

He blinked. "What?"

"The Costello kid. Tomorrow afternoon. You going?"

He nodded.

"Said it was an animal."

Scott knew. Though descriptions were sparse, the official word was that some animal had caught Joey on the riverbank. The autopsy showed that the boy had been drunk, and had been found facedown in the water, battered, cut, death from loss of blood. The police had spotted something that night, had fired at it, but it had escaped. Prints, long gone now since most of the snow had melted, proved that at least it hadn't been human.

No guess.

Just an animal.

"Dog," Relbeth said, picking the cleaver up, turning toward the meat locker. "You get 'em in winter. Hungry as shit, they'll go for anything they figure is helpless. This damn cold weather isn't helping, of course." Relbeth stopped at the door. "And turn on the lights, will you, for Christ's sake? People'll think we're closed."

Scott did, and squinted at the unnatural brightness, shuddered at the way the neon buzzed in the window. Then he looked toward the locker, looked toward the street, grabbed his broom and swept the floor. Straightened the shelves. Counted the money a sixth time and scribbled the amount and time on a sheet of paper he slipped under the tray.

He hadn't thought about the funeral much, or the way Joey had died; he tried not to think about it now. Tomorrow would be soon enough. Tonight all he wanted to do was sit in the tub and let the hot water put him to sleep. With luck there'd be no more dreams. With luck he'd be able to convince himself he was wrong, dead wrong, that the police were right, that Relbeth was right, that it really had been some kind of hunger-crazed animal who had caught Joey at the wrong place at the wrong time, had chased him until he'd slipped on the frozen bank and stunned himself on the rocks, had savaged him while he'd been helpless. If he could do that, sleep would be a cinch.

If he could do that, he thought, putting on his jacket, he'd be able to teach elephants to fly.

He pounded on the locker door and yelled a goodnight to his boss, heard a cursing response, and left with a half-smile that remained even when the night wind cracked against his cheeks, dropped his hair into his eyes, slithered down the back on his neck to stiffen his spine.

"Jesus," he muttered.

Traffic was heavy. People leaving town for the malls and mall theaters, for shows in New York, for parties in other towns. The street was dry, the tires hard and high-pitched, and it took him a while to find a break large enough to allow him to cross in the middle of the block. Once on the other side, he debated walking up to the diner, gave it up, and started home.

And once off the Boulevard he saw the man across the street.

Dark coat, dark hat, keeping pace with him without a sound.

"Screw you, Barnaby!" he yelled.

He jammed his hands into his pockets and hurried on, the wind nudging him from behind now, bringing with it the sounds of the cars behind him.

The man kept walking. Stiffly. As if he had not one, but two false legs.

Barnaby, dammit, he thought, I'm going to kick your ass, you keep this up.

The man kept walking.

At his corner, temper surging, heat tightening his jaw and his stomach, Scott stopped.

The dark man stopped, under a streetlamp.

The dark man raised his head and took off his hat.

The dark man had no face.

Scott backed away, knowing it was trick, a stocking pulled down to Barnaby's chin, a mask, something like that.

But the dark man had no face.

Eyes, yes; nose, yes; brow, cheeks, mouth, chin—yes.

Yet the face was still blank.

And the dark man had no shadow.

The wind rose, fell, rose again and danced with the bare branches of trees and shrubs.

A car horn blared.

Scott turned and hobble-ran when the dark man put his hat on and stepped down off the curb. There was no ice to be cautious of, only cracks in the pavement, sections that had been lifted and still had weeds poking out from underneath, a rock that could have tripped him if he hadn't seen it in time, his own shadow plunging ahead and falling back, pointing the way and, like him, refusing to look back.

The dark man made no sound.

Scott felt the wind chapping his lips, stinging his cheeks, pulling at his hair and turning it to fine whips.

The dark man made no sound.

Scott couldn't believe this was happening again. The same figure, the same flight, the same stumbling up the stairs and into the house, his mother coming out of the kitchen still wiping her hands on a towel, asking if he was all right.

He didn't answer.

He hurried into the living room and stood at the window.

This time the dark man was still there. Across the street now, by a telephone pole.

"My god, who is it?" his mother asked over his shoulder.

He shook his head. He didn't know.

"Well, I'm calling the police."

He felt her turn. "Don't."

"Don't be foolish, Scott. That could be—"

"He's gone."

He was.

There. And gone. Blended into shadow, leaving only the pole behind.

TWENTY

In all his dreams, his legs were as they were, and he could not run, and so Blade Murtaugh scooped him up and raced together down a year-long alley, the Queen of Foxriver running at their side, giving her blessing to the rats and the worms and the beetles and the slime, the hat that looked like a turban wobbling side to side until it finally fell off and he saw that she was bald; and when she saw that he saw, she told him not to worry, that none of her knights had any hair either; and when his hand touched his head, he knew that it was so, and it was so with Blade as well, and with the rats that fell from the walls onto his stomach, with the dogs that began to chew on his leg despite the speed Blade managed to hold, and with the cats that ran past them, bits of Slap in their mouths; and when the Queen of Foxriver finally began to fall behind, he looked over Blade's shoulder and saw something huge looming there, the dark man ten times as tall and oddly shaped and oddly running; and when the Queen saw it, she began to laugh; and when Blade saw it, he began to laugh too.

And Scott sat up in the middle of the night, eyes wide, the screams that he heard clinging to the dark.

His mother.

In his haste to get to her, he fell from the bed, used the

mattress to get back up, and hopped to the door, threw it open, and hurried down the hall, past the bathroom on his left, the stairs on his right, to his mother's door where he knocked as hard he could without pounding.

"Mom!"

He leaned against the wall.

"Mom!"

A light under the door, a grumbling, and she opened it, peering at him as he squinted back.

"Are you okay?"

"Scott, for god's sake."

"I heard you screaming."

She pushed her hair back with the flat of her hand and gave him a look that told him, flatly, she didn't appreciate the interruption of her sleep. "Scott, you were dreaming."

He looked past her into the bedroom. There was nothing wrong that he could see, and he felt suddenly awfully stupid.

"You were dreaming," she repeated.

"Yeah," he answered, not arguing when she took his shoulder and turned him around. "Yeah, I guess I was."

It wasn't until he reached his own bed again that he realized he'd been wrong.

The Queen had been laughing.

What he'd heard was a scream.

TWENTY-ONE

Large patches of grass pockmarked the hillside cemetery, making what was left of the snow look whiter than it was, making the bare trees look almost attractively grim. The headstones seemed more clean, sharp-edged. Angels prayed and wept, copper and brass gleamed, cherubs directed their pious gazes toward heaven.

Ice daggers hanging from branches hidden from the light dripped rapidly from their points.

Sparrows pecked at the bare ground, crows strutted, a cardinal balanced on a twig, vivid and noisy.

The sky was clear.

The sun was bright.

It was not, Scott thought, wishing he'd brought a pair of dark glasses, the right day for a funeral. There should be rain, or sleet, or at least a few clouds. And it should be cold, bitter, the way it had been the week before, not just about warm enough for him to take off his suit jacket.

It was wrong; all wrong.

Joey, he believed, deserved more of a proper mood. He deserved that at least, since Eddie had gotten nothing.

But he was pleased at the number of people who had shown up, both here, and earlier, at the church. The Costellos stood and were seated under a stiff canopy beside the gravesite; it seemed as if there were hundreds of them, black suits, black hats, black dresses, black coats with dark buttons. Laine sat with Mrs. Costello. Al was white-gloved in his policeman's dress uniform, as were a number of his off-shift friends. Detective Jorgen was there as well, off to one side, standing alone, his hat on but his hands held reverently in front of him.

Snow glittering in the sunlight, white and silver gems trapped beneath the surface, winking at the dead.

Scott stood with the Pack on the fringe of the assembly. They had arrived one by one. Solemn. Saying nothing. Dark suits and coats. Katie kept herself between Fern and Tang; Pancho stood next to Scott, fidgeting, Barnaby just behind and muttering under his breath. They listened to the overweight priest, to the responses, to the sniffling, the muted sobbing, to Mr. Costello swear at God once and angrily until Al put a hand on his shoulder without looking down. They watched the flowers placed on the coffin—roses, carnations, a spray of baby's breath; watched Mrs. Costello so odd without her apron stand at the edge of the grave for so long, so rigidly, they feared she might throw herself in; watched two figures standing beneath a distant tree, small people, one with an arm around the other, the other wearing a turban; watched the line of automobiles and limousines whose windows fired back the reach of the sun.

Black.

Everything was black except the sky.

The snow.

And when it was over, prayers and silent weeping, when the priest and his acolytes stood aside, when friends and strangers began to drift away after paying their respects to the family, when the relatives huddled around Joey's parents, Scott made his way to the coffin and looked at the flowers, the brass fixtures, the polished dark wood.

Damnit, Joey, dammit.

A touch of a breeze; the petals fluttered.

Damnit, it's not fair.

He wondered if he should try to say something to Mrs. Costello, and decided against it. She had already noticed him at the church, had given him a brave smile, a grateful nod. It was enough. As long as she knew Joey's friends hadn't forgotten him, it was enough.

He returned to the Pack and they moved as a pack up the rolling slope, avoiding the paths now clogged with escaping traffic, making their way toward the main road that would bring them out onto the street behind Town Hall. They didn't walk over the graves; they found the spaces in between. Fern groped for and found his hand. Tang shifted to Pancho and Barnaby. Katie walked on his other side.

None of them said a word.

Until Barnaby muttered, "Shit, what the hell are those stupid farts doing here?"

Scott looked to his right over Katie's head wrapped in a dark kerchief, and saw Blade and the fur-coat-wrapped Queen still huddled beneath the tree where he'd seen them before. On impulse he headed over, Fern not protesting, the others reluctantly falling in behind. It startled him for a moment, their silence, their following, but he was more intrigued by Blade's not moving away, not trying to leave when he realized he'd been spotted.

Scott nodded a greeting as he approached.

Blade nodded back, collar up, head bare, wool cap crumpled in one hand. "Sorry to hear," he said, wiped his nose on a sleeve.

"Thanks for coming."

"My knights," the Queen said with a tremulous smile.

"Jesus Christ," Barnaby said in disgust.

Scott turned on him, glared at him, chest abruptly tight with rage. "Shut up, Garing, okay? Just shut the hell up."

"Hell?" Pancho said.

Scott grinned.

Blade cleared his throat as he smoothed on his cap, tucked the tips of his ears under. "You gotta know something, Leg, you gotta know." The Queen tugged at the black man's arm, but Blade brushed at her hand impatiently. "He gotta know."

"Know what?" he said.

A car backfired, and the Queen jumped.

"I ran away."

"Yeah, so I noticed."

Blade wiped his face hard with a palm, glanced up at the branches overhead. "I ran because . . ." He cleared his throat, looked sheepish. "It wasn't you. It was . . ."

"You heard," Scott said quietly.

Startled, Blade nodded.

The Queen took a step back.

"You're shitting me," Pancho whispered.

Scott shook his head. "He's right. I was there. I saw."

Feet in the snow then, shifting nervously, the Pack breaking up in several directions at once, but not running away, not leaving. Barnaby was the only one who didn't move; he glared at the others as if forbidden access to a secret.

Tang, her hair loosely bunned, making her face look too thin, said, "Last night, I—"

"Last night," Katie echoed. "God, yes. Me, too."

Scott remembered his nightmare.

Blade nodded jerkily. "Somebody, I don't know who."

"Oh, man," Barnaby moaned, flapping his hands. "This is nuts. You guys are frigging nuts."

Scott checked at his watch, waited a few seconds for his vision to steady. "The diner, okay? Tonight. Eight or so."

"Hey, look," Garing complained, "who the hell made you king, huh? You can't even wait for them to put Joey in the ground, you son of a bitch?"

Tang gasped.

Fern said, "Screw off, huh?"

"Oh, dry up."

"Knights and ladies shouldn't use coarse language," the Queen scolded without raising her voice.

Katie giggled.

"Christ, bitch," Barnaby said, "mind your own goddamn business, okay? You ain't nothing but a—"

Scott took a single long step to stand in front of him, cutting him off, making him stare and finally look away. "Barnaby, zip it. Just . . . zip it, okay? You don't have to come if you don't want to, that's okay, but in case you hadn't noticed, we've got a problem here. Unless we're all going nuts, we're all hearing things. And when we hear things, people die. Three of them."

"Five."

He spun around.

They all did.

Laine stood above them, stark as a desert shadow in her black dress, black veil, black shoes belonging on a woman forty years older. So pale her minimal lipstick was a vivid smear of blood, her eyes too deep, her hands clasped white-knuckled at her waist.

The breeze stirred again.

The veil pushed against her face.

"What . . . what are you talking about, five?" Pancho asked.

"Al told me this morning." Her voice was flat, but she had to swallow several times. "Last night."

Scott immediately looked back toward the grave, searching for Jorgen. The detective was gone.

Laine's voice quivered. "Dale heard."

"Jesus, Dale?" Katie yelped, then quickly covered her mouth.

"I'm scared, guys," Tang said, reaching for Barnaby, who sent her to Pancho with an exasperated shove that didn't touch her.

Blade hustled around them, stopped when Laine held up a hand. It was clear she wasn't sure about him. He ducked his head, lifted a shoulder. "Who?" he said gently. Smiling. Flipping his collar down as if to prove he was harmless.

Laine looked at Fern. "Mr. Tobin."

"Jesus," Fern said, and grabbed Scott's arm.

"He was with Arlette Bingham, Al said. In the Island. Both of them in one chair." She took off her hat, a shake of her head that freed her hair.

"How?" Katie asked.

"I don't know. He didn't say." She glanced at Blade, then faced him squarely. "They think, now, your friend was a victim too."

Blade shrugged. "Know that. Hat Trick Boys don't fall asleep in the park. Not in the cold."

"Please?" the Queen said, not quite calling to Murtaugh.

They all talked at once then, demanding answers, asking questions, loudly and quietly. Scott felt it, the fear, and let it roam for a while, confused because he realized he had somehow taken over the Pack, confused because taking over had been the furthest thing from his mind, confused because the Pack, and Blade, and the Queen, and a little kid had heard people dying.

"Please, Blade?" the Queen said.

When he saw the tears in Tang's eyes, Scott said, "All right," and they shut up.

Just like that.

Even Barnaby.

It scared him.

But not as much as the faceless dark man had.

He had no idea what to say, and didn't like the looks he received, the expectation he felt. Hope for a solution, and doubt that he had it. This wasn't what he wanted. This wasn't the way it was supposed to be. But: "Let's go home, change, do what we have to do."

"So why don't we just go now? Pancho asked.

Scott gestured down the slope toward Joey's grave. Men in heavy coats were taking the flowers from the coffin, taking the canopy down. A few yards away a backhoe waited to fill the grave as soon as all the mourners were out of sight. "This isn't the time. It sure isn't the place." He looked at Blade and the Queen. "Will you come? To the Starlite tonight?" Amazingly, there was no protest from the Pack.

Blade nodded, then shook his head quickly, fearfully.

"Hey, it's all right." Scott nudged his shoulder, thinking as he did that it was the first time he'd touched him. "It's on me. But you've got to be there, man. We need your help."

"Rats," Blade whispered fearfully. "They got—"

"We shall cleanse ourselves at the Mission," the Queen interrupted. Her eyes were puffed, slow-moving tears on her cheeks. "We shall prepare for our trip to the warm place."

"Bonita," Blade said from the corner of his mouth, "this ain't no—"

The Queen hushed him angrily. Raised a hand in imperious

farewell to the Pack. Turned and walked slowly away toward a stand of evergreen floating on its own shadow above the snow. Blade watched her, looked to Scoot, and wiped his face again.

"No kidding, it'll be fine," Fern reassured him. "We practically own the place."

Without answering, the little man ran off, clumsy in patches of deeper snow, hailing the Queen, who didn't turn around.

Weird, Scott thought; this is really getting weird.

When he looked away at last, the girls had surrounded Laine and were leading her away. Barnaby was on his way as well, stamping up the hill, shaking his head like a bull who needed to charge and had no target.

"He doesn't hear," Pancho said then.

Scott stared. "Say what?"

Pancho took a deep breath. "Eddie knew it. Eddie told Joey, and Joey . . ."

Scott waited, barely patient. He knew Joey had said something to Panch about Eddie's death; he'd just never believed it had been important. After all, how could Eddie know, and how could he tell Joey?

"You okay?" Pancho asked as Scott pushed himself up the hill, nearly slipped and threw out a hand for balance.

"Yeah."

At the road, a single wide-lane blacktop, they walked faster, black creeks of melted snow meeting them on the way. The girls were already gone. Barnaby paused at the open iron gates, kicking at the air before vanishing around the brick wall that marked the cemetery's boundary. He didn't look back.

"Saw Jorgen," Pancho said, chin tucked into his chest.

"Me too."

"Maybe we should tell him."

"Tell him what? We hear people screaming? He already thinks we're on dope and stuff, for god's sake."

"Stuff?"

Scott laughed. "Shit, okay?"

"Okay." He poked Scott's arm. "Okay. But don't say it again, man, it sounds dumb coming from you."

Scott wasn't sure if that was a compliment or not, but he was sure about talking to Jorgen. His mother hadn't believed him about the dark man chasing him, hadn't believed him about the screaming either when he told her. The cops sure as hell wouldn't. Why should they?

"Poor Mr. Tobin," Pancho said when they reached the gates, stepped out to the sidewalk. Fern waited a few yards away, Laine with her. Tang and Katie had already reached the distant corner.

"Yeah," Scott said.

"Bugs," Laine said as they joined the girls and headed up the street.

"What?" Fern exaggerated a shudder, but nobody laughed.

Laine ignored the others, looked at Scott. "When the cops found them, they were covered with bugs."

Fern stopped.

Scott passed her before he realized she wasn't with him.

"What bugs?" she demanded.

"Hey, Fern, take it easy," Pancho said.

"What bugs?"

Laine twisted her hat in her hands. "I don't know. Al said the heat was turned way up, they came out from the walls. Cockroaches, I guess. They were all over the place."

"Oh, gross." Pancho grimaced. "Jesus."

"Beetles," Fern whispered. "They were beetles."

Laine shrugged, moved on, Pancho hurrying after.

Scott waited, but Fern didn't move. And he didn't like the way she kept looking at the cemetery wall, the gutter, the street—as if waiting for something to jump out and scare her. He tried a smile. It didn't work. He held out his hand. She didn't take it.

"Hey," he said gently.

"Beetles," she repeated. "Oh, god, Scott, they're real."

He shook his head, took her arm, forced her to move with him. "With heat like that, on a day like this, sure there's going to be bugs. You think they want to stay outside?"

"Scott—"

"No," he said. "Fern, look, your beetles, the guy I think keeps following me . . ." He laughed softly. "Katie's giants, for god's sake. They're monsters, man, and they don't exist. Not really. Not that way, anyway." He pulled her close; she didn't resist. "Like you said, remember? Kid stuff." He looked up at the back of Town Hall, feeling the slope pull at his leg. "You grow up, you learn different, right?"

She didn't answer.

He tugged. "Right?"

She didn't answer.

TWENTY-TWO

Oh man, Blade thought as he walked Bonita Logan to her home; oh man, this ain't right, this ain't right. We're gonna die, all them rats, Jesus God, we're gonna die.

He knew why Bonita wept as they walked. There wasn't much he didn't know about his friends. It pained him to see her that way, head up, gaze straight ahead, tears dripping from her chin. She wouldn't let him touch her, wipe them away. That was all right. The almost-smile she gave him was enough for the time being. She knew. It was all right. She knew.

His stomach growled.

"You must promise me you'll go to the Mission," she said as they headed down the Boulevard.

"I will, I will."

"There will be a banquet this evening. We must not appear ill-prepared for our guests."

Oh Bonita, c'mon, just once, knock it off.

The tears stopped.

They kept to the east side of the street so he wouldn't have to cross the mouth of is alley. There was a uniformed cop in the doorway of Sunset Books, the sidewalk blocked off by saw-horses.

Bugs, Blade thought; Jesus goddamn.

His head itched fiercely under his cap, and he scratched it just as fiercely until, when they reached the park's wall, the place where Slap had sold his pictures, trying to get out, she grabbed his wrist to make him stop. Then he took her hand and wouldn't release it, forced her to look at him, forced her to blink, forced her back until she leaned against the stone and, finally, sagged.

"Bonita, this ain't a game no more." He tugged her arm once. "We're not playing no games now. This is real life here, y'know?"

A slow and defeated nod, the trap of a sob in her throat.

"Your ticket out is gone, you know that, right? You know that, he's gone? Ain't gonna get you away, ain't gonna get me away. Slap, he says he's gonna get out, and he didn't. And we ain't, Bonita. We ain't going nowhere."

"Those children—"

"—are okay, don't you worry about that. Okay, for kids." He could feel her trembling, could see the desperation begin to cloud her big beautiful eyes, eyes that sometimes put him to sleep in the spring because they kept the damn rats away because they were magic. Something like that, anyway. Something like that.

"You gonna be there? Tonight?"

"Blade, I don't know." She looked helplessly up the street toward the bookstore. "I didn't count windows today, you know. It could have been the day."

God damn. God . . . damn.

Big house on Long Island, fancy car all filled with leather, and now all he's got is this—an alley that talks to him, and a crazy goddamn woman who's crazy one way this minute and another way that minute. Best buddy's feeding worms. Hell of a thing. He started walking, pulling her along gently. Hell of a thing, and the hell of it was, it didn't seem any different than any other day, these days. Except the Hat Trick Boys had been reduced by one, the Pack by two, and goddamn frigging Tobin finally got his, and that bitch too. Justice sometimes, but it was sometimes too scary.

She whispered, "Blade," as they walked. Every fifth step. "Blade."

Now ain't that a thing, he thought, shifting his grip to her elbow. Hundred years, the only time she calls me "Blade" is when Slap's dead and can't hear it, goddamnit. Jesus. Hell of a thing.

When they reached the old Cape Cod, dollhouse tiny, a door on the side that led to the basement apartment, he stopped her.

Her eyes were still wide. Too wide.

He took her hand, and he kissed it, and the eyes closed a little, and the trembling stopped, and her shoulders rose as she took a slow breath.

"Gotta polish my armor," he said, holding his breath.

"You do that, Lord Murtaugh."

He almost laughed his relief.

"Until the banquet hall."

He grinned and watched her go, the grin snapping off the second the door closed behind her. Then he turned to the front window where he'd seen Calvin Nobbs standing, and watching, and he flipped the old fart the finger, and cackled when Calvin stiffened in rage and raised his cane in return.

Sometimes, he thought, even bad days got good times.

'Course, now he had to go and keep his promise, clean himself up, shave, dust off his coat, and probably have the ladies praying over him the whole goddamn time.

He started off when the front door opened, was a good ten yards past the house when a woman's voice called to him. Not by name. The voice said, "Sir? Sir? Blade, would you wait, please?"

When he looked around, he saw Erma Vollt hurrying as best she could down the stairs, wearing a too-large cardigan and hugging herself. This one he liked. She'd given him odd jobs during the summers, mostly tending the lawn and her shrubs which she never could figure out how to water without rotting the roots. Very patient, she was. She had to be, living with the old fart and the shrew.

"Blade," she said breathlessly, swiping hair from her eyes, visibly suppressing a shiver though it wasn't all that cold.

"Ma'am," he said, touching a finger to his cap.

"I'm worried about Miss Logan."

He didn't know what to say.

Erma checked the house, waved to Calvin, who remained stationed in the window. "She's been having nightmares."

"Yeah, well—"

"You seem to know her pretty well." A gathering of the sweater across her neck. "Is she . . . that is, is there anything I can do?"

He saw it in her eyes, dimmed but not blind, and he half turned to run away. He didn't want to know who else heard the screaming. Bad enough for the kids. Bad enough for him. But it was too late. Skinny fingers reached for his arm and pulled away, not quite begging, not quite telling. She didn't have to. So he looked at the house and shook his head.

"Go away," he told her.

She looked ready to cry.

"Go away," he said again. "Get away. Can't stay here, can't stay there, can't stay anywhere you stay around here."

"Blade, surely—"

"You leave her alone, you nigger freak!" Calvin yelled from the doorway. "I'll call the police!"

Murtaugh grabbed her arm, yanked her close, ignored her fear. "Take him, take the fat one, and you get away, lady. Hat Trick Boy ain't got blades anymore, can't stop the puck, can't use the stick. Take him away before the rats come."

And he ran.

Thinking that he could spend the night in the alley by the police station, it would be safer; thinking that staying near the cops didn't do the kid with the greasy hair any good, the kid's brother was a cop; thinking that in broad daylight, sun out but going down, shadows not yet ready to take over the streets, he could hear the rats massing behind the houses, the stores, down in the sewers; thinking his heart would explode before he got to the Mission and the cleaning and the ladies doing all that praying, and it might not be so bad, hell of a thing, goddamn, if his heart did decide to give it up, stop the race, because then he wouldn't hear the screaming anymore or the rats or see the shadows that moved against the wind.

Kids hear.

Old people hear.

He ain't so old yet, he hears, and Bonita.

Slowing down after colliding with a trash can that nearly trips him.

Holding his side as he cut through the park to the Mission.

Hoping he'll be around to see his ducklings again, come spring.

Wondering what Leg can do about stopping the noise at night.

Nothing.

Hell of a thing.

Hell of a thing, but he knew, he *knew,* there weren't nothing anyone could do.

What the hell.

Free meal, warm place to sit, what the hell, he'd seen worse, how bad could it be?

Standing in front of the First Methodist Church, fists in his pockets, humming to himself, swaying side to side, shaking his head because if he went in there, he'd have to come out, fetch Bonita from the house, bring her to the diner. They would talk, and he would hear things, and none of it would matter.

They were going to die.

As sure as he stood here, feeling his bladder begin to loosen, they were all going to die.

PART FOUR

WHAT WE FORGOT

TWENTY-THREE

But in the dark, child,
  Something stirs.

TWENTY-FOUR

Winter rain.

A light fog that rose over the surface of the snow, knee-high, unmoving.

The snow itself bleeding into gutters, slipping off roofs, retreating to ragged islands beneath shrubbery and steps. Snowmen toppling soundlessly. Slush on the Boulevard pushed by sparse traffic into the storm drains or down the western slope into the river.

Winter rain that lasted hard for an hour, a shower for another, a drizzle that threatened to last all night.

"Laine?"

"Dale, not now, okay? I have to go out."

"I like your horse hair."

"It's a ponytail, honey. They call it a ponytail."

"Who?"

"Me, that's who. Now beat it, little creep, before I pluck out your freckles."

"How come you're wearing that coat? You said you weren't ever going to wear that coat again. It's black. I don't like black,

Laine. It's a spooky coat. How come you're wearing that spooky coat?"

"You know, for a kid who's supposed to be thinking about going to bed, you sure ask an awful lot of questions.

"How come your shoes have two colors? Mine don't have two colors."

"Dale. Please."

"You gonna see Joey?"

"No, dear. Remember what I told you? Joey . . . oh God . . . Joey's in heaven now."

"Oh. Yes. I'm sorry, I forgot. He gets to play with angels now."

"That's right."

"And I gotta play with you."

"Hey, watch that mouth, kid. I'm bigger than you."

"Where you going?"

"Out. I told you. Out."

"I wanna go."

"Dale!"

"Don't care."

"Dale, c'mon, now, you can't go with me, you know that. It's late. Too late."

"I can tell time. It's only eight o'clock."

"So?"

"So take me with you, Laine, please?"

"Dale, honey—"

"It's bad out there, Laine."

"What? What did you say?"

"It's bad out there, Laine. I gotta protect you."

"Dale—"

"Take me, Laine, please take me. I'll be good. You can buy me a sundae and I'll be good and I can take care of you."

"Mom'll kill me. Us."

"Bad, Laine. If Joey's with an angel, all you got now is me."

Barnaby decided he wasn't going to go. It was dumb. It was stupid. The goddamn gimp was trying to take over. It was bad, this shit. Something, maybe Eddie and Joey dying like that, it was making them all crazy. Besides, didn't anybody even listen to the weather? They were supposed to have another damn snowstorm tonight. The report said flurries; the way things were going, it would probably be a blizzard. All this rain was going to turn to snow. And he'd be damned if he was going to get himself lost in a damn blizzard.

He marched through the house, much too large, touching things, turning lights off and on, listening to his heels on the bare hardwood floors, looking for someplace comfortable to sit. He couldn't find it. He walked on.

Those geeks will probably show up, he decided, turning into a living room he knew was almost as big as the gimp's whole damn house, and what the hell did Byrns think he was doing, asking them to the clubhouse? Eddie would shit. No. Eddie would think it was funny. But not him. He thought it was stupid. Scott was an asshole. He was making big deals out of nothing, talking to scum, talking to *him* like he didn't care about keeping his head on his damn shoulders. Asshole.

In his bedroom he couldn't decide what tape to play, what show to watch, didn't want to practice his electric guitar, the keyboard, and left. Rubbing his hands and arms though the house was perfectly warm.

What he'd do is, he'd call Pancho, have him sleep over, they could go to school together tomorrow. Panch loved coming to the Heights. They could sneak over to Tang's, rap on her window, shit like that, scare the shit out of her. The trouble was, the way the dumb shit had been acting today, he'd probably want to go to the diner. Hell, he was probably already there. But shit, what good would it be, on the other hand, hanging around here all damn night, the whole place empty, the old man down in Florida for the weekend; the place was too big.

Shit.

Maybe he would go.

He looked at his black jacket, hanging in the closet. Touched it.

Maybe he would.

One more time.

It wasn't like nothing was weird, that's for sure. Maybe Byrns . . . what the hell. There was nothing better to do. He could walk. Keep himself in shape. He'd been eating too much crap since Thanksgiving, this would help keep the lard off. But if the frigging gimp thought he was going to take over, make the Pack into something stupid, a bunch of scaredy-cat wimps, he was wrong.

Dead wrong.

The little shit.

The goddamn little shit.

"Katie dear?"

"Yes, Gram."

"Katie, you can't go out tonight. It's raining, silly, can't you see that? And that terrible jacket isn't nearly warm enough. My goodness, child, you'll catch your death."

"Gram . . ."

"My back hurts."

"Gram . . ."

"It's cold, Katie. For goodness sake, please close the door, you'll let out all the heat. We can't afford to let out all the heat."

"Gram, I have to go."

"My back hurts."

"It's . . . it's like it's going to be a wake, Gram. Joey wouldn't want us to just sit around like we were going to jump off the bridge."

"He was a good boy. I remember him. He shoveled our snow last year."

"I know, Gram."

"Well, maybe it is a good thing."

"Thanks, Gram. I love you."

"I love you too, dear. And be careful. Stay in the light. There are people sneaking around out there tonight. Stay in the light."

"People?"

"My back hurts."

"Gram, what do you mean, people sneaking around?"

. . .

Pancho crunched down in the front seat, folding his arms over his chest, tucking his chin into the black leather jacket, not wanting to see the way Tang drove. She was crazy. Nuts. Traffic rules were made, she believed, for the rest of the poor slobs of the world, not her, but he hadn't remembered that little fact once she had called, gabbed for a while, finally asked if he'd like a ride to the diner. He didn't remember until she took the first turn, at probably a hundred miles an hour, and bumped over the curb, nearly clipped a telephone pole. The trouble was, if he said something, she'd look at him. He didn't want her looking at him; he wanted her looking at the road.

"Panch, are we out of our minds?"

"Nope," he said, wincing at the way the car slid on the road, seeing from the corner of his eye the way her hands flew over the beveled steering wheel.

"Only crazy people hear things, you know."

"We're not crazy. Jeez."

Streetlight flared in and out of the front seat, a strobe effect that made him close his eyes for a moment, open them again when she muttered, "Damn," and they thumped over something he hadn't seen in the road.

"What?"

"A branch," she said tightly. "Just a branch. God, Panch, lighten up, okay? I'm not going to kill us, you know. I know how to drive."

On a racetrack, maybe, he thought glumly.

"You think those people will come?"

"Huh?"

"You know. Scottie's friends. Those street people."

He shrugged. "I don't know." And he didn't much care.

"She's pretty." They sped onto the Boulevard, narrowly missing the back of a steaming bus.

"Yeah, I guess so."

"She's not old, either. What's her name?"

"How the hell should I know?"

"Well, excuse me for living, Mr. Touchy Duncan." Through a stop sign. "I only asked. God."

A cruiser pulled in ahead of them. She slowed down, cursing softly to herself, thumping the wheel impatiently with the heel of one hand. Pancho sat up and smiled prayerful thanks to the police, took a few deep breaths, rubbed one eye with a thumb.

"Who killed Joey?"

He stared at her, mouth open. "What?"

"It wasn't some dog." She glanced at him, face distorted in the dashboard's glow. "You know it. I know it. It wasn't some stupid dog."

He was too amazed to say anything. But she always amazed him, something new every day. Half the time, she looked as if she were visiting from another planet. Spaced. Tuning in only when the girls talked about clothes or boys. The rest of the time floating through town on automatic. Even the other night, in the car, when Joey died, it was as if she hadn't been there, as if the body he'd been exploring belonged to someone else. Like she was watching an experiment. Interested, but not very.

"Well?"

"I don't know what you're talking about," he answered sullenly.

"Bullshit." Her voice was old. Older. Not pleasant at all. "Bullshit, Duncan, that's bullshit."

Fern waited on the stoop, huddled beneath the slight overhang above the front door. Scott, she figured, would have to come by soon, if he was coming at all. And he would. It was his idea. He wasn't going to chicken out. He'd be there. And to be there, he'd have to pass here, and she wasn't leaving until he did. No way was she going to walk to the diner alone. No way in hell.

A car sped past, taillights flaring as it approached the intersection.

Water dripped from the eaves, landed in what was left of the snow.

Sounding like something crawling.

Something big.

A giant beetle.

She shuddered, hunched her shoulders, drove her hands deeper into her jacket pockets, stamped her feet lightly though it wasn't all that cold.

Mr. Tobin had been covered with bugs. Maybe they'd been eating him and Miss Bingham. Maybe . . . she shuddered again, sorry he was dead and just as sorry Laine had told them how he'd looked. She had already dreamt about it several times, waking up cold and drenched, slapping at the covers to keep all the . . . Okay, enough, Bellard. That's enough.

A glance up at the sky invisible beyond the streetlight's glow. Snow tonight. Right. Flood, maybe, but no snow.

A man across the street, walking a tiny dog, carrying an umbrella. She could hear him talking to his pet, urging it to hurry up before they both drowned. She smiled, checked the length of the block, and prayed that Scott wouldn't try to talk his mother into driving him, because of the weather. Another smile. No, it wouldn't work that way. She would do all the talking, the insisting, and he would be the stubborn one. As long as she had known him, he'd been incredibly stubborn. Scots stubborn, he'd say with a grin whenever someone called him on it. Pigheaded is what it was; damn pigheaded. If it were snowing all to hell tonight, he'd want to walk just to prove he could do it. Be like everyone else.

A movement down on the cement walk, a furtive skittering from one side to the other.

She looked, swallowing, and saw nothing.

Imagination.

No bugs, Fern. Take it easy. No bugs.

C'mon, Scott, c'mon.

And when he rounded the corner, she fairly leapt from the stoop to the sidewalk, the hell with being casual, *hey, what a coincidence, now we can walk together, okay?* and grabbed his arm almost before he realized she was there.

"You took long enough," she scolded, leaning into his side.

"My mother," he answered. "I had to tell her this was

something Joey would have wanted. No tears or anything like that. Ice cream all around. Just like Eddie."

She giggled. "I told my father the same thing."

"He buy it?"

"Sure." She showed him the Fern-smile, the daughter-smile her father had never been able to resist, except when it came to buying her a car. "See? No problem. It's the freckles. I think they're magic or something."

He grunted and they walked on; when they reached Summit Boulevard, she could almost feel the temperature begin to drop as the drizzle began to fade. It still wasn't cold, not for this time of year, but it made the mist on her cheeks feel too much like ice.

"Scott."

"What."

"Do you know what's going on? I mean, are we being paranoid or something?"

Half a block toward the Strip before he cleared his throat and answered: "We hear things, we see things, people get killed." His look made her stare at the sidewalk. "It's Eddie, you know."

"Huh?"

"Eddie. It's him. I don't know exactly what it is yet, I'm going nuts trying to figure it out, but it all goes back to Eddie."

She wished he hadn't said that.

She wished he had said sure, Fern, we'll all going nuts, it's the season, and it's just a string of shitty luck, that's all.

It happens.

Shit happens.

No, she thought; not with us, it doesn't. Maybe sometime, but not now.

Eddie.

He was right.

It all came down to Eddie Roman.

It all came down to the screaming.

TWENTY-FIVE

In the Starlite dining room, bright lamps on the paneled walls and no shadows, five long windows overlooking the parking lot; a corner table, round and the only one in use, where Scott sat restlessly, left heel tapping, hand absently grabbing at his thigh. In the center, a ceramic napkin holder in the shape of a Christmas star, salt and pepper shakers the same, and the squat stub of a striped candle floating on water in a clear-glass bowl. Opposite him sat Tang, flanked by Barnaby and Pancho; Fern slouched on his right, Dale Freelin and Laine on his left. He didn't know what to make of the boy, who grinned at everyone, laughed when Barnaby stuck out his tongue, applauded when Pancho lit the candle, kept asking his sister where all the ice cream was. It was strange. This was supposed to be one of those battle plan sessions, where the generals and the colonels all get together to figure out who the enemy really was and how to fight him, defeat him, so they could get on with things. He glanced around again—they were even in their uniforms. But there were no children. There were never any children. Just all the generals. But Laine hadn't apologized when she walked in with her brother, or made explanations.

"Where the hell is Katie?" Barnaby complained. "Jesus."

Where were Blade and the Queen, Scott wanted to know. He

twisted around, checked the front, the few booths he could see and the curve of the counter, sighed and sat back, shook his head slowly. Customers out there were staring at the Pack, at their black jackets, collars raised, their hairstyles gleaming, ponytails and ribbons, probably wondering what the hell things were coming to when Karacos let hoods take over the place. Bad enough they were in front half the time. Now they were in the back, where all the gentlefolk dined.

The waitress had already come and gone, scarcely bothering to listen to the orders since they were always the same— hamburgers and chocolate malts, and a banana split for Dale.

"I'm starving," Pancho complained.

Tang sneered at him.

He shrugged. "I'm a growing boy. Jesus."

"Stupid," Barnaby muttered, pushed well back from the table, his chair tilted and resting against the wall. "This is stupid. I just want you guys to know that. Stupid, okay?" He glared at Scott. "So?"

Scott felt like a complete jerk. Earlier, at the cemetery, all this had seemed like a pretty good idea, the best idea, and he'd opened his big mouth without thinking the idea through. Now, for some reason, they were actually here, waiting for him to say something, and he hadn't the vaguest notion what to do next. Jerk. Idiot. He might as well tell them what Fern said, that it was monsters, creatures from outer space, things that went bump and snarl in the night.

"For Christ's sake, Byrns, get your head out of your ass, huh?"

"Barnaby . . ." Tang waved a disgusted hand; it wasn't worth the effort.

The hamburgers arrived, and the banana split.

Dale laughed in delight. "You want the cherry?" he asked Laine. "You can have the cherry if you want."

"Jesus," Garing muttered, and glared out the window.

Laine smiled at her brother, took the cherry and bit it off its stem, flipped the stem into an ashtray.

Dale laughed and began to eat.

Scott looked at his plate, at the fries, the pale tomato slice on its bed of curled lettuce, and suddenly didn't feel very hungry anymore. The others, however, weren't as reticent, and for the moment he was off the hook as they started to eat. A silent prayer of gratitude, and another check of the front. Then he pushed away from the table.

"Be right back."

"Don't hurry," Barnaby said.

"Be nice," Dale scolded.

They laughed.

And Scott felt a little better as he made his way past the other customers, not many, leaning into an empty booth by the cash register and checking the street north and south. The rain had stopped. From the looks of the pedestrians, it was getting colder, fast. But no Blade or Queen, and for that matter, no Katie, either. His leg hurt. His stomach lurched with acid as he hurried to the pay phone near the restrooms, fumbled for a quarter, and dialed Katie's number.

No one answered.

Ten rings.

No one answered.

He hung up and checked the street again, returned to the table and took his seat. Fern smiled tentatively at him, Dale asked him for a couple of his fries. Tang argued with Barnaby, their voices low and hissing. Pancho just sat there, chewing automatically, staring at the table, at the salt and pepper shakers.

Scott decided this was as good a time as any.

"What did he say to you, Panch?"

All but Dale quieted abruptly; the boy asked for more fries, and Scott, without shifting his gaze from Duncan, shoved his plate over.

"We . . . we were on South Bridge," Pancho said, sitting stiffly, still staring at the shakers.

The diner went away.

No conversation, no music, no scraping of silverware on plates, no traffic, no chime when the register opened, no muffled carols from the outside.

It was gone.

The lights bright, faces washed now and without depth; like mannequins, Scott thought until he shook the thought away.

"Hanging out, you know?"

Dale busily creating a raft of french fries atop a mound of catsup.

"Joey . . ." Pancho cleared his throat with a harsh cough, glanced at Laine, looked down at the candle. "He was talking about . . . We were just kidding around, you know? Throwing rocks, shit like that."

"The boy," Tang whispered

Dale began to hum, no tune, the notes high and sweet.

"He was talking about . . . stuff." Pancho sniffed, rubbed a hand around his neck. "You know, kid stuff."

Scott looked quickly at Fern, looked away. Her lower lip was pulled between her teeth; the cheek he could see was sucked inward, pulsing.

"So what the hell did he say?" Barnaby demanded.

"Voices."

"What?"

"Hey!" Dale said, slipping out of his chair before Laine could stop him.

"Voices," Pancho insisted. "In the river." He looked around to see who already knew. Most of them did, about the fear Joey had, but Scott could see that only Laine knew what Pancho was really talking about.

"Hey, wow," Dale said, pressing his nose against the window.

"He was little or something, nearly drowned, and he told Eddie . . ." He looked uncomfortable. Scott smiled, nodded at him to go on. "He kind of believed something lived down there. Scared him half to death." Pancho laughed quickly, forced, grabbed a spoon and began polishing its bowl mindlessly with his thumb.

"So big deal," Barnaby said, rolling his eyes. "What the hell does that have to do with the price of apples."

"Snow, Laine," Dale said gleefully, tapping the window with one finger. "Look. Snow."

"A little while ago," Pancho said, ignoring Barnaby, looking straight at Scott, "Eddie called him and told him he was right."

"Oh crap," Barnaby declared in disgust.

"Snow, Laine," Dale repeated.

And thunder. Faint, but enough to distract Scott's attention to the wall of windows. His eyes widened when he saw the flakes flat and wet falling heavily, in no single direction as a wind began to rise. Despite the damp ground, he knew it wouldn't be long before things started to cover over.

Thunder again, still distant.

Dale backed away.

"Hey, it's okay," Laine reassured him, taking his arm gently and guiding him back to his chair. "It's all right, Dale, it happens sometimes."

Thunder a third time, and the lights went out.

"Swell," Fern said, almost angrily. "Swell."

Nervous laughter from the front, and calls for Karacos to bring out the lanterns. Scott leaned forward to look around Laine, and saw that the streetlights were gone as well. There was nothing beyond the windows but black and slashing white, nothing in the room but a few flickering candles.

"Laine?"

"It's all right, Dale."

"Sure," Scott agreed. "No sweat. Somebody probably skidded and hit a pole, that's all."

Dale gripped the edge of the table and said nothing.

Scott didn't touch him, but he knew the boy was trembling.

"Maybe we'd better go," Laine suggested, hugging her brother lightly.

"Eddie," Pancho continued, as if nothing had happened, "told Joey, and Joey told me, that Eddie was trying to find . . . I don't know . . . something in his closet."

"Oh really?" Barnaby said. "Like what? A lost jock? A chick? A new tube of grease for his hair?"

Pancho shook his head. "I don't . . . a monster."

Garing gaped, then laughed hysterically, slapped Pancho across the back. "Oh Jesus, get a life, man." He thumped the chair down, stood up, leaned across the table. "Look, gimp, this is all shit, okay? Eddie was bouncing off the walls before he killed his old man. We all know that, right? Fucking bouncing off the walls." He slapped a palm on the table, and Tang jumped, uttered a cry. "I don't know what the hell he was on, but c'mon . . . something in his goddamn closet? Christ, he was doped to the gills, you could see it."

"Scared," Pancho contradicted. "He was scared to death. And so was Joey."

Barnaby snorted, looked around the table, threw up his hands and walked away. "You guys are nuts," he called, turning to walk backward. "You're out of your mushhead minds! Jesus, next thing you know, you'll be saying Eddie believed in the goddamn boogyman."

Hanging a caustic laugh behind him, he left, bumped into the counter, and snarled at a man who told him to watch it.

Fern picked up a bread stick from a straw basket by the candle, held it up, snapped it in half. Everyone jumped, and she grinned. "See?" She pointed with one half while she nibbled on the other. "Look what's going on here. You got a dark room, a candle, snow, and you're scaring each other half to death." A poke at Scott's arm. "He's right, you know." She looked to Pancho. "He is, really. Eddie couldn't have meant that. Not monsters, stuff like that. Nobody believes in that anymore. My god, we're practically in college, for god's sake. We know better." No one answered. "We do!"

Of course they did, Scott thought. Like you outgrow your toys, you outgrow whatever monster plagued you when you were young. Some kids sooner, some kids later, but it always happened. One night, for no reason at all, you got the nerve to look in the closet, or under the bed, or behind the hedge, or in the cellar, or wherever, and you learned that there wasn't anything there at all. Just imagination, and shadow, and sometimes a quiet noise that didn't belong to the house. Which meant Eddie had to have been talking about something else, something he was trying to tell Joey and failed, something Joey had misunderstood. So Mr. Roman died, and Eddie dead, and . . .

He frowned.

Slap died.

Joey died.

The wind changed again, and snow scratched at the window.

Mr. Tobin and his lover died.

He pinched the back of his hand, squeezing until the pain made him stop, woke him up.

"Laine?" Dale said.

Tang had pulled her ponytail over her shoulder, twisted it aimlessly with her fingers. "Then what about the screaming?"

"I don't know," Fern said. "Some kind of psychic thing, maybe, like Katie claims." She scowled. "How the hell should I know? And why isn't she here yet, anyway?"

"Laine?"

"Hush, honey, we're going soon, don't worry, we're going." She gathered her brother's hands into hers, pulled them into her lap. "Joey," she said, "was scared too, like Panch said. He wouldn't tell me why. He was just . . . scared." A quick glare toward the front. "And it wasn't dope. Not with Eddie, either. I don't know what's with Barnaby, but it wasn't dope, no way."

Silence then.

A moist scratching at the window.

Low voices in the booths.

A siren that passed the diner.

The lights flickered, died, flickered and died.

"So what are you saying, Laine?" Tang smiled, but only briefly. "That Eddie made his monster come back or something? He did a Tinker Bell thing? You know, clap your hands if you believe in fairies?" Her laugh was almost genuine.

Scott's left heel tapping.

Fern biting into the bread stick.

Tang spread her hands. "So . . . ?"

Scott saw them all, faces danced with shadow, expressions changing each time the candle's flame moved, waiting for someone to tell them it was all stupid, ridiculous, they were only a bunch of kids sitting around a campfire scaring the hell out of each other with ghost stories they claimed really, honestly, happened to someone they knew. All except Tang Porter. He knew the look on her face; he had seen it a million times in math class when she'd lock onto a complex problem that had stumped everyone else, knowing she had the solution and was just waiting for the words to come.

The wind punched at the window, shimmering the glass.

And then he saw it himself, and grinned almost smugly, and Tang blew him a kiss.

"Okay," he said, "listen up. This is the way it is."

Which was simple when he finally got around the candlelight and the storm and Pancho's story about Joey and Eddie. There was, he said, no denying that something weird was going on. The screaming, for instance. They all heard it but Barnaby, and he thought that might be because Barnaby didn't have much of an imagination. Which is what it all boiled down to—having an imagination. Eddie maybe really had been trying to resurrect a childhood monster, and, knowing Eddie, it wasn't such a farfetched thing for him to try. He hung on to an idea like a dog on a fresh bone. It excited him. It made him jumpy. Energized, something like that. The Pack, since it was tied so closely to him, fed on that energy, felt it, followed it, grew its own. Like when they joined the Pack in the first place. Eddie might even have done it, found the monster in the closet, but the most likely explanation, the probable explanation, was that he *thought* he had done it.

And in thinking it, believing it, had gone over the edge.

And in going over the edge, nearly dragged the rest of them with him without them realizing what was wrong.

Fern's weird beetles.

Katie's giants.

Laine's cellar.

"Monster bees," Pancho admitted with a lopsided smile, when Scott stalled, trying to remember what the halfback shied away from. "They could even talk, shit like that. I used to think they lived in the walls and were trying to get into my bedroom. My dad says it's because I was stung when I was little. I mean, real little. I'd have fits every time a bee came near me." He thumped himself on the forehead in mock admission of something silly. "Even now Barn can get me, put a dead bee on my tray, something like that. The bastard."

Dale pointed at the window, nearly fully coated with snow. "Laine?"

Embarrassment lifted one of Tang's shoulders. "They live behind trees and bushes. I don't know what they are, but they were after me all the time. Couldn't stand to go into the yard at night." A plea, then, not to laugh. "They wanted me. I don't why, but they wanted me."

"Exactly," Scott said with an *I told you* grin. "We got all this stuff coming down, that cop bugs us, we get nervous, we see things, we get more nervous . . ." He leaned back. "Simple."

"So," said Fern, "the guy who followed you home twice isn't real?"

Under the streetlamp.

Faceless.

Without a shadow.

"No."

Pancho dropped the spoon on his plate. The clatter made them start. "So what killed Eddie, then? Him? You really believe he killed himself, you really believe Joey cut himself up?" He looked at Scott. "You really think that guy, Slap, he froze to death and some cats ate him?"

"Laine!"

"Damnit, Dale, what do you want?"

Dale slipped out of his chair, stood behind Scott, shifting from foot to foot. "Bad, Laine."

Scott watched as Laine's face paled. "It's all right," he said to the boy. "Hey, it's okay, pal."

Dale shook his head quickly and pointed at the window. At the snow. Lower lip quivering. "Bad out there." A tear slipped from one eye. "Real bad, Laine. I'm scared."

He's retarded, Scott thought as something cold touched the back of his neck; he doesn't know what he's saying. The lights, all this talk about monsters . . . we've scared him. That's all it is. He's a kid. A little kid.

The wind punched the diner again, and all he could think of was Katie's giants.

Stupid; this was stupid.

He stood up slowly, easing his chair back to move Dale aside, moving to the window to watch the snow pull its blanket over the cars down in the lot, top the fence that hid the houses across the way. The blacktop was still mostly uncovered, though it wouldn't be long before the cold changed all that. Dale stood beside him, and he put a hand on the boy's shoulder.

The lights danced on, dim but steady.

"Pretty, isn't it," he said.

"Bad," Dale answered. Then he touched a finger to the pane and said, "Hey."

"Jesus," Scott said, "it's Katie!"

She ran.

don't be late, dear.

i won't, gram, it's just to the diner for a couple of minutes.

She ran.

be careful, it's starting to snow.

i will, gram, i will.

She had been a block from Midhill Avenue when she felt the dark begin to grow behind her. Refusing to look lasted only a few paces. Just long enough for the flakes to take the cold and sting her cheeks, make her squint, make her wish sourly that she'd thought to bring her mittens.

Then she looked.

Then she ran.

Skidding around the corner onto Midhill just as the lights went out.

Confusion turned her in the wrong direction, heading down-hill instead of up, realizing her mistake when the footing became precarious and she felt herself slipping, sliding, landing on one knee, crying out at the hammer-blow when she struck the concrete, still sliding as she kicked and thrashed her way back to her feet and turned the next corner.

It was back there.

Growing.

Formless despite the snow, filling the gaps between the flakes with a dark that had never belonged to the night.

Her first thought had been to get back to the house, hide in her room where she knew the giant couldn't get her, it never had; but Gram was there, and this was different, and the wind had grown strong enough to slow her to a fast trot. Quickly, then, she cut through two yards, back to her own street, crouching beside a fence until she was sure the way was clear.

Running.

To the Pack.

She had to get to the Pack, because they would know what to do.

Up the avenue this time, knee throbbing, her jeans soaked, snow clinging to her hair and eyelashes like spiders that tried to claw their way into her eyes.

It was back there.

It had turned.

The wind began to howl.

A window shattered somewhere.

A streetlamp screamed as it twisted to the ground.

She ran, veered off the sidewalk and ricocheted off a telephone pole. She sobbed as her left arm dangled uselessly, the tingling racing across her shoulders, replaced by pain, replaced by numbness. The collision had spun her around, and she faced the giant for a second, watching it fill the gap between the curbs, still without features but there nonetheless. In that second before she turned again, before she tried to scream and couldn't, she told herself there was no such thing as the thing swatting aside a parked car, its windows exploding, its hubcaps spinning off, passenger door crushed when it came up against a tree; no such thing since she had been a little girl.

Another car was kicked aside.

She ran.

No such thing.

Please, God, no such thing.

Feeling returned to her arm, and the sudden needled agony nearly brought her to her knees.

A siren.

Here and there the lights returned, none of them fully bright, but the glow caught and spread by the snow allowed her to swerve into the parking lot behind the Starlite. There were places to hide here, alleys between stores, people who could help her, and she ran headlong past the diner while the wind tried to pull her apart and the shadowgiant behind her tore apart the fence and a hand grabbed her arm and yanked her off her feet.

As Scott ran for the exit, the others, standing or half out of their chairs, saw Katie race past, limping, clutching her left arm to her side, saw the fence down at the end lift and shatter into splinters, saw an automobile's front end crumple as if it had crashed against a boulder. Then the last window in the dining room imploded, glass and snow and wind shrieking over the tables that lifted and toppled along with their chairs, while napkins and placemats flapped into the air.

Scott grabbed the back of a counter stool, spun around as the stool spun on its post. Someone yelled, "Katie," and he ran for the door.

The next window blew in.

The others were right behind him, soon passed him, and they battled through the customers in the front who were trying to see what had happened back there. A woman cried out, the cry shredded by the wind; the third window shattered and snow funneled furiously toward the booths and counter. Scott took an elbow in the ribs, a foot lashed against his good leg as the crowd turned from curious to frightened and reversed its rush. He lashed out when someone tried to grab his arm, saw an open-mouthed Barnaby step in just in time to have Pancho grab his jacket in a fist and yank him outside again.

Once on the street no one stopped.

The wind had already knocked over all the newspaper dispensers, had begun to rend the newsstand awning next door.

Another siren, and the hoot of a fire engine.

Scott did his best to follow the Pack south, cursing his leg, cursing the slick layer of wet snow that had settled on the sidewalk and made running, even for the others, precarious at best. He didn't see Laine or Dale, but Fern dropped back to grab his hand, look at him long enough to tell him she didn't think either that the wind had done all this.

Between a record shop and a card shop was a narrow alley, a pedestrian walkway to the parking lot in back. They spun into it one by one, Scott the last and breathing hard through his mouth, tasting snow, smelling wet stone and blacktop, suddenly yanking on Fern's hand when a black cloud passed the alley's mouth at the far end, killing the light for just a moment.

The others had stopped as well.

When the cloud had gone, the light returned, there was nothing left but the sighing wind, the drip of snow from a fire escape somewhere overhead.

And a sobbing in a shadow that pulled away from the wall.

Katie, huddled in the arms of Blade Murtaugh.

Dale, in the arms of his sister.

Crouched under the table where she had dragged them when the first window exploded, as if someone had taken a bat to it from the outside.

Sobbing now, her face streaked with running blood, glass around them, in her hair, stuck in her sweater, her jacket.

Sobbing as she pulled a blade of glass from her ankle.

"Dale."

His face freckled with blood, his hair matted darkly, his eyes closed.

"Dale."

Yelling for help when the wind died.

Karacos kneeling beside her, gasping and swearing when he saw them, trying to pull the boy from her arms, but she wouldn't let him go, couldn't let him go, he wasn't even supposed to be here and it was her fault, all her fault, just like Joey's dying had been her fault because they had had a fight and he had gotten drunk and if he hadn't gotten drunk he never would have gone down to the river.

Her fault.

"C'mon, kid, let the boy go."

She rocked, and wept, and tasted blood.

And when Karacos finally pried her arms loose, she looked at him, pleading, and he only smiled when she said, "Bad."

TWENTY-SIX

Abruptly the wind settled, the snow retreated to flurries, the
street- and floodlights regained their purpose and kept the alley
and parking lot free of most of the dark.

"We gotta get out of here," Pancho said uneasily, snapping
his fingers, dancing toward the street, dancing back. "C'mon,
guys, we can't stick around."

Out on the Boulevard Scott could hear a fire truck's blare,
cruisers, caught a glimpse of an ambulance van flaring away,
with a patrol car right behind.

"Right," Tang agreed. "We can't stay here. We gotta get
moving."

Katie broke away from Murtaugh then with a hasty, grateful
"thanks," and Blade nodded as he wiped his face with a sleeve,
opened his mouth but said nothing. He tried a smile, tried a
frown, threw up his hands and, before anyone could stop him,
sprinted away. Scott reached out to grab him, hold him back,
but the little man dodged nimbly, whimpering, and vanished
into the parking lot.

"Outta here!" Pancho insisted.

"Go!" Tang said.

They turned toward the street, stumbling at first, then
running slowly, herding Katie into the center. Not looking

back. Not asking questions. Scott considered trying to get Murtaugh back, realized it was futile before he even started, and took a dozen steps after the rest of the Pack before a bonfire suddenly erupted in the meat of his left leg. He gasped loudly and fell against the alley wall, pushed off with his right arm, and fell again, this time to the ground.

The burning cramp brought instant tears to his eyes, familiar and hateful ones, as he tried to sit up and grab for the thigh, knowing why it had happened, knowing this time he would have to ride it out because there was no way he could get the prosthetic off. Not here. Not now.

He fell back, clenched his fists, and tried again.

A dark figure blocked the boulevard light.

He stiffened, panting, shaking the tears away.

Oh god, he thought; not now, please not now.

"You hurt?"

It was Barnaby.

"My leg," he gasped. "Cr-cramp." The fire spurted. He groaned. "Jesus!"

"You ran, you dumb shit," Garing said flatly, kneeling beside him, grabbing hold of the thigh to knead it roughly. "You're not supposed to run, you know that." His hands worked. "You know that, asshole."

A siren screamed to silence.

Scott squirmed around to prop himself against the wall. "That won't work," he said when Garing rocked back to flex his fingers. His mouth dried, his throat tightened. "Gotta get it off."

"You're shitting me."

The cramp eased, and returned.

"Oh *god*!"

"All right, so take off your damn jeans, idiot."

Scott glanced to his right, as a crowd of the curious began hurrying down the alley to examine the parking lot, voices echoing off the stone walls, freak storms, freak tornado, some kind of gang on the rampage.

"Jesus, man, c'mon!" Barnaby snapped. "We ain't got all night, y'know."

A scrambling at his buckle, the zipper down, and he eased the pants off his hips, just far enough to be able to get at the straps that wound toward his groin. The moment the upper leg was clear, Garing cursed and stripped off his jacket, dropped it over Scott's lap, grinning without humor.

A woman paused and watched with concern.

Barnaby snarled at her, told her to mind her own fucking business, get lost, and her eyes widened, her mouth opened, as she moved on, looking around for someone to help her.

"Grab the shoe," Scott said.

Barnaby did.

The straps fell away, the cup around the stump eased off much easier than he thought, though not without a stab of protest, and he sighed, sagged, when Garing pulled the plastic limb away, through the jeans leg. The cramp eased almost immediately, and he clenched his teeth in anticipation as he leaned forward to pull the jeans back up.

Barnaby held the leg away from his body, straps dangling. "C'mon, Byrns, for god's sake."

"A minute," he asked. "Please. Just a second, okay?"

"No time." Barnaby reached down, grabbed his arm, hauled him upright without apology. "So now what?"

Scott grinned. "You'll have to be my crutch."

"Christ!"

An arm around the fullback's waist was good enough to get him to the street. Awkwardly. Twice he stumbled, nearly fell, until they found a reasonable rhythm. And as they moved, Scott wished he could kick at something, throw something, yell at someone for making him this way—almost but not quite good enough to pass for normal.

"Dumb shit, running like that," Garing muttered as they turned down the street. "You know better, asshole. Christ, you're heavy."

"So what was I supposed to do?" he demanded heatedly, gulping air, forcing the residual pain to go back where it came from. "Fly?"

Barnaby grunted, pushed them to one side as a gang of young kids in football jackets raced up the Strip, yelling to each other, dodging and laughing into the street where the traffic had been stalled by a fire engine and the cruisers.

Scott's right heel began to ache, his side grew a stitch. "Wait up," he said before they'd gone half a block. "Not so fast. Gotta rest."

Garing stopped, the false leg rapping impatiently against his side. Then he sniffed, looked around. "Byrns, what the fuck *was* that?"

Scott just looked at him until he turned away, moved on, practically dragging him along until he recovered the rhythm. "Where'd they go?"

"I don't know. Tang's car's in the next lot, she found a place behind the Apollo. Maybe there. Panch went to find Laine and the kid."

People stared.

Barnaby glowered at them, daring them to comment, forcing them to veer around them as if they had the plague.

Scott noticed and, for the moment, didn't mind. He was too busy trying not to fall. He couldn't fall. If he fell, he'd be a cripple. Helpless. And helpless fed a slow growing anger that tightened the muscles of his neck, his jaw, promising another cramp if he didn't calm down. Helpless, and feeling as though he weighed no more than a gnat in Barnaby's grip.

A siren whooped and died.

What had he seen?

A stiff flurry of flakes slapped his cheeks, made him duck his face into Barnaby's arm. The smell of fear there and damp cloth.

What the hell had he seen?

A man tried to stop them, ask what had happened, but Barnaby waved the leg in his face, straps whipping the air between them, and snapped something about getting the hell out the way of an emergency, was the jackass blind or what?

Scott almost giggled.

If he hadn't been so scared, he might have even laughed.

The wind kicked once, scrambling a torn tabloid cover into Garing's legs. He growled at it, kicked it away, and had to sidestep to avoid losing his balance. Scott yelped, positive he was going to fall, throwing out his right hand to grab at something that wasn't there. When the threat passed and he could breathe easier, he looked up to ask a question and saw Barnaby checking over his shoulder every few feet. It wasn't the crowds, or the converging police cars; he was looking up.

"It isn't there," Scott told him.

"Hell it ain't."

A voice called their names.

"It's gone."

"Hell it is, gimp."

Scott jammed his heel into the pavement, startling Barnaby into stopping. "Damnit, will you stop calling me that?"

Garing's eyes narrowed.

"God, if you don't like me so much, why did you come back?"

He felt the grip loosen, and grabbed Garing's coat more tightly.

"It doesn't have anything to do with who likes who, Byrns."

The call a second time.

Scott nodded, and concentrated on keeping up. It had been a stupid question, at least from Barnaby's point of view. They were part of the Pack; no other explanation needed.

They managed to reach the corner without having to stop again, without speaking, and were forced to wait while a patrolman funneled what vehicles he could off the Boulevard, away from the activity behind him. Beyond the cars, the grumbling trucks, Scott spotted Katie standing under the Apollo's marquee, waving her arms wildly, beckoning, turning to walk away and turning again to wave again. White light falling around her. More a shadow than a girl.

"There," he said, pointing.

Barnaby looked, and nodded, and stepped off the curb.

"Hey, you want to get us killed?"

Garing grinned. "No sweat." He swung Scott in front of him and waved the leg over his head. "Coming through," he bellowed. "Move your ass, jerks, we're coming through."

I'm going to die, Scott thought in dismay as a car braked less than inch from Barnaby's left knee; my god, I'm going to die.

"Hurry up!" Katie yelled.

She was midway down the block, but Barnaby yelled anyway: "Jesus Christ, hold your water! He can't fly, you know!"

Scott laughed.

Barnaby stopped without warning in the middle of the street.

"Hey." Scott tried to pull him on. "Hey, C'mon, man, we—"

Barnaby pointed with the leg.

He pointed up.

Scott looked.

As traffic complained loudly on the street and the patrolman puffed his cheeks and used his whistle, white-gloved hands pointing and directing as he stepped side to side in increasing frustration.

As customers leaving the theater watched and stood in uncertain groups, some wandering immediately off to see what all the commotion was about, others not so sure and hanging back, keeping their distance from Katie, rising up on their toes as if that would provide them proper height.

Scott saw it all, and saw Katie.

As the wind returned, grabbing hats, toppling trash bins, snapping awnings and their fringes, he saw something monstrous press down out of the night sky, piercing the dome of the light the shops and theaters and streetlamps had thrown up. He didn't know what it was—a hand, a claw, a foot, an insect's leg—but he saw it.

And he yelled.

Katie grinned and nodded vigorously, yanked on her cap and started toward them.

Barnaby began to run, was pulled up by Scott's weight, and yanked him off his feet, carrying him one-armed, tilting sideways, until they reached the curb, where he dropped Scott against the hood of a parked car.

"Katie!" he bellowed.

Scott couldn't see properly, there was too much movement, too many panicked people in the way.

But he could hear the sudden groan and crack of masonry, could hear a man's voice cry out a sudden panicked warning.

Seconds later, sparks exploded from the corners of the marquee as wires and cables were exposed and snapped in two, bulbs popped before blacking out, mortar dust and shards of brick flew from the theater's upper facade. Streamers of white fire reaching into the sky. Veils of white falling to the sidewalk, a fireworks display, crackling and steaming.

Scott threw his arms up to protect his face just as the marquee ripped away from the building.

The last thing he saw was Katie waving to him even as she looked up at the white, coming down.

Scott sagged against the car, didn't care when he felt himself sliding.

There was a great silence on Summit Boulevard, an instant of stunned immobility.

Even the wind had temporarily lost its voice.

But not its vigor.

Fire convulsed in it; sparks became dervishes; branches on the far side of the park wall clawed their way over; the snow increased and marked its currents.

Barnaby turned to him, lips working, hands fluttering.

When sound returned, it came with screams.

Garing picked him up, he didn't complain, and ran down the side street and flung them into the parking lot. They could see the others racing toward them from the other end. Barnaby howled a warning, Scott punched at them to turn around, get away, for god's sake, run. Pancho, back from the diner, was the first to understand and grabbed the girls to stop them.

Tang instantly retreated.

Fern stood there, fighting Pancho's hands, slapping at them, twisting away from them, calling Scott's name above the wind that filled the air with smoke now and the stench of burning wire.

It's gone, Scott realized then, feeling as if he'd been slammed in the stomach with a log; Katie's gone, and now it's gone too.

It is, he answered himself.

Katie's nightmare is gone, but it isn't over.

TWENTY-SEVEN

Blade Murtaugh ran.

He didn't stop at his bedroom alley.

He didn't stop when a cruiser's spotlight tried to pin him to the ground.

He was crazy.

He didn't want to be crazy. Not like Slap. Not like Bonita. But he was crazy. He was sure of it now. If he wasn't crazy, then he was going to die and the Hat Trick Boys wouldn't even be a memory.

The Queen of Foxriver sat primly on her bench at the station, hands carefully folded, turban placed just so, just right, knees together, coat properly buttoned. A regal muffler around her throat. Regal boots on her feet.

Two lights beneath the platform roof, a handful from the houses across the way, beyond the trees that dodged the wind kicking at the railbed gravel.

She didn't mind not having the sun, and the occasional snowflake that brushed against her face was a comfort, a soft caress, a kiss from the season that seemed to have arrived too soon.

But she didn't mind.

The train would be here shortly.

She was sure of it.

Despite the din that rose above the park from far, far away, and the pandemonium it signaled, despite the occasional puzzling flares of brightness that made the shadows duck like guilty children behind their posts, she knew her train would arrive before she knew it. She checked her watch; it was only just after nine. Any minute now. Any minute.

And when it came, when it slowed, when the engineer greeted her with a salute of the train's horn, she would rise and count the windows, the train would stop, and she would be on her way to the warm place.

Blade would understand.

Though he had expected her at the banquet hall, and she had as much as given her royal promise to be there, she had a feeling he would understand that things had changed. With Lord Tobin no longer around to protect her, to fill her coffers, she was forced to protect herself.

As she had just after sunset, when that disgusting, fat serving woman had forced her fat way into her private quarters, yelling all sorts of things, foul things, obscene things, and the Queen had no recourse but to punish her.

Execute her.

Then make her way through the rest of the cold castle, the knife close to her side, searching for the rest of those who conspired against her benevolent rule, against the faithful Blade, against the dear Lord Tobin.

She felt a tear.

She swallowed.

The tear never fell.

They had been surprised, those unfaithful others, but were too weak from living softly under the Queen's command, too bereft of purpose. They made no rational attempt to deny their complicity, their fear of her, and only the old, foul-mouthed retainer tried to defend himself with his sword. A pitiful weapon. The Queen took a single blow to her shoulder, and delivered a blow herself.

The castle was hers.

And now it was hers no longer.

Blade would understand.

He would miss her, no doubt, but he would understand, and forgive, and perhaps once in a while think kindly of her in his dreams.

And her knights, of course; her dear sweet knights all dressed in black armor, would have to find someone else to serve.

The rails began to hum.

The Queen began to smile.

Blade ran.

Cold air slicing his lungs, threatening a headache, cleared his mind, cleared his eyes, relieved him of the notion that he was going, had gone crazy.

He knew it was so because the rats were coming.

They had disguised themselves this time, the little bastards, dressing like some kind of weird shit creature from the movies he remembered from when he was a kid. He had seen it almost squash that little girl, the one who ran with the Pack. She'd been lucky tonight. Lucky he'd been in the alley, trying to make up his mind if Leg had really asked him inside. It was so different, so unexpected, he hadn't been able to think two straight thoughts since the funeral, walk two straight blocks without turning around and walking back, just to be sure he had done it, just to be sure he wasn't lost.

Then the wind came.

And the darker piece of the night.

She had been lucky, the little girl.

Tomorrow would be different.

But for now there were the rats.

And they were going to kill him.

He ran across the plaza in front of Town Hall.

His shadows scrambling up the pots that held the flowers long dead, up the stairs as he swerved by them, filled the narrow gap between the Rotunda and an office building with no windows on this side, fled into the street when he left Town Hall and almost left him behind.

It was the long way around to the train station.

It was one of his secret ways.

But he had to get there without the rats ambushing him because he knew the station was where she was. Waiting for her dumb train. Sitting in the cold. Going to freeze to death like the Hat Trick Boy. Trying to get out.

Always trying to get out.

Ain't nobody gonna get out this time.

Nobody.

The town was going to die.

He didn't want to die with it.

A dog chased him.

He kicked at it until it ran in the opposite direction.

A cat paced him.

He spat at it until it spat back and disappeared.

Staying out of the light. Always in the dark. Using the shadows the way the shadows used him, teased him, taunted him in his dreams. Crawling at one point under the low branches of an evergreen tree, shuddering at the needles prickling across his neck and cheek, freezing when he heard footsteps, closing his eyes and waiting until the footsteps receded. Moving. Fast when he could, and when he could barely move anymore, using lampposts and shrubs and mail boxes and hydrants to propel him along, to keep him on his feet.

Sweat in his eyes.

His legs half-filled with lead.

Finally reaching the tracks where they indented the street and hurrying south along them, slower by necessity, head down to make sure the ties didn't trip him.

Despite the cold wind, more sweat dribbled into his eyes, stinging, not warm at all.

The night filled with his panting, and with sirens, both sounding so distant he wondered if maybe he was really dreaming after all, that he hadn't yanked the little girl away from the creature he couldn't really have seen, that he hadn't run away when all Leg had wanted to do was talk to him, thank him, that the Queen was still back at the Mission, standing on the sidewalk as he walked out, cleaner than a baby's washed ass and grinning just as dumb.

Getting out.

God damn.

Stumbling over one of a partially splintered ties and falling forward, crying out and landing on his hands, one on each rail, feeling like a jerk because he was still on his feet. Straddling the bed. Staring at his shadow.

Cold iron; too cold.

Carefully he pulled his right hand away and paused to catch his breath, easing down a little, not quite kneeling, mouth wide open to catch snatches of the wind.

Feeling, then, the rail began to vibrate, softly.

He ran.

He had no choice.

There were no trains this hour, and the rails began to sing.

Hat Trick Boy on the move, down the ice, faster than spit, faster than the wind, catching up to his shadow and leaving it in his dust.

Faster than the snow that fell heavily again.

"Ah," said the Queen of Foxriver.

She smoothed her coat, touched at her muffler, made sure her turban crown was firm against the wind.

"Ah," she said.

Blade saw the flickering headlamp of the train that shouldn't have been.

He saw the Queen rise from her bench and move to the edge of the platform.

He couldn't run any faster.

Not even when he saw the first rat.

TWENTY-EIGHT

On the way out of the lot, tires skidding as they tried to find traction in the wet new snow, Tang sideswiped another car, but no one made her stop, no one yelled when she spun the sports wheel right and nicked another vehicle's fender.

Pancho in the front seat, hugging himself, muttering that sounded more like incantation; Barnaby behind her, staring blankly out the window, his left hand level with his cheek, palm against the glass; Fern in the middle, an arm around Scott's shoulder and wishing she'd never left the house tonight. She could be home now. Safe. Dad watching TV, Mother complaining that all the shows were about nothing but sex and killing, and she would be curled in her chair, wondering how long it would be before Scott got the hint and decided to call.

Katie. Dead.

The car shot down the slope toward the river.

Laine and Dale, Pancho had said, taken to Foxriver Memorial on the north side of town, where her father did his out-of-clinic surgery; most of the other victims on their way to St. Francis, closer in the South End.

Dark and light swept through the inside as it passed under the streetlamps. Light and dark.

The windshield wipers scraped and thumped the snow away,

bunching it on either side, turning it to ice, smearing it until Pancho leaned over and turned on the blower. The rear window was already covered.

A great shudder made Scott sit upright, and Fern held him more closely, smelling the fear in him, mixing with wet wool and damp leather. She didn't want to read his mind. She didn't look at the prosthetic lying across his lap.

The car's engine hummed steadily, not changing pitch, barely stuttering when Tang reached Bank Road and turned right, shifting gears.

No one told her to slow down.

Light and dark.

Scott fumbled for Fern's free hand, and she let him take it, squeeze it, watching his profile, the hair that bounced slightly over his forehead whenever the automobile swerved, hair that looked white now, ghostly, even in the dark. Watching him think though his gaze never shifted from the back of Pancho's head. She didn't want to read his mind, but she knew what he was thinking; and she didn't doubt for a second that Katie's monster had really killed her. No accident. No freak of nature. No wrong-place-at-the-wrong-time. Katie Ealton was dead, and something huge had done it.

It was true.

No bedtime story this time.

She didn't know why it was, why she believed it, why there were no angry questions, no denials. It just seemed . . . right. Horribly right. To think anything else, now, would mean everything since Eddie's dying had been nothing more than insanity taking seductive hold of her, cradling her, whispering to her. Touching her.

Which meant that the guys had been right about Eddie somehow wanting to conjure a childhood monster; and wrong. Because if all that energy Scott had talked about was real, if the Pack really did absorb all that Eddie Roman had created, it should have been gone by now. Eddie was dead. The energy should have died too. There should be nothing left to hold the Pack together.

There should be nothing left to call their nightmares back.

The increasingly slick roadway forced Tang to reduce her speed as she approached South Bridge, the lights planted here and there along its skeletal superstructure blurred and rung by haze. There were no cars here. The headlamps drove the snow ahead of them, swirling it across the blacktop, and what didn't stick gathered on the shoulders. She couldn't see the river, but she knew it was black.

"Stop," Scott said.

"Jesus, man," Pancho said, wriggling lower in his seat, "we gotta get away, Scottie. We can't stay here. We—"

"Stop."

"Shit on that! We gotta keep moving, man, this ain't a game, Katie's dead."

"Tang."

Without argument she pulled over, thumped over the curb, and came to a halt in the middle of the block, in the unlighted fan between two distant lampposts. Only then did Fern hear her choked sobbing.

The engine grumbled; the blower melted the snow.

The wipers, thumping back and forth.

Fern eased her arm from his shoulders. "What, Scott?"

He used the back of Pancho's seat to pull himself forward, leaned down and across her to stare out the opposite window. His hair was darkly wet. She wanted to touch it, instead tried to see what he saw and saw only bare trees. A quick inhalation then—this was where Joey had died. Had been killed. "Scott—" A sideways glance cut her off. She looked outside again, half expecting to see those goddamn beetles swarm over the snow-bank.

"Eddie," he said quietly. "That sonofabitching Eddie."

Pancho groaned.

Tang lowered her forehead to the steering wheel.

Scott held up a hand, not pointing, though she couldn't stop herself from following his finger up, out, up again and gone into a loose fist.

"He . . . *his* monster. It vanished, or something, as soon as he died. That's why the cops couldn't find the killer."

Warm in the car.

Fern felt the sweat gathering between her breasts.

Barnaby's head turned slowly, his face barely seen.

"Joey," Scott said, pointing now toward the river. "The cops shot at something." He looked at Garing. "It disappeared before they could find it, or see it. Because Joey was dead." His hand dropped from the seat, he eased back and slid down, staring at the roof. "Probably the same for Slap."

"Longer each time," Barnaby said.

Scott nodded.

Fern looked from one to the other. "Why?" She couldn't think of anything else to say.

"I don't know."

Without thinking, nerves and temper taut and close to snapping, she grabbed the front of his coat, and when he took his wrist gently, she glared. *What the hell do you mean, you don't know why? What the hell kind of an answer is that, you creep?* He shook her wrist just a little. She stared at it, opened her fingers. Then she told him what she'd thought, how the energy should be dissipated by now, that none of this—especially Katie—was right, if Scott was.

"I know," he said. "Don't you think I know that?"

"For Christ's sake, drive!" Pancho yelled, a fist slammed to the dashboard. Tang's head snapped up. "Jesus, guys, who the hell cares, huh? I mean, this shit ain't real, and it's killing us off, you know?" He grabbed Tang's arm. "Goddamnit. will you drive?"

"Where?" she said flatly, not looking at him. "Where do we go?"

"How the hell should I know?" Pitch rising. "Just keep going north, shit, I don't know."

"Canada?" she said.

"Tang—"

"The North Pole?" She whirled on him, punching his hand away. "Where the hell are we going to go," she yelled, "that those . . . things aren't going with us?"

Pancho wiped his face with the crook of his elbow. "Tang, I don't know." He sounded ready to cry, and Fern didn't blame him. "Can't we just—"

Scott's head rolled to the side, and Fern felt him stiffen suddenly, hold his breath. "Tang, he's right. You'd better get moving."

"At last!" Pancho said, applauding.

The car moved.

Fern looked over Scott's head and saw the dark man on the sidewalk. Standing just beyond the reach of the nearest light.

They're ours, Fern thought as Tang drove slowly into the dark; Tang's more right than she knows—they're all our monsters, there isn't just one, and they won't go away until we're all dead.

A prolonged gust buffeted the car.

Just like Katie.

She didn't give a damn when the tears began to fall.

Scott didn't look to see if the dark man had been left behind. It didn't matter. He would be there, anywhere, not long after the car stopped again.

Bad Dale had said.

He grunted a bitter laugh. Poor kid didn't know what he was talking about, and he was right anyway. Of all of them, somehow he *knew* when things would be bad; somehow he knew *before* it happened.

"You know," Barnaby said dully, still looking out his window, "I know what I saw, I was at the funeral, but I can't get a grip on this. I feel like . . . like I'm sleepwalking or something."

No one answered.

"I mean," he went on, "I don't feel like I'm gonna die."

No one answered.

And suddenly Tang wailed, "All those people! God damn, all those people dead because of us!"

Scott sat up so hard he had to grab the back of his neck to ease a sudden sharp pain.

"What?" Fern asked.

He ignored her. "Tang, go to the hospital. Memorial."

The car didn't turn.

"Tang, damnit!"

Pancho threw an arm over the seat, his hand catching him on the cheek. "Shut the fuck up, Scottie! We're getting out of here. Just shut the fuck up!"

Tang made the next corner, started up the hill, and Pancho slapped her. Raised a hand to slap her again, and Barnaby lunged forward and grabbed his arm.

"Barn, don't, man. Don't do this."

When Fern tried to pry them apart, Scott elbowed her and nodded at the plastic leg as he fumbled with his belt buckle. "Hold it."

She blinked stupidly.

"I can't walk without it, Fern."

Pushing deep into the corner, he wriggled his jeans down for the second time that night, glad for the dark that hid what he knew would still be an angry flush of skin where the stump protested. He was glad too she didn't seem to react, though he didn't look at her face. Instead, he wiped the inside of the prosthetic's cup as best he could, then slipped it on, made sure it gripped properly, and began winding the straps around.

At the next intersection they crossed, the dark man took off his hat.

Barnaby sat back again; Pancho rubbed the feeling back in his arm.

"Tell me where I'm wrong," Scott said, still working on the straps around, setting them in place. "Eddie got his monster, right? I mean, he brought him out. Joey got his, probably from listening to Eddie."

"Clap your hands," Tang said. She was crying.

"Something like that. Maybe. I don't know yet. But it's real. We know it is."

Pancho groaned his despair.

"But we're not the only ones they've hurt. If it was all phony, all in our minds, Mr. Tobin, the others, they'd still be okay."

The car skidded. Tang's hands darted across the steering wheel to bring it straight again.

So it didn't necessarily follow that each of them would have to die for their respective childhood nightmares to die with them. The things were real. And if they were real, they could be hurt. Maybe driven away. Maybe destroyed.

"Right," Pancho said sarcastically. "We'll just call up the army, let the tanks take care of them."

"No," he said. "We talk to Dale."

Fern slapped his arm. "Are you out of your mind?"

"Well, who better than a kid?"

Dark and light.

They crossed the boulevard.

He checked south and saw the lights spinning, the lights flashing, the lights reaching into the storm but not high enough to catch the clouds.

"Clap your hands." Tang giggled.

Scott put a fist to his chin and pressed, hard. There was something missing, and he couldn't figure it out. He didn't even know if it was important. Hell, he didn't even know if anything he'd said was even right. But he was glad for one thing—he was glad no one had asked him about screaming, why they heard it, why them, and Blade, and no one else.

"Clap your hands."

"Tang," Pancho said. "God, I'm sorry."

"Clap your hands. Here we are."

TWENTY-NINE

Like Town Hall, Foxriver Memorial was set back from the street behind a concrete plaza, though this one was more narrow, more stark, less shrubs, no trees at all. A snow-covered, free-form steel sculpture on a raised concrete island. An overhang to protect the ambulances and visitors. It was a six-story building, square and modern, strips of dark-masked windows along its face that made it resemble a square layer cake. Tang had to park a block away, and by the time they reached the entrance, they were too cold to talk. The snow fell in smaller flakes, harder flakes, but the wind hadn't abated, jabbing at them, covering their hair, their shoulders before they'd left the car's shadow.

The lobby was bleak—all plastic chairs and plastic flowers, warning signs and welcome signs, hidden lighting, indoor-outdoor carpeting and a reception desk in the center.

"Visiting hours are over," the woman sitting there said. Pink smock, white hair, expression sympathetic but adamant when Fern explained about Laine and her brother. "It's almost ten. I'm afraid you'll have to come back tomorrow."

On the wall behind the desk a bank of elevators.

"Can we stick around for a minute?" Barnaby asked. "It's awfully cold out there, ma'am."

"Of course." A finger to her lips. "Just keep it down, all right?"

He smiled and nodded, returned to the others standing in the middle of an open visitors area, and said, "No sweat. She likes me. Who's gonna go up?"

Scott pointed at himself.

"Who else?"

"Me," Fern said.

"No," Scott told her. "Just one. It's easier to cover that way."

A soft chime announced an arriving elevator. The doors opened without a sound, and Dr. Freelin stepped out, buttoning a hunting jacket with one hand, the other holding his glasses.

"Magic," Scott said, and they hurried over, ignoring the receptionist's rise to protest.

The doctor was surprised to see them, but Scott was glad to note he wasn't annoyed.

"Laine's okay," the man said before they could ask. "Just a few cuts, a couple of bruises." He looked at them one by one. "Dale's lost a lot of blood, but he'll be all right too. Thank God. He's already had a transfusion. Nothing to do now but build up his strength." He blinked, replaced his glasses. "Thanks for coming, kids. I . . . Thanks."

"Can we see them?" Fern asked.

Scott saw her flash "the smile," tried not to laugh aloud.

Freelin shook his head regretfully. "Sorry, but they're about bedded down for the night."

A low mumbled chorus of regret, a steady, respectful barrage of promises just shy of pleading to only peek in, grin, wave, let her know they're all right too. Except for Scottie, whose leg was killing him but he came anyway because he was so worried. And Laine must be worried about them too, right? She hasn't seen any of them since . . . the windstorm. She'll sleep better, no kidding, Dr. Freelin, and he knew them well enough by now to know they wouldn't disobey him. Just a quick look and a wave and they'll go home and get a good night's sleep, come back tomorrow, swear to God.

No one said a word about Katie.

No one asked about the casualties at the theater.

Fern gave him "the smile" a second time.

Freelin fussed with his jacket. "Look, I know you mean well, and it's true that Laine's been worried sick—" He glanced over their heads at the receptionist. "Oh hell, why the hell not." He turned, but Barnaby had already pressed the "up" button. "Confident, aren't you."

Barnaby shrugged. "Laine's our friend."

"We'd sneak up anyway," Pancho admitted. "Then we'd just get into a lot of trouble."

"They'd probably arrest us," Tang assured him. "No kidding."

"And it would be all my fault, right?" Freelin said.

Scott saw the lips twitch before the doctor pulled the smile back. It was clear he was moved; and for a moment, Scott felt like hell.

The doors opened and they hustled in, stood in the back and didn't look at each other.

Scott watched the digital numbers glow and fade, tried not to smell the antiseptic, prayed that Dr. Freelin wouldn't ask any more questions. He had enough of his own.

On the fourth floor the doors reopened, and they followed Laine's father out. He went directly to the nurse's station, whispered something, then beckoned them over.

Whispers in the halls stretching away from the station.

A creaking cart.

"One at a time," Freelin ordered gently. "Third door on the left." He pointed. "Dale's in Pediatrics down the hall, but you can't see him, okay?"

They agreed.

Scott took off before a visiting order could be established, looked back and watched the Pack carefully herd the doctor into the tiny waiting room next to the station. Pancho, behind his back, gave him the thumbs-up sign.

Sure, he thought; now all you have to do is send me a stupid army.

He pushed the swinging door open without knocking, said, "Hi," when Laine sat up with a start in her bed. She was by the window; the other bed was empty, its mattress folded up at the foot. The only light on was over her headboard, and he could see that her hair was still in its ponytail, her cheeks plastered with bandages, her forearms lightly bandaged as well. A bruise in the center of her throat. Another one, larger, on the back of one hand.

"Got a minute?"

When she started to cry, he sat beside her and held her, patting her back self-consciously, flinching when he felt bare skin through the opening of her short-sleeved hospital gown. When she was done not long after, sniffing and grinning, cheeks ablaze and chin trembling, he told her they didn't have much time, held his breath a moment before telling her what had happened since Katie's giant had blown in the Starlite's windows. He gave her no time to react, only begged her to believe him when he said that he needed to talk to Dale. It was important. He couldn't exactly explain why, but her brother held some sort of answer, and the dumb part of it was, he wouldn't know it until he heard it.

Laine didn't laugh, nor did she protest. "I knew it," was all she said. "Damn, I knew it."

Then she slid out of the bed, winced and grabbed her arm—"Bandage pulls, god, it's a bitch"—and led him to the door. Poked her head out, pulled it in. "Pancho's trying to turn him around. He's not falling for it."

"Smart guy."

She ducked her head, shrugged. "I guess so."

A second check of the hall, and she hissed at him, slipped out, and he followed, not looking toward the waiting room, hurrying down the corridor into the pediatrics wing and ducking into Dale's room so rapidly he nearly trod on her heel.

Dale was by the window.

His face and neck were wrapped in bandages, leaving only a band that exposed his eyes and eyebrows, his mouth and part of his right cheek; an IV tube fed solution into his arm, and the one hand lying on his stomach with a mesh of pale scratches.

Laine touched his arm. "He's okay, Scottie. It looks worse than it is."

"God, I hope so."

Dale stirred, opened his eyes. "Laine!"

"Hush," she said, finger to her lips. "It's a secret."

"Daddy's gonna be mad. This is the kids' place. You're not supposed to be in the kids' place."

She tiptoed to the bedside, bringing Scott with her. "Got a surprise for you, kid. Look who's here."

Dale stared at him. "Hi." Uncertain.

"Hi."

Laine kissed the boy's cheek, whispered something that made him giggle. "Quick," she said then. "Be quick, Scottie, he's tired."

Scott hesitated. Now that he was here, now that he had the chance, he didn't have a clue as to what to ask. But Dale had known, somehow, that it had been "bad" outside the diner long before Katie had run by. And that thought made him lean over, smile, and ask how he'd known.

Dale frowned. "Because."

"How because, pal?"

"My arm itches, Laine."

"Dale, how because, honey?"

"Because there's monsters out there."

"How do you know that?"

"Because there are."

"He believes it?" he asked Laine.

"My arm itches, Laine. Will you read me a story?"

"Not now, honey."

"I want the one about the teeth in the attic."

"Dale, please."

Scott felt helpless, and in feeling helpless, angry. He'd disturbed the kid for nothing, and now Dale was wide awake, demanding stories when he should be sleeping, healing. He looked heavenward in self-scolding and turned to the door.

"Tell me, Laine," Dale said groggily.

"Oh, Dale."

"Please?"

Scott paused, looked back.

"Okay." She tucked him in, smoothed his hair, kissed his forehead. "No dragons," she whispered.

"No dragons," he whispered back.

"No witches."

"No witches." Dale yawned in the middle of a grin that showed his teeth, and those gaps where they were missing.

"No bad guys."

"Okay."

And Scott had it.

"Will I see you guys tomorrow?"

Laine was back in her own bed, Scott poised at the door. "Count on it."

She stared out the window.

He blew her a kiss she didn't see and returned to the waiting room. He wanted to get the rest of them out of there, forget talking to Laine, but he couldn't. Fern had already left to see her, and Pancho, standing by the entrance, was next.

Tang dropped onto the plastic couch beside him. Her look asked him *Well?*

He nodded.

She paled.

Barnaby snapped his fingers while Dr. Freelin talked to him about the football season past, the Thanksgiving clobbering of Port Richmond, the football season to some. He seemed to think Garing was already ready for the pros.

Scott bit softly on his tongue to keep from screaming.

"Who's driving?" Dr. Freelin asked, down in the lobby.

Tang raised her hand.

"You be careful," he said sternly. "The roads are getting bad."

She promised.

He smiled, thanked them again for seeing Laine, and with a wave to the receptionist, hurried down a corridor, out of sight around a corner. A janitor worked by the elevators, mopping the floor. Scott jerked his head toward the exit, led them outside though he could see a desperate command in Tang's expression, a plea in Fern's.

The wind swatted him.

A lull in the snowstorm allowed him to see as he hurried toward Tang's car. Ignoring their protests. Their demands. Thinking furiously, shaking his head, glancing up at the hospital facade and wondering what would happen if he was wrong.

Stupid question.

He would die.

Barnaby snared his arm just as they reached the car. "Goddamnit, gimp, you tell us the fuck what's going on!"

Scott shook him off. "Clap your hands," he said, grinning at Tang.

"Oh fuck!" Garing said, groaning. Yelled it. Spun in a tight circle and would have thrown a punch had not Pancho stepped between them.

"Scott," Fern said.

"You were sort of right, Tang," he said, "and I was sort of wrong."

The wind flung snow into his face from a bank beside the car. He sputtered, wiped his face on a sleeve, reached for the door handle, but Fern stopped him.

"Look," she said.

Down the block, near the corner, the dark man waited.

"I'll kill him," Barnaby declared loudly. "I'll kill the sonofabitch."

Scott started walking.

Fern ran after him, but he wouldn't look at her.

"Stay close," he said, loud enough for the others to hear. "But stay away." He did look then. "Stay away, Fern, I mean it."

"He'll kill you!"

He said nothing.

"Pigheaded bastard!"

"Scots stubborn." And he grinned.

Walked.

While the snow tried to trip him up, falling again but not heavily, just enough to slash the dark with grey, with white, once in a while a glint of silver; while the wind talked to him, taunted him, twisted his hair into his eyes, his ears, his mouth when he realized he was breathing with it open; while his legs began to ache.

Walked with his hands fisted in his pockets.

no dragons

Wrong and right: they hadn't learned that monsters weren't really real. They hadn't learned that at all. No one had. What they had been taught was that the monsters couldn't hurt them if they weren't afraid.

no witches

How many times had his mother crooned as she rocked him out of a nightmare's clasp, "It's okay, hon, it's okay, they can't hurt you, don't be afraid."

So he grew up. And so did Barnaby, and Tang, and Katie dear god Katie, and they weren't afraid anymore.

Because they no longer believed the monsters were there.

no bad guys

He squinted into the snow and saw the dark man. Waiting. Standing this side of the nearest streetlamp. Standing rigidly. Waiting.

Growing taller as Scott approached.

I can kill you, he thought, slid on ice, and waved the others back without looking to see if anyone had tried to help him; I can kill you, and you know it.

The dark man moved.

Scott stopped as the shadowfigure stepped off the sidewalk and into the deserted street. And waited.

Bright light behind it, spreading its form, hiding its features. Blurring it here, making its edges sharp there.

Scott hesitated, stomach leaden with fear, before sliding between two parked cars himself. He had no choice. He could have run, but he was tired, and he ached, and he didn't want the dark man walking into his house.

Closer.

no dragons

Dale believed in monsters.

Dale hadn't learned, but he was learning. Not that they weren't real, but that he didn't have to be afraid that they were, that they would hurt him. He was learning to doubt their existence.

The dark man took off its hat.

Faceless.

Patiently waiting.

Scott heard the wind, heard his footsteps in the snow, heard the Pack ranged behind him, at a distance but coming on to watch his back.

So this, he thought, is what terror is like.

All because of Eddie's own terror, deliberately embraced. Scott knew it, remembered it, all of them did—the wonderfully chilling sensation of scaring himself to death when gruesome monsters and unrepentant evil bad guys, snarling dragons and cackling witches, spooks and shadows, crawled across the pages of a book, the face of a screen large and small.

And the magic words to fend them off: *don't be afraid, they won't hurt you, they aren't really there.*

He stopped suddenly, heard the others stop behind him, yards away, he didn't turn.

No.

Jesus, no, he was wrong.

The dark man took a step forward, and he heard someone muffle a cry.

A branch snapped off a tree to his left, rattling to the ground. A gunshot crack that made him think of glass breaking, mannequins escaping a boulevard display. Coming for him. Get him to join them.

The dark man lurched toward him another step. Stiff-legged. The hat still in one hand, untouched by the wind that lashed the snow and lashed his face.

Scott licked his lips, bit them.

A second cry behind, this one of startled pain, quickly followed by one of rage. He whirled and saw Fern down on one knee, something large and shining worrying at her foot.

Barnaby was stomping on it, Pancho trying to get close, Tang vacillating between running away and running toward him.

Real; he could smell her blood.

Real; he could see the marquee as it came down on Katie's head.

Fern called his name.

The dark man husked his name.

He spun back and lost his breath; the dark man was less than ten feet away, and though there was no face, he knew it was smiling.

"Kill it!" Fern screamed. "Kill it! Kill it! God, it hurts, kill it!"

no dragons

yes there are

It had been so simple, maybe simple-minded. All he had to do was face the dark man and tell it he didn't believe it existed, not anymore. It was nothing more than the dregs of his imagination, carried to the surface by the energy of fear Eddie had set loose. The energy the Pack had sustained simply by being together.

The dark man reached out, and Scott stumbled back, heard Fern scream again, heard Tang join her, and with a cry of his own lunged at the black mannequin, cried out again when his hands closed on the dark man's throat, cold, freezing, burning, giving like supple flesh, holding like stone, while the dark man's arm wrapped around his shoulders and they fell to the street. Rolling over, Scott's head slamming against the black-top, stunning him, loosening his grip, and the dark man rolled away, staggered to its knees and grabbed hold of Scott's foot.

"No!"

And pulled.

"Jesus, no!"

He lashed out, struck something, struck nothing, and bellowed when his leg pulled away from its mooring.

The dark man laughed, the laugh multiplied by the wind.

Eyes flooding tears, Scott rolled to his side and kicked out with his other foot, screaming pain, kicking out, screaming rage, kicking out, pushing himself to his knee and throwing himself at the dark man's throat again.

Searing cold.

Flesh blistering across his fingers as his rush brought the dark man to its back and he straddled it, used its head to pound its head against the street. Again. Again. Its arms trying to envelop him and slipping off, legs thrashing clumsily, Scott sobbing because nothing had happened, it wouldn't go away and it wouldn't die and it was laughing at him and cursing him and slapping the hat across his face. Stinging. Burning. Throwing his leg away, Scott unable to stop himself from watching the mangled prosthetic skid and slide across the snow.

The dark man bucked and Scott fell backward, grabbing a leg as he reached the ground.

The wind, biting.

Scott pulled.

The dark man screamed.

Scott bared his teeth, braced himself, and pulled again.

The leg came off.

A mannequin's leg.

He scrambled to his belly and grabbed the other one before the dark man could right itself and flee.

Pulled it off.

The dark man floundered.

Beat away the arms and pulled them off, one by one.

The dark man sighed.

Gripped the head in both hands and pulled it from the torso.

The dark man vanished.

Scott lowered his head and sobbed, raised a fist above his shoulder to claim his triumph, and changed his mind.

"Scott!"

Clap your hands, he thought bitterly, you stupid son of a bitch.

"Scott!"

He gasped for air and sat down, hard, facing up the street. Fern limped toward him, the others standing where they were, staring at the ground.

"Are you all right?" She dropped beside him, cheeks glinting with frozen tears. "Are you . . . Oh god." She saw the empty trouser leg. "Oh god." A check of the street. "I'll get it," she said. "Hang on, I'll get it."

"No." He grabbed her arm, pulled her close. "Don't bother, it's wrecked, I couldn't use it if I wanted to."

She cupped his cheeks with her hands, then brushed the snow from his hair. "It tried to kill me."

"Tell me about it."

"Barnaby squashed it. It was huge. It was . . . awful."

She wept without closing her eyes, without shifting her gaze from his face. And he wondered what she saw there when she finally looked away, swiping at her eyes with the backs of her hands, refusing to turn back when he touched her chin with a finger.

He didn't ask.

He thought he knew.

Learning to doubt, then deny, their monsters' existence didn't make them less real. They just hid, that's all. Impotent until doubt returned. And fed them.

Bumps in the night.

Shadows in the corner.

Pancho crunched past them to fetch the prosthetic. Cursed when he held it up to the light.

Until the energy of fear was strong enough to give them form.

That's what Dale would eventually forget: that his dragons and witches never really went away.

Barnaby and Tang followed soon after, Tang helping Fern to her feet, Barnaby slipping his hands under Scott's arms. "Well, Byrns," he said gruffly, "at least we got the goddamn hospital right here."

No one laughed.

The snow thickened as the wind died.

"Scott?"

He was exhausted, had nothing left, and didn't care.

"Scottie?"

He couldn't even blink the flakes from his eyes when he

slipped from Barnaby's grasp and fell to his back, stared at the sky.

He didn't care.

The dark man was gone.

Now it was his time to hide, and he didn't care at all.

THIRTY

Blade sat forlornly on the edge of the platform, legs dangling, a hand beside each leg as if ready to lift him. His head was cold, something had happened to his cap, but it didn't make any difference because he could be inside a furnace and he'd still feel made of ice.

He was alone.

The rest of them, all them uniforms and smartass guys and the goddamn guy with the notepad who asked him a hundred questions and didn't write anything down, they were all gone. So was the police car; so was the ambulance. Nobody asked if he had anywhere to go. They left him sitting there, dangling his legs, thinking about Slap and the Queen and thinking about waiting for another train to come along.

Gonna get out.

No way in hell.

Even the rats knew that, goddamn goddamn, they had run away when he'd run past them, squealing like baby pigs, back into the sewer mouths that opened along the tracks, back to get ready for when he came back to the alley.

They knew he wasn't gonna get out.

They knew it all along, goddamn little shits.

Bonita had tried. She had reached out to touch the express,

and it had sucked her onto the tracks. No time for screaming. Not even his. After staring a while, scratching his head, he'd just trudged across the park and talked to one of the cops by the ruined Apollo. An hour later, they came. Less than an hour after that, they were gone.

Getting out.

Murtaugh cried, blew his nose, cried again and prayed he wouldn't hear the screaming anymore.

If he didn't, he'd get out.

Like hell.

That's the way it was.

He sniffed and turned away when the snow clawed at his face, reached out beside him and pulled the Queen's turban into his lap. Thumbed the silver diamond as if it were a magic lamp. No more screaming, he'd get out. Take a bath. Take a job.

Hat Trick Boy.

Goddamn.

THIRTY-ONE

The acoustical tiles in the ceiling looked like they hadn't been changed in a thousand years, and those damn tiny holes were probably filled with a secret nerve gas that kept the patients quiet whenever the nurses weren't around to torture them, give them shots, feed them the garbage that pretended to be food, wake them up to give them a sleeping pill, tell them to get some rest in the middle of the afternoon.

He had figured that out yesterday.

He had been ready to go home the day before that, when he first woke up and found himself alone, the second bed empty.

So far, however, no luck with figuring out how to get out of here before he went bananas.

"Scott," his mother scolded with a laugh in her voice, "if you don't stop twitching, I'm going to strap you down, you hear?"

"Well, what's taking them so long, Mom? God, it isn't like they have to make one from scratch. It's only a temporary one, until the new one gets done."

She rose from the chair by the window and walked over to the bed, fussed with the sheet, sighed, and walked to the open door and looked out.

"See?" he said, gleefully vindicated. "See?"

"Oh hush up."

He chuckled.

He swung his leg over the side of the bed, rubbed the side of his neck, and stared out the tinted window. As far as he could tell, the sky was clear, the air was cold, and it would probably be a white Christmas.

Big . . . deal.

"You know," she said, leaning against the frame, "I'm surprised the kids haven't visited you more often."

He shrugged.

"It's not like them. Especially Fern. She's only one floor down."

He refused the bait.

The radiator snapped at him.

"Well, if you're okay, I'm going down there to see what's taking so long. They were supposed to be here an hour ago."

"Okay, Mom."

"You'll be all right?"

"Sure. What am I going to do, fly?"

She left.

He didn't see or hear her go; he felt her absence.

As he felt someone walk into the room a minute later, felt someone stand at his back until he turned around and grinned.

"Hey, Dale."

Dale, his face uncovered, unsightly tracks where most of the stitches still lay, grinned back. "You looking for Santa?"

"Something like that."

Dale leaned over the radiator, his nose close to the window. It reminded Scott of another time, too long ago, and he touched the boy's shoulder to move him back.

"I'm okay, really. I'm not gonna fall." He pointed at Scott's hip. "You gonna get your leg today?"

Scott grunted.

"Can I see it?"

"Sure, why not?"

A nurse wheeled in a cart to take his temperature, blood pressure, suggest that perhaps Mr. Byrns would like to lie back for a while, until the doctor and therapist arrived. Scott said he'd rather sit up, he'd been on his back too long already, he was about ready to scream. Dale agreed. The nurse shrugged and left with her equipment.

A bird flew by the window.

He waited for it to come back.

Dale left to take his nap.

His mother returned with the day's newspaper, scowled at the headlines, scowled at the weather report, probably would have scowled at the obituaries if he hadn't begged her to stop. Besides, he didn't give a damn about the news. He'd already read about the Queen jumping in front of a train—the story stuck way the hell in back like nobody cared—had already made himself a promise to find Blade as soon as he got out, no matter what his mother said.

He only hoped the little guy wouldn't die on him before he did.

When, despite his best intentions to cover it, he yawned and she caught him, he was ordered into bed.

"Rest," she commanded, closing the door behind her.

Right, he thought.

The door opened again.

"God, Mom—"

It was Fern. On crutches.

He sat up hastily, not sure what to say. When Barnaby had led the Pack back to the hospital that night, it had been Fern who had come up with the story that fooling around on the street had caused the injuries they'd taken. That she had been bleeding herself, her shoe nearly chewed off, gave credence to Pancho's addition that they'd attracted some dogs who'd gone after them, and run away when Tang scattered them with her car.

If there were doubts among the staff, they hadn't been mentioned.

"Hi," she said, still on the threshold. "Can I come in?"

"Sure." He didn't know what else to say. "Sure. I'm going nuts in here."

She sat on the empty bed and lifted her foot to rest on the mattress. "I'm getting out in an hour."

"Hey, that's great."

"Your leg?"

He nodded. "This afternoon. A temporary. Dr. Freelin's got some connections or something, he's going to fit me with one of those motorized jobs when the stump heals."

"Motorized?"

He grinned.

"Creep."

She looked great. A little pale. But her eyes were bright, her voice strong and steady.

It tore him apart.

"Scott—"

He waved her silent.

"No," she said. "I can't. This isn't right."

But it was, and they both knew it.

During the only time the Pack had come to see them, the only time Scott would see them, he had told them what they wanted to know, what they hadn't wanted to hear. Pancho hadn't slept because he was afraid his walls would open up one night and let out the bees. Scott told him it wouldn't happen, not if the Pack broke up. For good.

It was the only way, he told them while they turned their heads, tried not to weep; it was the only way to break the energy chain Eddie Roman had created.

Soon enough, he had reasoned, all that fear would weaken, all that terror would subside. Soon enough, it wouldn't be any worse than anyone else's vague feelings of unease. Soon enough, they'd be strong enough to let in some doubt. And the other people, the ones who'd never known was what going on—Blade and Slap and who knew who all else—soon enough they would barely remember a thing.

They would never be totally free, but neither would they be endangered.

The monsters were real, but if they didn't scare you—

Soon enough.

"What if you're wrong?" Fern asked tearfully, almost stuttering in her anger. "You were wrong once, suppose you're wrong again? Suppose some frightened little kid, or some guy's who's about to lose his life savings, suppose they tap in before it's all gone? Suppose—" Angrily she grabbed the crutches and hauled herself up. "The hell with it. I don't care."

He yelped and shoved back against the headboard, pointing at the floor. "Jesus, a bug!"

She didn't move. "Big deal." She looked around, only mildly perturbed. "So where is it, I'll squash it."

He grinned smugly. "See? You're learning already."

She didn't return the grin. Instead she came to his bed and leaned over it, frowning. "I don't want to never have to see you again, Scott. I mean it."

"Me neither," he answered truthfully. "But for a while—"

"Yeah, yeah." She turned away. "Right." At the door she stopped, and he saw her back straighten as she took a slow breath. "We killed them, Scott. Katie's dead and Joey's dead, but we both killed our monsters. It's supposed to be a happy ending."

"It will be," he promised, closed his eyes, made a wish. "Swear to God, Fern, it will be."

She left without responding.

He lay back and stared at the ceiling, counted the holes, said nothing when his mother and the doctors finally returned and fussed and fitted with his new prothesis; said nothing as he test-walked the halls and ignored the twinges and fire in his leg; said nothing but a mumbled "goodbye" when visiting hours were over and his mother finally left him alone.

He watched television.

He walked a little more.

He stopped at Dale's door, remembering his promise.

The boy was on his knees on his bed, testing its bounce and laughing. When he saw Scott in the doorway, he clapped his hands and said, "Will you say the magic for me? Laine's not here. She probably forgot."

"Oh, I don't think so, pal. It's kind of late, you know."

"Bedtime."

"Just about."

"No dragons."

Scott grinned. "That's right, no dragons."

"I know that sometimes. Really I do." He scrambled under

the covers, pointed at the television on its stand bolted to the wall. "Watch cartoons with me?"

"Hey, you think I'm stupid? It's too late for that."

"Pretend cartoons, Scottie. Boy, you're silly."

Scott watched him settle in, and wanted to cry again, and wanted to laugh. Thanks, buddy, he thought as he walked across the room, holding the hospital gown up so Dale could see how the leg worked; thanks, I needed that.

"Neat," Dale decided sleepily.

"I think so." He perched on the edge of the bed. "So, what's on?"

"Bugs Bunny."

"Good. Cool guy."

Dale nodded.

Scott watched the blank screen and saw Fern, saw Tang, saw Barnaby and Pancho. For a brief moment he felt like a murderer, almost ran from the room to find the nearest telephone.

Dale giggled.

Scott relaxed.

"No witches," Dale whispered.

"No witches," he agreed. And: "Always," he added.

"Dragons, sometimes, though," the boy mumbled, shifting to lie on his side.

Scott tickled him, rearranged his covers. "What do you mean by that, you little punk?"

Dale looked at him like he was stupid.

Scott crossed his eyes.

The boy giggled again.

"Okay," Scott conceded, "so I'm stupid, okay? So what do you mean, dragons sometimes."

"Well . . . sometimes."

"Sometimes what?"

Dale sat up then and looked out the window. "Sometimes they get waked up, Scottie. And they get mad when they get waked up, you know, really mad."

"Well, so would I, somebody wakes me up when I'm sleeping."

"But I bet you don't yell."

Scott saw their reflection, and Foxriver through it. "No. No, I guess I don't."

"Well, *they* do. And they sound just like people."

Scott eased off the bed, turned off the light. Through the open door, he heard a moaning drift down the hallway.

"Can't you hear them, Scottie?"

He stood in the dark and looked out the window.

"Can't you hear them?"